MW01196671

FROM NEAR EXTINCTION

A Dystopian Novel of Survival and Adventure
By

VICTOR ZUGG

FROM NEAR EXTINCTION

© 2018 by Victor Zugg
All rights reserved.

No part of this book may be reproduced in any form
or by any electronic or mechanical means, including
information storage and retrieval systems, without
permission in writing from the author.

This is a work of **fiction**. Names, characters,
businesses, places, events, and incidents are either the
products of the author's imagination or used in a
fictitious manner. Any resemblance to actual persons,
living or dead, or actual events is purely coincidental.

VictorZuggAuthor@gmail.com

ACKNOWLEDGEMENTS

Many thanks to Brandi Doane McCann for the cover design. Her creation belongs in a gallery. And equal thanks to Tamra Crow for the professional editing. They both made the book infinitely better.

Brandi: **www.ebook-coverdesigns.com**
Tamra: **tcrowedits@yahoo.com**

CHAPTER 1

The tall, dark, elderly looking man stood in line midway up the passenger loading stairs as he waited his turn to board. He wore a white-collared shirt, blue suit coat, wrinkled, with trousers to match. The square end of his red tie stopped several inches short of where it should have, for a man his height. Though his shoes were polished, the many creases, nicks, and scars betrayed their age. His head and forehead glistened with sweat, and beads streamed down his face and neck, dampening his collar.

Most would have blamed his condition on the midday, hot Nairobi sun. The skin of those around him gleamed as well. Dark patches of sweat stained their shirts. Several women used hand fans to supplement the light breeze across the tarmac.

But for the tall, dark man there was something more. He didn't look well. His sweat was profuse, and his shoulders slumped. Laboring to breathe, he clung to the railing for support. His hand on the rail also held a white handkerchief, which he used often to mop his forehead and neck, and to muffle his frequent coughs. A small valise occupied the other hand. Every step he took resulted in an audible exhale, followed by a raspy inhale, and then a shallow cough.

Finally, at the airliner's entrance, he ducked to enter. He returned the pretty female flight attendant's smile with a much weaker version of his own before he turned to enter the passenger compartment. The people ahead of him shuffled slowly down the aisle as they waited on others to secure their bags in the overhead bins and take their seats.

The much cooler air that filled the cabin did little to abate his sweating. He pulled at his cinched collar frequently and continued to mop the sweat from his head and neck. Each time he palmed a headrest as he moved along, he left a damp handprint behind.

Toward the back of the plane, he pulled his boarding pass from his inside coat pocket and checked his seat number. He continued until he stood in front of an empty aisle seat next to a young man and woman already planted. They both peered out the woman's window and didn't seem to notice as the tall man sat and placed his bag under the seat in front of him. He leaned back, stuck the boarding pass back in his pocket, and reached up to his air vent. He adjusted the nozzle so the air would hit him directly in the face. He looked around at others buckling their seatbelts, so he did the same.

With nearly everyone in their seats, the same pretty flight attendant made her way down the aisle as she checked each of the passengers. She stopped several times to answer a question, or to ask that something be done. When the attendant reached the tall man's seat and glanced at his seatbelt, he made eye contact and offered a weak smile.

"Would it be possible to get a glass of water and some aspirin?" he asked in a heavily accented voice.

"Are you okay?" she asked.

"Just overheated, I think," he said. "And a bit of a headache."

"Will Tylenol be okay?"

The man nodded.

"As soon as we're in the air, I'll be back first thing," she said, as she smiled and continued down the aisle.

The man laid his head back and closed his eyes.

Soon the cabin's door to the outside closed with a *thump*, the air from the vent slowed, and the plane rocked. The engines whined and then fell into a steady drone as the plane began to move.

The man's head rocked with each bump and turn as the plane proceeded down taxiways. At the main runway, the plane sat for several minutes before the engines finally whined and then roared as the plane accelerated, pressing everyone back against their seats.

Just when the plane would surely run out of tarmac, the huge mass lifted and the sound of wheels locking into their up position filled the cabin.

The man opened his eyes and adjusted the air vent's flow against his face. Despite the steady stream of cool air, sweat continued to bead on his forehead and run down his face. He mopped the wetness with the handkerchief and turned his attention to the attendant headed his way, holding a glass of water.

She handed him the water and a small packet. "I hope you're feeling better soon," she said with a smile.

"Thank you," the man said, as the attendant turned to leave. The man opened the packet, dropped the two white tablets into his mouth, and washed them down with the entire glass of water.

"Is New York your final destination?" a voice to the man's right asked.

The tall man turned his head toward the voice. "It is," he said in a raspy voice to his fellow passenger.

"You know, you don't look so good," the woman next to the window said.

"Just a headache," the tall man said. He coughed into his handkerchief. "I'm sure I'll feel better soon."

The man and woman nodded, smiled, and turned back toward the window.

The tall man coughed and then used the handkerchief to wipe his mouth. He saw a spot of red contrasting sharply against the white cloth. He folded the handkerchief to cover the stain.

Hours later, the tall man exited the terminal and ambled toward a line of taxis waiting at the curb.

One of the drivers approached, "Need a taxi?"

"I do," the man said.

The driver opened the rear door and motioned for the man to enter.

The tall man scrunched himself into the seat and sat his valise next to him.

The driver closed the door, ran around the car, and got behind the wheel. He started the engine and slapped at the meter. "Where to?" he asked, as he stared in the rearview mirror.

The tall man handed the driver a piece of paper. "Do you know this hotel?"

"I do," the driver said, as he turned the wheel and pulled out. "Nice hotel. You in town for pleasure or business?"

"I was invited to a convention." He coughed into the handkerchief and then leaned forward, placing his hands on the back of the front seat. Given his height, his face was only inches from the driver's head. "Farmers from all over the world," he said, after clearing his voice.

"Where you from?" the driver asked.

"Kenya." The man wiped his mouth with the handkerchief. "I have a small farm there."

"And they invited you to a convention in New York?" the driver asked, as he glanced back at the tall man.

"All small farmers," the tall man said. "I was selected by my village to represent the region."

"That must have been an honor," the driver said.

"A great honor," the tall man replied.

"Are you feeling okay?" the driver asked. "You don't look so good."

"I will feel better when I get to my room and lie down," the tall man said. "Tomorrow will be a big day for me and my village."

The driver nodded and then turned his attention to the road ahead.

The tall man leaned his head against the window glass of his door as the buildings raced by.

The tall man entered the large convention hall, filled to the brim with mostly men. Their form of dress indicated they were from all over the planet. For one day they were there to learn how to quadruple the output from a small farm in one year.

Despite looking worse than the day before, the tall man made the rounds in his blue suit. He shook hands and conversed as best he could with people from all over. The meet-and-greet, as they called it, was to last two full hours, followed by a series of lectures from government experts and representatives of several large chemical conglomerates.

Halfway through the second hour, chilled to the bone and shivering, the tall man had had enough. He took a seat alone in the back of the room, too weak to stand a minute longer. He slumped forward, chest almost to his knees, and coughed from deep inside his lungs. Copious amounts of blood covered the wad of napkins he held in his hand. He shivered uncontrollably. Suddenly he turned his head to the side and vomited the bagel he had eaten that morning in the hotel dining room, before entering the convention hall. Liquefied bread, mixed with dark blood, saturated the thick, gray, pile carpet.

Everyone around the tall man stopped in mid-sentence and turned toward the spectacle. Two men rushed to his side as most of the others resumed their conversation as though nothing had happened.

The tall man coughed and spat a large clump of coagulated blood to the carpet.

The two men jumped back, their faces speckled with red.

The tall man then, almost in slow motion, rolled off the chair and crumpled to the floor in a heap. He took two labored, shallow breaths, followed by an extended exhaled. He took no more breaths after that.

Within days people poured into emergency rooms. There were reports that the same was happening at several large cities around the globe. All the patients complained initially of profuse sweating and weakness, followed closely by coughing and fever. A non-itchy red rash could be found on most of them, usually on their torso or chest. For a lot of the victims, onset to death took only a few hours. For some, it took longer. Some were found to be carriers, with no symptoms.

Before most of the major epidemiologists succumbed to the disease, they had determined the cause. It was a form of the plague bacteria, the pneumonic plague variety, which affected the lungs. It was the only type of plague that could be passed from person to person through the droplets in their breath. It was similar to the bacterial infection that killed thirty to sixty percent of the population of Europe in the fourteenth century.

But there was a big difference this time. Those that survived back then probably did so because their immune systems were strong. The same couldn't be said of the more recent outbreak. The overuse of pesticides, herbicides, hormones, and especially antibiotics, in the food had reduced the human immune systems over time, making modern people much more susceptible. That, and the routine over-prescription of antibiotics for every conceivable ailment, made the plague bug itself completely resistant to even the most powerful antibiotics. There was nothing anyone could do to stop the epidemic; they could only try to make the patient comfortable.

Early news reports blamed it on a really bad worldwide flu season. But then the season pressed into spring, and then summer. Summer of death they called it. July was the worst. People died faster than they could be buried, cremated, or even pushed into a hole by a bulldozer. Of course society stopped moving. Everyone remained in their homes as long as possible. When they finally ventured out to scavenge mostly empty shelves, they returned home infected. With no one to work the various facilities, soon the power was out, water stopped flowing, and the sewage backed up. People who might have survived the epidemic ended up dying of dehydration, starvation, dysentery, or typhus. An extremely hot summer didn't help matters.

Scientists from the CDC were just getting started with their investigation when they ran out of time. Start to finish, it took nine months. The depopulation reduced once-bustling cities to empty hulks. Empty, except for the dead bodies that lined the sidewalks. And the stench. The reek of decomposing bodies never seemed to dissipate. Not completely. At least not from the cities.

Two years later, the dead no longer littered the streets. The few survivors, apparently immune, had managed to burn or bury the lifeless. But for the living, life remained far from normal.

CHAPTER 2

Leroy Tubbs scrambled up the barren hill of North Texas sand, stone, and calf-high scrub grass in the hot, dry air. A cloud of dust trailed behind his advance. At the top, he stood up straight and waited for the dust cloud to waft past him before he took a deep breath and surveyed his surroundings. Between him and the horizon in every direction he saw flat, dry land, covered with the squatty brown grass. Heat rising from the surface caused the landscape to shimmer in the distance. There were almost no trees, which meant no shade. The only signs of civilization were the twin ribbons of concrete interstate highway less than a mile to the north. Both ends disappeared into infinity, east and west.

He lifted a half-full, one-liter water bottle from the canvas satchel on his left hip, twisted the top off, and took two swigs. He replaced the cap and bottle and then removed his floppy boonie hat from his head as he glanced at the cloudless, blue sky. The sun sat only a few degrees off the crest of the western flatlands. He extended his fist, twisted his arm, and counted the number of knuckles between the horizon and the sun. Four. Fifteen minutes each gave him an hour before sundown. He dropped his fist and looked back toward the eastern sky.

"I'm forecasting another hot, dry day tomorrow," he said to himself. He snorted as he returned the hat to his head and adjusted the cord dangling under his chin. He then scanned the horizon again, in all directions. Nothing of interest captured his attention. He gazed at the dry streambed in the gully, fifty yards below where he stood. He rubbed the stubble on his face and shook his head. At least the streambed would provide good cover for the night. He stuck his thumbs under the backpack straps at his shoulders, shifted the weight, and then started down the incline, careful where he placed each foot. He was well aware that a broken ankle would mean certain death. The only person he could rely on for help was himself.

Leroy made his way into the streambed and partially up the other side of the gully until he found a semi-clear area large enough for a camp. He slung the backpack to the ground and set about collecting twigs and branches for a fire. He deposited the wood at one end of the area and then retrieved a small foldable camp shovel strapped to the outside of his pack. He made his way back into the streambed and then walked about, kicking the sand in various places. Finally, his eyes locked on a bit of foliage greener than the rest. He dropped to his knees at the spot and started digging.

Down a foot, the sand turned a darker shade of brown. Another foot, the sand turned even darker and more moist. Another ten inches, and Leroy sat back on his calves and watched water trickle into the hole. He shoveled a couple of more scoops, which increased the flow.

Leroy got to his feet, walked back to the camp area, and rummaged through his pack. His hands came out with a stainless mug, a stainless cook pot, a handkerchief, an empty sixty-four ounce stainless water bottle, and a Katadyn microfilter. He returned to the hole, dropped to his knees, and peered at the accumulated water at the bottom of the hole. About five inches worth.

He dropped the filter, cooking pot, and water bottle to the ground beside him, and then draped the handkerchief over the top of the mug. Holding the cloth tight around the entire rim, he dipped the mug into the water. After a few seconds, he raised the nearly-full mug, lifted one side of the handkerchief, and poured the brownish water into the cook pot. He repeated the process until the pot was full. He then picked up the filter and attached two tubes. He ran the end of one tube into the water bottle, and the end of the other tube into the pot. He took hold of the filter's handle and pumped.

Soon, clean, filtered water streamed into the water bottle. When the pot emptied, he repeated the entire process until the large water bottle was filled to the brim. He then took the smaller bottle from his hip, removed the cap, drained the contents into his mouth, and proceeded to fill the smaller bottle. It was well after sundown when he gathered the filled bottles and the rest of the items, got to his feet, and ambled back to the camp.

He returned the items to their respective spots and then moved over to the pile of branches. He assembled the stack with twigs on the bottom and larger branches on top, and used a lighter from his pocket to light the twigs. Flames worked their way to the top of the pile until fully engulfed. Leroy added a few larger branches and watched the flames jump higher. The glow lit the camp.

After a few seconds of staring into the flames, mesmerized by the colors and shapes, he stepped back to his pack, unbuckled a bundle strapped to the bottom, and unrolled a Snugpak personal backpacking tent. It was the one most favored by army troops in the field. He flattened the layers of material on the ground a few feet from the fire. It took only minutes to assemble the tent, complete with the rain fly and all sixteen stakes.

Leroy didn't expect rain during the night. The tent was to protect him from scorpions and snakes that claimed the ground as their own. He included the rain fly to protect against the morning dew.

Too tired to set up his camp stove and cook something, Leroy opted for a package of beef jerky. With the tent up, the fire blazing, and a mouth full of jerky, Leroy chewed as he took a seat in the sand and leaned back against a rock. He stared at the flames and listened to the crackle as he pondered the end of another day.

Screams in the distance pierced the night-time quiet. A woman's screams.

Leroy blinked his eyes open to find the interior of his tent still pitch black. He raised his left arm and glanced at the dull green glow of the hands on his watch. Two-thirty. Unsure of whether he had been dreaming, he remained flat on his back and listened. He heard a pop from the fire's dying embers. The stridulating chirp of a male cricket started up, and then just as suddenly went silent. Something scrambled through the dry scrub-grass near his tent. Probably a lizard. A woman screamed. Though in the distance, it still drowned out all the other night sounds.

Leroy unzipped the section of tent mesh near his head and the corresponding section of the rain fly. Still dressed in multicams and Garmont tactical boots, he slid his one hundred and seventy pound, five-foot ten inch frame through the opening, dragging his backpack. He sat the pack on the ground and then reached back into the tent. His hand came out with his Glock 17 pistol, secured in a Kydex holster. He slid the holster's quick clip inside his waistband, slipped his arms inside the pack straps, and slung the pack to his back as he stood up straight. With another series of screams, he turned his head to the north, toward Interstate 40. He stepped off in that direction along the streambed.

Stars and the moon provided enough light as Leroy traversed the sand, rocks, and dry vegetation in stealth mode. He stepped fast and kept low, making sure to never silhouette against the lighter sky. Moving quickly, but pausing frequently, it took fifteen minutes to cover the distance to the highway. He heard screams twice more along the way. He went prone against a mound of sand, only forty yards from the highway, and carefully raised his eyes above the crest.

Headlights from a car illuminated the median and the scene. Five men and a woman. One of the men had the completely nude woman bent over the hood, raping her from behind. The man's pants gathered at his ankles. As flesh slapped against flesh, the woman pressed her face into the hood and winced with each thrust. Two of the men cajoled the rapist to hurry up. Apparently they were waiting their turn. The fourth man watched quietly, the corners of his mouth were turned up in a smirk. Leroy figured he had already finished his turn. And the fifth man, the largest of the five men, stood back from the others. He held the arms of two children, a boy and a girl. Both appeared to be under ten years of age. Both were crying.

Twenty yards or so behind the car, Leroy spotted what appeared to be a sixth man. He was face-down on the pavement, lifeless. It appeared the five men had come across an entire family, or vice versa. It was unclear whether the car belonged to the family or the five men. Didn't really matter. Leroy also thought it odd that an entire family had survived the epidemic. How did they do that? Where did they live? Leroy wagged his head back and forth. The hows and wheres didn't matter either at this point.

Leroy's scrutiny turned back to the five live men. Three wore sidearms. Leroy had no doubt that all five had access to weapons, including rifles, most likely.

The visuals of the family being accosted were actually mild compared to other things Leroy had seen over the prior two years, but just the same, murder and rape were still wrong.

Leroy contemplated his next move. In his mind's imagination, he saw himself scramble over the fence that lined the highway. He ran directly across the pavement, gun drawn. Then what? Any gunfire would likely result in a couple of dead men, maybe three. But the woman and the kids were just as likely to get hit. The remaining men would likely get some rounds off. With no cover, Leroy would be a sitting duck. A dead duck. Tactically, it was a bad move.

He then saw himself circling around to the opposite side of the group, and approaching from the north. But then he imagined the crack of a limb under his boot, or the scuffling of a rock. Either was likely and would alert the men. Plus, moving around and in from the north would take time. It was no better than approaching from the south. Worse, really.

Leroy ran through various scenarios, but each time he saw himself dead or wounded. One man with a pistol, against five armed men in the open, amounted to a lousy chance of success, unless suicide was the goal.

The family being caught in the open was exactly why Leroy opted to travel parallel to, but well off, the highway. He glanced at the car. After two years of no production, gasoline capable of running an internal combustion engine was a precious commodity. Leroy estimated they were sixty miles outside of Amarillo, in the middle of nowhere. Either the five men were traveling somewhere, or the family was. Where and why, again, didn't really matter, so Leroy didn't dwell further on the possibilities.

Leroy had survived the last two years by staying low and not getting involved, no matter how incensed he might have gotten over the depths to which humanity had sunk. The United States, the world probably, had devolved to a time before civilization. Without the means or inclination to enforce rules and laws, man had reverted to his darker nature. Some men; not all. Leroy watched what amounted to another example of just that.

Leroy reconciled himself to the fact that he couldn't help these people. The odds were too much against him. He would simply end up dead if he tried. Leroy had survived the last two years by avoiding stupid, like traveling down the middle of a highway in the open, in the midst of an apocalypse, with still too many unrestrained men and women with guns.

Snickering grunts, the woman's pathetic groans, and the children's whimpering continued from the median as Leroy back-crawled into the streambed. He got to his feet and stepped off toward his camp. Twenty minutes later, as he stopped next to his tent and dropped his backpack to the ground, he heard three gunshots. Leroy turned toward the highway and then shook his head as he dropped his chin. A couple of minutes later he heard the roar of an engine and saw the light from the headlights move east. As the sound of the car's engine melted into the night, the staccato chirping of a lone cricket started up. Leroy slid back into his tent.

CHAPTER 3

Leroy couldn't help but feel some guilt as he stared down at the man, woman, and two kids in the early morning light. The man and woman were in their late thirties, ten years younger than Leroy. Based on their clothes, they had likely been members of the upper middle class, with good jobs and a nice home before the sickness. A family. But that was then. Now, they lay in the sand alongside a desolate highway, each with a single bullet hole in their head. Leroy rubbed the stubble along his jaw and chin, shook his head, and tightened his lips. He closed his eyes and hoped they could now find peace. At least they were together.

Leroy took a deep breath as he looked up and scanned the horizons. Seeing nothing moving, he slid his pack off and dropped it to the ground. Remaining in the open for too long was a risk. But it was a risk Leroy felt compelled to take. It was the least he could do. He removed the small camp shovel from the pack and stepped a few feet farther into the median, where the sand was softer. He started digging.

An hour later he stared at the four mounds of darker soil. He stood for a moment in silence. He then strapped the shovel to his pack, slung the pack over his shoulders, and stepped off to the south with one final glance at the graves. He crossed the fence and marched through the calf-high scrub-grass until he was about a mile off the highway. He adjusted his hat, shifted his pack until it felt more comfortable, and then headed off toward the sun.

He stepped carefully, mindful of where he placed each foot. Rattlesnakes were common in the area and they blended with the brown grass. The last thing he needed was a snake bite, so he kept his eyes peeled.

He had only a general idea of where he was headed. East. Months earlier, before he left California, he heard rumors of a movement back east to reestablish some form of government. Leroy didn't know who, what, or where, but if the rumors were true, at least someone was trying. He was sure the military, or what was left of the military, would be playing a part. Leroy thought he could help. Since his only goal was to survive, he thought he might as well move east while he did it.

Leroy wasn't the only one headed in that direction. He had seen all manner of transport along the highway. Mostly people walking. Lots of walkers, just like Leroy.

Some pulled wagons, but most just carried their belongings. Men, women, and children. He had also seen the occasional bicycle, decked out with the usual totes and bags of a trekker. He had even seen a horse or two. Rarely, like the night before, he saw a car or truck. Word of something happening back east had gotten around. People were migrating, looking for a better life. Unfortunately, many would be culled by the harsh environment, or the nature of bad men that seemed to exist everywhere. Leroy thought of the four graves he had just dug. There would likely be more.

As Leroy stepped to the crest of a small hill, he paused and peered north, through the shimmering bands of heat rising off the land and the concrete highway in the distance. He made sure to check his distance from the highway from time to time, to make sure he didn't wander too far south. Without a point of reference as he traveled, it would be easy to get lost in the wide open landscape, where each hill looked like the last.

The corners of his mouth turned up slightly as he thought of how ironic it was that he would be migrating, along with other people, east along this section of Interstate 40. It was along this very route that people migrated west to escape the dust bowl of the nineteen thirties. This was their primary route. Back then it was only two lanes, but it had an iconic name. Route 66. It stretched from Chicago to Santa Monica. The 1960s television show with the same name came out a full ten years before Leroy was even born, but he knew of the show. He had even watched an episode or two on Youtube. Leroy closed his eyes and bobbed his chin in beat with the show's theme song.

Suddenly he opened his eyes, removed his hat, and glanced up at the sun. *Heat must be getting to me.* He smoothed his hair with one hand and replaced the hat. He looked off to the east and started walking.

As he walked, his mind drifted. He found himself ticking off the food left in his backpack, and how many days he could continue before he would be forced to replenish. He had several cans of beans, a couple of cans of chili, one tin of tuna, and two cans of peaches. He also had some beef jerky and beef sticks left. He could travel several more days before he would have to start looking. Water was the bigger problem. In this parched section of the country, sources of open water were few and far between. Luckily, his army survival training had taught him how to find water, if there was any to be found. So far, he had found enough.

Leroy paused at the top of a sand hill and scanned his surroundings as he lifted the water bottle from its satchel. He held the bottle up and contemplated the contents and his level of dehydration. Only a quarter was left. He twisted the cap off and drained the contents into his mouth. He replaced the empty bottle as he continued walking.

He was daydreaming about swimming in his California home's pool when the rattle penetrated his consciousness. The sound of a grass hopper or cricket was similar, but the rattle of a diamondback's tail was distinct. It was the latter that immediately brought his mind back to the here and now, and his gait to an abrupt halt. The rattling droned on but less intense, which meant that Leroy's stop had an effect on the snake. He was close. Somewhere off to the right. As the rattling ceased all together, Leroy checked every patch of brown grass within ten feet. He saw nothing, until his eyes caught the slight movement of the snake's head. He was eight feet ahead, slightly off the right side of the small animal trail Leroy had been following. If Leroy had kept walking, he would surely have been struck.

Based on the circumference of the snake's curled body, he was big. He looked mean, with his head lifted off the ground and his dark, piercing eyes watching Leroy's every move. The brownish diamond patterns along his body matched the surrounding grass perfectly. This was his terrain.

Normally Leroy would simply bypass the creature, but in this instance, the snake represented a food source. It offered considerable protein to Leroy's mostly bean diet. Since he didn't want to waste a bullet, and didn't want to alert anyone within miles to his location, Leroy reached across his body with his right hand and wrapped his fingers around the handle of his Bark River Golok in its sheath just behind the water satchel. Much longer than a knife, but considerably shorter than a machete, Leroy wasn't sure the twelve inch blade was the right tool. The snake could strike a lot farther than twelve inches. He thought of the shovel strapped to his pack, but folded out, the shovel was only an inch or two longer than the Golok. He needed a long stick.

Leroy glanced around at the treeless surroundings, devoid of anything longer or thicker than a twig. If Leroy hadn't needed a branch, he was sure he'd be tripping over them. Since he needed a branch, there were none to be found.

While Leroy continued to think, the snake started up his rattling again and raised his head higher. More ominous. He obviously wanted Leroy to move on.

The next best thing to a long stick was a large rock. Leroy scanned the ground and saw plenty of pebbles, but no large rocks.

He then gazed at the snake. "This is your lucky day, my friend," he said, as he removed his hat, scratched his head, and then replaced the hat. He stepped off in a direction that gave the snake a wide berth. He kept his eyes glued to the ground while he thought about how well the snake blended with the grass. He also gave some thought to walking on the highway where snakes would be much easier to spot. He finally decided he was just being paranoid. Remaining off the highway was tactically the better option.

Despite his growing fatigue, his mind remained ever vigilant as he jerked his head back and forth along the animal trail. It took some time to shake the feeling that snakes lurked in every patch of grass just waiting for

Leroy to get closer, but finally his mind relaxed and he thought of other things as he walked.

A few miles farther on, Leroy came to what looked like an abandoned farm. Walking a mile or so off the highway, Leroy often came upon farms and ranches. For the most part he avoided both, even if obviously abandoned. It was always possible someone could be lurking with a rifle and an itchy trigger finger.

The fields, arranged in large circles making them easier to water, were obvious in the dirt, despite their lack of greenery. The sprinkler system pipes, raised above the fields, looked as though they hadn't been used in years. This particular property looked more abandoned than most, so Leroy decided to walk through, rather than around.

Each strike of a boot against the baked dirt field brought a cloud of dust that swirled around his pants legs as he pressed on toward a structure in the far distance. While most farmers didn't actually live at their fields, there was always a shed for storing tools and to house the pump for the irrigation system. Leroy was sure that such a shed was what he saw in the distance.

The sun, shining from over his right shoulder, lit the white building in stark contrast to the dark ground. The open door swung side-to-side in the light breeze. Off to the right a few yards was a round, metal trough about twice the diameter of a child's blow-up swimming pool and three times deeper. Some rain did pass through several days earlier and it was possible water had accumulated in the trough faster than it could evaporate.

Leroy checked the shed first. He stuck his head in the open doorway and waited a few seconds for his eyes to adjust to the relative darkness inside. He didn't want to just blunder inside. The shed provided one of the few spots for miles around where animals and snakes could get out of the sun. The little shed, built over a concrete slab, was empty, except for an old full-sized shovel, an axe, and a plastic bucket. He could have used the shovel during his altercation with the snake.

He walked the few feet to the trough and was surprised to find it half-full of standing water. Clear water. It wouldn't be safe to drink directly, probably brimmed with bacteria, but it would be fine for his water filter.

He looked over his shoulder at the sun, still well above the horizon, and decided he had walked enough for the day.

He returned to the shed, slung his pack off his shoulders, and lowered it to the dusty concrete floor. He looked around the grounds until he spotted a couple of old boards lying in the dirt. He could break those up for firewood. Tonight he would have a cooked meal.

He thought about using the trough to wash his clothes and himself. Neither had been washed in weeks. But then he thought about the growing reports of flesh-eating bacteria he had heard about before the sickness. Such reports drove Leroy to avoid all bodies of water.

Most cases occurred in warmer climates, like Florida. And it seemed that particular bacteria lived mostly in brackish waters. People with compromised immune systems were most at risk. Another result of poor diets and the overuse of antibiotics. Leroy stared at the half-filled trough of water. He wasn't standing in Florida and the trough water wasn't brackish. Plus, exposing water to intense sunlight was one way to purify against bacteria. The sunlight had certainly been intense lately. Leroy decided to take the chance.

From his pack, Leroy retrieved the water filter, pot, and the nearly empty two-liter water bottle. At the trough, he assembled the filter, placed one tube in the trough, the other in the water bottle, and pumped. He found that it took much longer to filter the water, probably because the ceramic filter inside was clogged from the sandy water he'd filtered the day before. To work at its best, the filter needed to be cleaned often. He filled both water bottles to the brim and then filled the cooking pot. He drank his fill during the process.

He then disassembled the filter and used the water from the pot to clean the ceramic cylinder inside. The kit included its own scrub pad. Once cleaned, he let the cylinder dry before reassembling the filter.

Next, he obtained the bucket from the shed, a bar of soap from his pack, and the one extra set of multicams, along with underwear and socks. He carried everything to the trough, stripped off the clothing he was wearing, and proceeded to wash everything, one article at a time, in the bucket. Once cleaned and rinsed, he draped the clothing over the edge of the trough to dry.

He then used the bucket to dip more water, rinse off his body, soap down, and rinse again. He could have taken a bath in the trough. That would have been more refreshing, but he didn't want to spoil the water with soap. He figured there were plenty of animals that drank from the trough.

After a dinner of hot chili, he sat in the open doorway of the shed as the sun dropped behind the horizon. He stared at the fire.

This was the fourth full day since Leroy passed the outskirts of Amarillo. His goal was to cover at least twenty-five miles each day. Without GPS it was difficult to judge his mileage, but given the relatively flat terrain, the heat, and his twelve to fourteen-hour days, he figured he was maintaining his goal. His only travel aid was an old western United States road map he found in an abandoned gas station just after he started his trek. It didn't show a lot of the terrain features, but at least it included most cities. Plus, he had driven the Interstate twice in his life. Once when he and his wife drove from their home in St. Louis to California, and again, when they moved to California, before he joined the army. He, of course, remembered the larger cities, like Oklahoma City, Amarillo, and Albuquerque, but not the smaller towns. Except one. Sayre, Oklahoma. It was at that exit when a tire blew. The people at the truck stop there were able to replace the tire so he could continue his journey.

Leroy obtained the map from his pack and ran his finger along Interstate 40 from Amarillo to a sharp twist in the road, about one-hundred and twenty-five miles to the east. He figured he must be near that spot. He had no intention of stopping, but the place did bring back memories.

CHAPTER 4

A dilapidated group of three homes and their associated sheds, barns, and garages sat nestled in the southwest corner of the Route 283 exit off Interstate 40, just south of Sayre, a very small town in southwestern Oklahoma. The owners of all three properties deserted the buildings during the epidemic and never returned. For over a year after the epidemic the small group of buildings remained unoccupied, baking in the summer sun and freezing in the winter cold. All the buildings were single-story structures, except one. This lone structure differed from all the rest. It stood two stories on a twelve-foot by twelve-foot foundation, constructed of red brick and a metal roof. Yard tools and lawn mowers occupied the bottom floor, behind double metal doors. Outside stairs led to the top floor, which was crammed with a sofa, small desk, and two lamps. The room was without bath or kitchen facilities, and, like the rest of the town, now without power. For the previous owners of the property the building served as a studio office. Cramped, but functional. For the past year it had served as home to forty-two-year-old Laura Wilson and her twenty-year-old daughter, Cindy.

They remained inside and slept during the day as much as possible, despite the heat. Cindy took the sofa since she was shorter; Laura was left with the floor, on top of a pallet made of blankets and two sleeping bags. Two windows, each opened a smidge, provided a bit of cross ventilation. They went out most nights to scavenge or reconnoiter the nearby town.

Night had just descended when the door creaked open and Laura and Cindy stepped out to the landing. They followed the same routine almost every night: observe from the windows at dusk, exit when completely dark, and observe and listen from the landing for a full five minutes before descending the stairs.

As usual, they were both dressed in black, with nylon mesh, lace-up boots, black jeans, and a black long sleeved t-shirt. Laura tucked her blond hair under a crimson ball cap. Cindy left her dark hair loose at her shoulders. And they each wore a medium-sized backpack. The extra clothing and the packs were courtesy of the only clothing store in Sayre, a western outfitter. The only variation to their nighttime ensemble was a black puffy jacket and gloves they wore during the colder months.

Their method of operation once on the ground had served them well since their arrival in Sayre. They had never been caught or, to their knowledge, even been seen by the few people that still called Sayre their home. The plan this night was the same as usual: no talking, hand signals only, move fast, stay low, get what they needed, and get out. And since they had no weapons except a pocket knife each, it was paramount they avoid contact.

What they needed was what they needed every other night. Food. Canned and jarred were about the only food still edible. Peanut butter was still okay. Some packaged stuff was still good, chips mostly. And water. Water was the most important commodity of all.

Since food stores had long been emptied of anything edible, their target was abandoned homes. Ninety percent of the homes in Sayre were without occupants. At least, none still alive.

Laura knew this routine and way of life was not sustainable. Eventually, soon actually, all the homes would be pilfered and all the food would be consumed. At that point, she and her daughter would have to move on. But for now, it was okay. They were surviving.

With their surroundings lit only by the stars and a partial moon, Laura nodded to Cindy and then started down the stairs. The steps were quiet, except for one, the first one from the ground. It would agonize from a person's weight with a low-pitched squeak. Laura skipped that particular step as she planted both feet on the square concrete pad that formed the base of the stairs.

Cindy followed her mother step for step until she, too, stood on the pad beside her.

Laura swiveled her head in all directions for a final scan, ducked low, and scrambled north into the scrubby trees that formed a narrow barrier next to the interstate. At the north edge of the tree-line she pulled up behind the thick trunk of an oak tree and took a few seconds to survey the area. Satisfied that all was clear, she glanced at Cindy behind her, and then sprinted across the county road that paralleled the interstate. At the fence running along the north side of the road, designed to keep small animals off the highway, Laura placed one hand on a fence post and used her momentum to propel both legs up and over the fence, without losing stride. Both feet were already moving when they hit the dirt and scrub grass on the other side. She heard a slight *oomph* from Cindy behind her, followed by the sound of two feet hitting the ground. Without looking back, Laura knew Cindy was close behind, matching Laura step for step.

To see a vehicle, or even a person, on the interstate would be a rare event, but just the same, Laura scanned up and down the highway as she scurried across the exit lane and the double lanes of the main highway. She leapt the short, four-strand, steel median barrier fence, accelerated across the west bound lanes, and then hopped the north fence with a fast, fluid one-handed pivot from the top of a post, a motion that even seasoned gymnasts would envy. At full gallop, she crossed the paralleling county road, and immediately entered a small community of twelve homes, all dark and vacant. Months earlier, these were the first homes to be emptied of anything of value, so Laura did not slow her gait as she cruised through the community and out the other side.

Laura, followed closely by Cindy, low-trotted across the dry, flat landscape. They passed through an overgrown golf course, across a dry, sandy streambed, through a stand of trees and brush, until a mile later they pulled up against the south side of a metal building, the first of four that comprised the town's only self-storage facility. Only then, on the edge of Sayre's business district, did they pause for a breather.

Laura pressed herself against the building's metal skin, still warm from the day's heat, and inched toward the southeast corner. She peered around the edge and scanned up and down the four-lane highway, the main drag bisecting the town's east and west sides.

Her target was the southeast section of the town's main residential area, an eighteen square block section of homes immediately north of the business district. Laura made it a point to hit a different section each night in order to avoid establishing a pattern. Like Sayre as a whole, only about ten percent of the homes in this section were inhabited, which left a great many vacant houses. Most had already been pilfered by her and other residents of the town, but there were still houses with potentially rich resources.

The men remaining in town did most of their pilfering during the day. They had weapons, and they weren't afraid to be seen. A gang of sorts had formed. From what Laura had been able to observe, this gang consisted of about ten men. She had also seen a couple of women. The group was loud, boisterous, and sometimes drunk. They pretty much had the run of the place during the day and into the early evening. After that, most were passed out and asleep. That had been their routine since Laura arrived. Still, Laura kept to her stealth protocol, ever vigilant, and taking nothing for granted.

With her breathing under control, Laura glanced at Cindy, motioned with two fingers, and then darted from her cover. She raced across the four paved lanes and immediately entered a stand of trees that bordered the edge of town and wrapped all the way around to the courthouse complex at the southeast corner of the business district.

She moved fast through the trees, pausing frequently to listen, until she had the back of the county jail building in sight. The jail and the sheriff's department had long ago been vacated. Laura figured the deputies had died from the epidemic, died from battling people on the streets, went into hiding, or departed the area. Whichever it was, they were all gone.

Laura took a moment to scan the area and listen for any unnatural sounds. Satisfied no one was about, she raced forward in a low trot, circled around the jail building, crossed Main Street, and proceeded along the fence of the town's ball field. On the back side of the field she crossed some railroad tracks and then took a knee next to a clump of bushes.

Cindy dropped to both knees next to her.

Laura contemplated her next move, knowing that entering a house at night was the most dangerous part of the operation. Nine out of ten homes were mathematically vacant, but which ones? She scanned the side yards and homes of the southernmost line of structures in the community. The houses stood back to back on each block and each house faced a residential street. From her position, Laura could see two blocks in each direction, a total of eight homes. All of them were dark. Laura knew that dark didn't mean vacant. Just like she did, people covered their windows before lighting a candle or oil lamp. That left Laura only one recourse. She would have to approach each house, one at a time, and listen for any activity inside. The process would go a lot faster if she and Cindy split up, but Laura had no intention of letting her daughter out of her sight.

She studied the line of homes for a few seconds more and decided to start with the one directly in front of her. The house was older, of frame construction, and it needed a paint job. But the yard was in relatively good condition which gave Laura hope that the owner had managed the interior as well. She glanced at Cindy, motioned with her fingers, and then stepped from the cover.

She caressed the ground with each foot before stepping to the next, ensuring that her surreptitious approach remained quiet. Like she had done hundreds of times before, she first wanted to check the doors. A smashed door meant the house had already been ransacked. She eased to the front yard, using trees and bushes for cover, until she had a view of the home's front door. It stood intact. She then made her way to the backyard and found the glass sliding doors also intact. She noted that the glass doors were not covered from the inside, which was a good indication that no one occupied the structure.

Laura always felt edgy during these excursions, but she felt particularly so this night. For several weeks, actually, a feeling gnawed at the back of her mind that eventually her luck would run out and she and her daughter would be caught. Her anxiety had grown over recent days until now, staring at the dark glass doors, her hands shook.

Gathering food was important, but they had built up a considerable stock. Most nights they returned with more than would be eaten in a day, or even two. Laura estimated they had a couple of week's worth of food and water stored in the little room. Did she really need to enter this particular house on this particular night?

Suddenly, she jumped at the touch of Cindy's finger on her shoulder, obviously wondering why they weren't moving. Laura glanced back at Cindy, nodded, and then advanced toward the front of the house.

Cindy remained in the front yard, keeping watch, while Laura approached the front door.

She knelt on one knee in front of the door while she slid the pack off her back. She placed the pack on the concrete, unzipped the main compartment, and produced a medium-sized pry bar. Laura preferred to force a door rather than break a window.

With the pry bar in her hand, she stood, slung the pack to her back, and wedged the bar between the door and the jamb, near the knob. As quietly as possible she applied pressure while working the bar up and down. She heard the wood separating and felt the end of the bar making progress. When she had penetrated the wood far enough, she slowly pulled on the pry bar until the bolt separated from the striker plate. With minimal noise from splintering wood, the door gave way and swung open a few inches.

Laura held the pry bar high, ready to swing, as she listened a few seconds and then slowly pushed the door open until there was enough room for her to slip her head inside. She listened a full minute before looking back at Cindy and waving.

Cindy joined her mother as they both entered the pitch dark house.

Unlike many other houses, the inside of this one did not reek of decaying flesh, which was good. Laura hated dead bodies. The prospects for this house were looking better and better.

Laura closed the door and waited in the foyer until her eyes adjusted to the darker surroundings. Soon she was able to make out the dark clumps of furniture in the living room, highlighted by the starlight filtering through uncovered windows. The only sound she heard was Cindy's breathing.

She kept the pry bar high as she stepped forward, careful where she placed each foot. Every few feet she stopped and listened. Slowly, she made her way around the house until she had checked all three bedrooms and the two baths. She then led Cindy to the kitchen where they both started opening cabinets and drawers. They worked quickly and quietly as they removed the contents and stacked everything on the counter. Like most people, the previous occupants maintained enough for a few days only.

Laura was not able to read the labels in the dark, but based on her experience and the shape and size of the cans and jars, she had gotten pretty good at identifying the good stuff in the dark. Canned meats, like tuna, were squatty; vegetables and beans were fairly uniform; soup cans were smaller. Peanut butter, in a plastic jar, and jelly, in the small glass jars, were both prized. Sometimes she ended up with olives instead of jelly, but olives were okay too. Not knowing exactly provided a bit of anticipation for the next morning. It was a little like opening gifts on Christmas.

No matter how good the find, Laura never overloaded their packs. Being able to move quickly and quietly was crucial. Resource rich homes might merit a return trip, usually the same night, but never two nights in a row. This house turned out to be a good source, but it didn't warrant a return trip.

Laura loaded select cans and jars in their packs, along with six bottles of water each. Laura knew the bottles contained water because she opened one, sniffed, and then drank the entire contents. She ensured Cindy did the same.

With their packs considerably heavier than before, they each helped the other slide into the shoulder straps. Before they left, Laura wanted to check for one other commodity.

She led Cindy to the master bedroom and immediately started opening drawers, starting with the night stands. She felt inside each drawer, scattered items back and forth, and then moved to the next. She found magazines, socks, underwear, and other articles of clothing, but not what she wanted. She then moved to the closet. Without windows, it was pitch black inside, and she had to search by feel only. Her fingers touched linens, towels, and boxes of all sizes and shapes, but not the cold metal of a gun. She knew it was a long shot. For people heading out during or after an apocalypse, guns would be a priority. But it was always possible one would be left behind.

Coming up empty, Laura headed for the living room, motioning Cindy to follow.

Laura pulled the door open wide enough for her head, listened and looked for any movement, and stepped outside with Cindy close behind. Laura closed the door, took another look around, and then she and Cindy raced off in a low gallop.

CHAPTER 5

Dallas Gentry had been the police chief of Sayre, Oklahoma. Technically, he still was. But in practicality there was little left for him to police in a town devoid of all commerce, ninety percent of its citizens, and all four of his former police officers. Three of those officers had been taken by the plague. The fourth left the area months earlier, headed in the direction of Oklahoma City. He had an ex-wife and a daughter that resided there. Gentry had lost his wife, all three of their children, and a sister to the sickness. He didn't have high hopes that the police officer had found his family alive.

At six foot, two-hundred and eighty pounds, Gentry had been a big man. But that was before the epidemic, before the stress of his family and town dropping dead, and before beer became a scarce commodity. He no longer wore the chief of police uniform. Being a hundred pounds shy of his former weight, it no longer fit. Jeans and a t-shirt were the garb of choice these days. And his Chief's ball cap. That and his air of authority were the only aspects of his former life that he still had. It was only natural that many of what few men were left in town would gravitate toward Gentry. They all still called him *Chief*.

Most days he woke around eleven. He would eat something and then he and his men would set out to rummage through the homes in search of food. There wasn't much variety to find, canned goods mostly. Chief Gentry had come to hate green beans. Rarely they'd come across something special, like wine, beer, or canned meats, like ham.

Weeks earlier they started finding homes that had already been pilfered. Each one bore the same signs of entry. A forced door. This is why the chief figured a particular individual was competing with the town for the few resources left. Probably an outsider. And that wasn't right. The townspeople came first.

So for the last few weeks the chief had made it his objective to eradicate the interloper. He started out with daily two-man roving patrols. They came up with nothing other than the fact that the scavenging continued, despite the patrols. Next he tried to determine if there was a pattern. On his office wall hung a large map of the town. He tracked the pilfered homes, but was unable to determine a pattern. Targeted homes were random throughout the community. It appeared the person or persons made it a point to never hit the same area twice in a row. The chief did come to one conclusion: the attacks were at night. Based on that information, he started setting up stationary observation points throughout the town at night. He usually left that to his men, but occasionally, when he was especially bored, he would go out.

That was the case on this particular night. He sat alone on a living room sofa in the dark, peering out the front windows of a house in the southeast section of town. He had been there since well before sunset. He had done his best to keep his eyes open, but had to admit, there might have been some instances when they closed for a few seconds. He frequently found himself rubbing his whiskered face with one hand to stay awake.

In an effort to keep his eyes open, he played mind games. To himself, he recited all the states and their capitols. It was something his mother could do, so he taught himself well before his teens. He tried to remember all the movies in which a particular actor appeared. He could only remember a few movies and even fewer actors, so he gave that exercise up early. He thought back to his life before. He had been an effective chief; he enforced the law. He even managed to make a few extra bucks along the way, walking a thin line between right and wrong. Unfortunately, money had become pretty much worthless after the plague. About the only thing valued were tangible assets a man could use to stay alive. Food, guns, and ammo topped the list.

He had plenty of the latter two, but food was a problem. The prior summer he got the town's people to work on a municipal garden. They had seeds. But without decent irrigation, fertilizer, and weed control, the effort didn't amount to much. But even so, he wasn't that worried. He figured it was only a matter of time before the government would get the lights back on and he could resume his former life. But that might be a ways off. He just had to hang on until then, and that meant stopping the interloper.

Chief Gentry was about to call it a night and head for the comfort of his home when he saw two dark forms dart across the road in the distance. His eyes opened wide, his mind perked, and he scrambled closer to the window just in time to see the dark blobs hop the railroad tracks and race south. They were obviously headed for the wooded area behind the courthouse.

Gentry had figured the ones responsible for the pilfering probably lived by day in one of the many vacant Sayre homes. But that was apparently not the case. They ran away from all the houses. They either lived in one of the commercial buildings in town, or they lived even farther south, outside of town. The chief intended to find out.

He slung the door open and took off west. He knew immediately there was no way he could chase them down. They were way too fast. So he headed for Fourth Street, the main north/south road through town. Maybe he could make it to the middle of the commercial district in time to see if they crossed Fourth Street. If they did, it meant they were likely holed up in some dwelling south of town. If they didn't cross, it meant they were likely holed up in a commercial building.

Gentry hadn't done any actual running in years. His almost immediate huffing and puffing was prime evidence of how out of shape he was. Still, despite being winded, he pressed on with one goal—reach Fourth Street before they crossed.

At Broadway he skipped over the railroad tracks, and limped at a fast pace through a stand of warehouses. With only a block to go, he tried to take deep breaths in an attempt to maintain his pace, but it only resulted in a fit of coughing. He came to a complete stop only yards from the highway, placed his hands on his hips, and tried to breathe. After a few breaths he continued with a fast walk, until he finally reached the corner of Fourth Street and Maple. He rounded the edge of the southeast building and fell into a steady walk. He kept to the shadows as he headed south, along the store fronts. He stopped several times to regain his normal breathing, but kept his eyes locked on the distant darkness down Fourth. He had gone only half a block when he saw the pair's silhouettes race across Fourth, down around the self storage buildings three blocks away.

There were a few homes on the southwest edge of town, and a few sparse homes and buildings farther south, between town and the Interstate. Those would be the first areas he would search, but it would have to wait until daylight. He was done for the night, happy in the fact that he had at least laid eyes on the culprits.

He stood in his office in front of seven men, all talking at the same time. Gentry removed his cap, smoothed his mostly nonexistent hair, and waved the cap to get everyone's attention.

A tall, lanky, middle-aged man with his back to the group raised his chin toward Gentry and flapped his extended arms, palms down, until everyone stopped talking. "How many men did you see, Chief?"

Gentry returned the cap to his head. "I saw two people, but I'm not sure they were men. They were small. Could have been small men, or boys."

"Could they have been women?" a man in the back asked.

"We could actually use a few more women around here," another man said.

Everyone snickered.

"Could have been women, I suppose," Gentry said. "All I know for sure is, they were fast and they ran south."

"There's not much south of town," another man said.

"True," Gentry said. "That should make them easier to find."

"How do you want to go about it?" the man in front asked.

Gentry stepped to the map mounted on the wall. He pointed to an area on the southwest edge of town. "Four patrols, two men each. I want to start with the homes in this area. I want an inspection inside every building. That includes houses, barns, sheds, and anything else that could provide shelter. Make sure you don't miss any. From there, we spread out and move south to the Interstate."

"And when we find them?" the man in front asked.

Gentry stepped closer to the men. "Our main goal is to recover any remaining resources taken from our town. Beyond that, use your own judgment."

The men started talking among themselves again.

"Let's get to it," Gentry said in a slightly elevated tone.

The men quieted and filed out, all armed with rifles or pistols. Gentry nodded to the man in front before he joined the rest of the men. "Jim, you're with me."

"Will do, Chief," Jim said, as he stopped to let Gentry go first. Jim fingered the butt of the semi-automatic pistol holstered at his hip. The weight of the pistol pulled his baggy pants lower on that side. The excess of his black leather belt, cinched to the first hole, flapped free in front. An embroidered patch on his long-sleeved, tucked shirt, just above a spot of grease, read *Jim's Service Station*.

Gentry, followed by Jim, fell in behind the gaggle of men as they sauntered out the building's glass door.

The group stopped on the sidewalk along Fourth Street and waited.

Gentry stepped to the front of the men. "We'll spread out here into our patrols and head south along paralleling streets. At the tracks I want two patrols to follow the tracks a ways west, spread out and come at the houses from the west. Two patrols will come in from the east and north." He pointed to a man wearing dark gray work pants, a white t-shirt, and holding a Winchester lever-action thirty-thirty. "Sam, you and Freddie spread out a bit and take up a position south of the houses. The rest of the patrols will systematically work through the houses from the north, east, and west." He nodded at Sam. "Stop any runners."

All the men nodded and voiced agreement. One man raised a finger in the air to get Gentry's attention. "If we find anything interesting?"

"Fire a shot," Gentry said. "The rest of us will come running." He looked around at the men. "Any other questions?"

"Did you see any weapons last night?" a man wearing jeans and a red tank top asked.

"Nope," Gentry said. "If there's nothing else, let's get to it." He pointed to various men and motioned them in various directions. When all the other men were on their way, Gentry turned to Jim. "We'll head down Fourth," he said, as he stepped off down the sidewalk.

Jim caught up and matched Gentry stride for stride.

Wearing only a long, light-gray t-shirt, stained darker in spots from sweat, Laura extricated herself from the bedsheet tangled around her legs as she rolled to her back and rose from her pallet of blankets. She padded to the nearest window and pulled open the ocean blue tarp covering the entire opening.

She didn't wear a watch, but based on the sunlight and shadows she guessed it was around three or four. She pulled the tarp a little wider and scanned the area to the north of the tiny building. Being on the second floor gave her a much better view, which was one of the reasons she chose this particular structure. She was able to see over the thicker shrubs, through the few trees, and well past the Interstate highway. She scrunched closer to the window to increase her field of view west to east. Nothing moved.

She let the tarp flop closed, looked at Cindy still asleep on the sofa, and then stepped softly to the door. Might as well let her sleep.

She gently pulled the door open just wide enough for her body to slip through and closed the door behind her. On the landing, she pivoted her body in a complete arc, north to south, as she scanned the areas to the west. Again, no sign of movement.

With bare feet, she ambled down the steps, around the building, and across the brown, grass covered open area on the west side of the building. Without a bathroom, or even running water, they were forced to use slit trenches in place of toilets. Laura had enclosed a small area against the back fence with a tarp over a frame of branches and PVC pipe. It was a simple structure, but it served the purpose. Over the time she and Cindy had occupied the property she had moved the structure eight times. Each move required a new trench.

After using the crude facility, Laura returned to the base of the steps on the east side of the building and removed her long t-shirt, which left her standing nude on the concrete slab. Months earlier she had solved the bathing issue by positioning a plastic, twenty-gallon storage container under the downspout that ran from a gutter on the east side of the roof and down the northeast corner. The contraption did a good job of accumulating rain water from the occasional storms. There were still several gallons in the container from a storm that had rolled through ten days earlier. She and Cindy used the same water to wash their clothes, but only when the water was plentiful. Currently there was only enough for bathing, and, if it didn't rain again soon, there would not be enough for even that.

She used a small plastic pail to pour water over her head and then soaped down with a bar of Dial obtained during one of their nighttime jaunts. She paid particular attention to her hair, which she had not washed in over a week. Both she and Cindy kept their hair short to make it easier to wash, and easier to hide.

When finished lathering, she used the remainder of the one pail of water to rinse. One small pail to wash and rinse had been a real challenge in the beginning, especially for Cindy, but they both finally got it down to an art form.

Laura picked up the t-shirt and climbed the stairs. At the top, standing on the landing to let her body air dry, she soaked in the morning sun's rays as she once again scanned the surroundings. She could see the buildings of Sayre standing silently just like every other day. The Interstate highway and the connecting county road seemed out of place without traffic. She tried to remember the last time she saw a moving automobile. It had been weeks, if not months. She gazed at a single blackbird perched on the power line that ran along the county road only a few yards away. She thought about how the term no longer described the wire, since it had not carried electricity in nearly two years. She wondered when, or if, power would return. And she wondered how much longer she and Cindy could stay in this place. They were already competing with the few people left in town for the meager resources that remained. Eventually, probably soon, there would be nothing left. But where would they go? Anyplace west would mean a long trek across mostly barren land. Besides, she came from that direction and had no desire to return. To the east, Oklahoma City was a hundred miles; to the south, Dallas, Texas, was about double that distance. But cities, with more people and fewer resources, would mean more danger. She would love to be in Florida. There was plenty of fishing there, and it was warm during the winter. But it was also over a thousand miles away. One thing was for sure, she would have to make a decision soon.

Laura took in a deep breath and blew it out forcibly as she turned and placed a hand on the doorknob. Just as she turned the knob she heard a sound from far off. It sounded like a shout. She couldn't discern the words, but it was definitely human. She stepped back to the edge of the landing and peered to the north. At first she saw nothing. But then, in the distance, she saw movement. A black speck moved over the landscape at least a half mile away. She focused on the spot and was able to pick out the features of a man as he walked across an open field. She scanned to the right of that spot and saw more movement. Another man walked parallel to the first. They were about a hundred yards apart. Apparently, one had yelled to the other. They both walked in Laura's direction.

Laura jumped back from the edge of the landing which put the corner of the building between her and the men. Wondering if she had been seen, she eased her head forward until just the man on the right came into view. There did not appear to be any change in his speed, but Laura knew they were not out for a morning stroll. They were looking for her.

CHAPTER 6

Laura barreled through the door, closed it behind her, and went straight for her clothes. As she passed the sofa, she patted Cindy on the calf. "Get up," she whispered. "There are men coming this way."

Cindy's head bolted upright. "What?"

"There are men coming this way," Laura said, as she pulled some underwear up her legs, and a pair of khaki shorts. "We need to be ready to move."

Cindy pivoted on the sofa and put her feet on the floor. "What do we do?"

Laura slipped an olive-colored t-shirt over her head and sat on the empty end of the sofa. "Load your backpack with stuff you'll need if we can't come back here, along with as much food and water as you can carry." She pulled some socks on her feet, her boots, and stood up.

Cindy, wearing underwear and a t-shirt, jumped to her feet and began stuffing her backpack.

"You may want to dress first," Laura said. "They could be on this place in minutes."

Cindy stopped stuffing and started pulling her clothes on. "Why can't we just hide out here? Lock the door and stay quiet."

Laura moved to the window, knelt, and edged the tarp to one side, enough to see. Both men were still in view and still headed south, toward the building. They were closer, but still fifty yards from the highway. If they were going to vacate the building, they would need to do it when the men were a little closer. The tops of the trees would block their view of the building.

Cindy hovered over the top of Laura, trying to see out the window. "Are they still coming?"

Laura let the tarp flop back and stood. "They are. If we're going to leave, we need to do it in about four minutes." She scurried to her pack and started stuffing.

Cindy looked around the room at their clothes and the food and utensils they had accumulated over the months. "There's no way we can carry enough of this stuff. Plus, where would we go?"

Laura stopped fiddling with her backpack, exhaled sharply, and stared at Cindy. She was right. It was already too late. The landscape around the property south, east, and west of the trees along the interstate was so barren they would surely be seen if they tried to escape. And they would be forced to leave behind practically everything they owned. With no food or water, they wouldn't last long out in the open. Laura nodded and then scooted back to the window for another look. The men were almost to the highway. Would they cross? But then, why would they not cross? This building sat pretty much alone, and only a few more yards. To not search this building would be stupid.

Jack Jenkins—wiry frame, balding, wearing blue work pants and a long sleeve shirt—was getting tired, hot, and thirsty. He and his compatriot, Fred Nolan, had separated from the main group and left them to finish the search of the last concentration of buildings on the south side of town. Fred said something about checking one additional area. Fred was considered one of the wisest men left in town, and also one of the meanest. He lost his wife and kids to the plague and had been mad about it ever since. He was a large, imposing man, quick to rile. Jack preferred to steer clear of Fred as much as possible. But when Fred asked someone to do something, it was usually hard to say no. When Fred motioned for Jack to follow, Jack followed. They had been walking south ever since. Over twenty minutes. Walking a hundred yards from each other, Jack and Fred were too far apart to talk. That was fine with Jack. He never knew what to say to him, or what might send Fred into a rage.

Fred never said where they were headed, but the interstate highway was ahead in the distance. Jack knew of a couple of properties just the other side of the highway and figured that was Fred's destination.

Jack gazed at the highway and the trees beyond. The roof of old man Simpson's two-story room, a retreat he had called it, was just visible through the tops of the trees. The house and the rest of the property, including the retreat, had been cleared of anything of value well over a year earlier. Jack figured he and Fred were probably on a wild goose chase.

"Let's finish loading the packs, just in case," Laura said, "but I guess you're right. We don't really have anywhere to go."

Cindy stopped what she was doing and stared at the door. Her bottom lip quivered. "What do we do?"

Laura tightened her jaw as she stared at Cindy. Her gaze then turned to the single oak dining chair that occupied a corner of the room. She slid the chair over to the door and wedged the back under the knob.

"Will that work?" Cindy asked. Her voice shook with fear.

Laura blinked slowly, and moved her chin subtly side-to-side.

Cindy's eyes grew moist and her hands visibly shook.

Laura put her arms around her daughter and hugged. "Everything will work out."

Cindy pushed away. "You don't know that," she said in a raised voice, as she plopped down on the sofa. "I wish dad was here."

"I wish he was here, too," Laura said. "But he's not. It's just you and me."

Cindy looked up at her mother. "What will they do with us?"

"I don't know," Laura said. But actually she did know. These were desperate times. There were no societal constraints. Many people had lost their moral compass. Laura had observed enough of the remaining town's people to know that they, especially the men, were in that category. Laura also knew she looked nearly as young as her daughter, just as attractive, in a more mature way, and just as athletic. They both would be highly desirable to a bunch of men like these; most had probably not been with a woman since the plague. Over two years. She looked back at Cindy, and then she scanned the room for anything that could be used as a weapon. There was nothing. A can of beans wasn't much of a weapon. She rummaged through her pack and came out with her knife. "You have the pocket knife. Don't be afraid to use it."

Cindy wiped a tear away, tightened her jaw, and pulled her knife from her pocket. She got up and joined her mother in front of the door.

Laura looked around again, and then pushed Cindy to the other side of the room, directly opposite the door. She would be the first thing the men saw if they busted through the door. "I want you to stand right there." Laura then flattened herself against the wall to the left side of the door. She would be behind the door when it opened. "The sight of you should stop them in their tracks. That will hopefully give me the opportunity to slash one, or both. When I do, strike out at the one nearest you."

Cindy nodded as she took a stance opposite the door and opened her knife.

Laura wanted to take another look out the window, but was afraid the men might see the tarp move. It was always possible the men would not search the room. She didn't want to give them a reason if she could help it. So she stayed put, next to the door.

Several minutes dragged by. But finally, Laura heard voices from outside. The men were on the property.

Fred, followed by Jack, exited the Simpson house. They both walked to the middle of the side yard, between the house and the two story building. Fred stopped and slowly scanned the property.

"I figured the place would be empty," Jack said. "It's too far from town. Nobody would stay here."

"Uh-huh," Fred replied, as he continued to inspect the property. His gaze landed on the concrete platform at the base of the stairs leading up to the second floor of the retreat. "Looks damp."

Jack focused on the spot and nodded. He followed Fred as he stepped closer to the building.

"The concrete's had water on it recently," Fred said. He then focused on the twenty-gallon plastic storage crate positioned under the downspout. He turned his head toward the sound of flapping. He looked toward the back of the property and focused on the brown tarp draped over something to form a small enclosure. One corner of the tarp lifted in the light breeze. He then looked up at the landing on the second floor of the building. "This is the place," he said, as he stepped off toward the stairs. He flipped the safety to off on the AR-15 semi-automatic rifle he held in both hands, glanced at Jack and then, without pausing, started up the stairs.

Jack pulled his revolver from the holster on his hip as he fell in behind Fred and followed him up the stairs. "The chief said to fire a shot if we found something."

Fred abruptly stopped and jerked his head back to Jack. "We don't need the chief. Anything here belongs to us." He then resumed his ascent.

Jack nodded and followed, without responding.

When Fred reached the top of the stairs, he quickly moved to the left side of the door. He motioned for Jack, standing on the top stair, to remain back.

Jack stepped back two steps and raised his pistol toward the door.

Fred held his rifle by the grip in his right hand, finger on the trigger, as he reached with his left hand, turned the knob, and pushed in on the door. The knob turned, but the door didn't budge. He tried again with more force. The door still did not budge. He then stepped in front of the door, raised his right boot, and slammed the sole against the door with his entire two-hundred and forty pounds of bodyweight. The door cracked in the middle, but stayed closed. He kicked again, focusing the force on the crack. The door splintered down the middle and swung open a few inches. Fred put both hands on his rifle and used the barrel to push the door completely open. He stepped into the room, where he stopped dead in his tracks.

In front of him, directly across the room, stood an attractive young woman dressed in boots, tight jeans, and an even tighter white t-shirt. But her beauty was in stark contrast to the look of horror on her face as she pressed herself against the far wall.

Fred smiled, and kept the smile, as he stepped closer. Just as he cleared the edge of the open door, he sensed movement to his right and saw a flash of metal. As quick as a snake, he released his right hand from the rifle, and caught the woman's forearm before she could complete her downward thrust. The tip of the knife stopped just two inches from his neck. He immediately twisted the arm until the knife dropped from the woman's hand. The woman was just as beautiful as the other, maybe more so. Fred pushed the woman back as he released her arm.

She had to dance to keep herself from falling, and finally came to rest against the room's north wall. She glared at Fred as he stepped farther into the room.

Fred motioned for Jack to enter and then leveled the rifle. He swung it back and forth between the two women. The barrel came to rest on the older woman as she inched along the wall until she stood next to the girl. For several moments, Fred ogled the woman's pretty face and athletic frame.

Jack's eyes went wide when he stepped into the room and saw the two women. "Looks like your intuition was right. And it looks like we hit the jackpot."

Fred nodded, pointed the rifle barrel at the younger woman's face, and then at the hand still holding a pocket knife.

She dropped the knife to the floor.

He swung the barrel back to the older woman. "Is there anyone else around?"

The woman shook her head.

"You have a name?"

The woman raised her chin and took in a deep breath. She stared back, eyes fixed. No emotion. No fear. "Laura."

He moved the barrel to the younger woman. "And her?"

"My daughter, Cindy."

Fred nodded.

"Now what?" Jack asked.

"We take them into town," Fred said. "You can come back for the rest of this stuff."

"What about the chief?" Jack asked.

"What about him?" Fred growled. "Like I said, everything here belongs to us. We found it. Including these two."

Jack tightened his lips, nodded, and lowered his chin.

Fred motioned his rifle barrel toward Cindy. "You take her." He then turned his head and stared at Laura. "I'll take this one." He shifted the rifle to one hand and grabbed Laura by the wrist with the other.

"What about the others in town," Laura asked, as Fred pulled her toward the door.

Fred paused and looked back. "You're in my custody. You don't have to worry about anybody else in town."

"What about my daughter?"

"That's up to Jack," Fred said, "as long as he can hold on to her." He snickered.

Jack tightened his lips again as he looked at Cindy. He cocked his head to one side as if to say that it would be okay. He holstered his pistol and stepped forward.

Cindy shrank back, pressing herself against the wall as Jack approached.

As Jack reached out to grasp her arm, Cindy's foot shot out, catching Jack in the groin with all the force she could muster. It apparently hit its intended target.

Jack bent forward with a sharp groan. The wind left his lungs as his knees dipped to the floor. He rolled to one side and curled up in a ball.

Cindy leapt over Jack in one fluid motion and went straight for Fred.

With both of Fred's hands occupied, he could only duck and weave in an attempt to thwart Cindy's blows and kicks.

Laura tried to pull away as she kicked and scratched, but to no avail. Fred's grip held tight around her wrist.

"Get up you asshole," Fred yelled to Jack. "Get this bitch off me."

Jack rolled back to his knees while still curled over and grimaced as he tried to stand. He got one foot flat on the floor, but then his face contorted in pain and he fell back to the floor. He then grabbed the edge of the desk and tried to pull himself up.

Cindy continued her barrage of fists and feet and then tried biting the beefy hand wrapped around Laura's wrist.

Fred, still holding Laura's arm, jerked his hand back slamming Cindy in the jaw. Though the force was much reduced because of his hold on Laura, it still knocked her back. She stood dazed for a moment before her eyes cleared and she went forward with even more determination on her face.

"Cindy," Laura yelled, "get out of here. Go hide."

Cindy jerked her head toward her mother as she resumed her kicks at Fred. "I'm not leaving you."

"I'll be okay," Laura said. "I just need for you to get out of here. I can figure something out as long as I know you're free."

Cindy stopped kicking and looked back at Jack who was still bent over, but now on both feet.

"Go now!" Laura yelled.

Cindy took a final look at her mother and then bolted out the door.

"Go after her you idiot," Fred screamed. His face turned beet red as the veins in his neck expanded. "I'll clean the floor with your ass if you let her get away," he yelled.

Jack took a step, grimaced, and stopped. He tried to raise himself upright, but his face contorted, and he bent back over at the waist. He stumbled back and came to a stop against the desk as he sucked air into his lungs.

Fred dragged Laura to the open doorway, looked outside, and then looked back at Jack. "Forget it, dumbass. She's long gone."

Jack stumbled toward the door. "I'll catch her," he mumbled.

Fred visibly relaxed and the redness in his face immediately began to subside. He glanced at Laura.

"Don't bother. She'll walk into town on her own when she gets hungry. We still have her mother."

With her hand white from lack of blood, Laura gazed out the open door as she exhaled with a sigh of relief, and worry.

Cindy glanced back at the two-story building growing smaller in the distance as she ran full bore west across an open, dry field. Her destination was a mostly dry creek bed and a line of trees another half mile ahead. Her goal was to make it to the trees and hide before either of the two men exited the building. If she could get to the trees, they would have no idea where she was, in which direction she had run.

Breathing hard, she forced herself to run faster as she glanced back every few seconds. So far, there was no sign of them. The trees were only a few more yards, and it looked like she would make it to cover. In her mind, she agonized over her mother's capture. What would they do to her? The big man was obviously delighted at the capture. Would he protect her? Would he harm her? Cindy visualized her mother beaten and raped. That's when she gritted her teeth and made up her mind to help her mother, no matter what. But it would have to wait until dark. For now, she just needed to hide and stay hidden until then.

Running as fast as she could, she entered the tree-line as she glanced over her shoulder for a final look. Looking backwards is why she didn't see the tree root protruding from the ground. The toe of her right boot slammed into the root, she stumbled as she jerked her head back around, and then crashed head-on into a large oak tree. Her body crumbled to the ground and rolled into the dry creek bed. She came to rest in a cloud of dust, out like a light.

CHAPTER 7

The sound of a crackling fire was Cindy's first sensation. The sound was distinct, but distant at first. The sound grew closer as her mind clawed up from the murky depths to the surface of consciousness. Her next sensation was a pounding headache. The worst she had ever had. Reluctant to open her eyes for fear of increasing the pain, she kept them shut as she tried to remember. What was the last thing she could recall? Searching for memories was like walking through thick smoke. Slowly, images floated forth. Her mother struggling, two men, Cindy running, and now, this moment. Her mind went back to her mother struggling and she blinked her eyes open. Pain shot through her temples and she closed her eyes again, but not before she caught a glimpse of darkness, a fire, and a man.

Then she heard a man's voice. "Looks like you might live after all."

Cindy opened her eyes again, winced, and immediately raised a hand to her head. She felt a wet cloth draped over her forehead. Through the cloth, she could feel a goose egg at the hairline. She turned her head slightly and tried to focus on the man kneeling beside her. An image of the two men and her mother struggling popped into her mind and she immediately recoiled. She raised both hands as if to protect herself.

"It's okay," the man said. "I'm not going to hurt you. I found you this way."

Cindy focused on the man's face and realized he was neither of the ones who accosted her and her mother. She relaxed a little. "Where am I? Who are you?"

"Leroy. Leroy Tubbs. And you?"

Cindy stared at the man's face, his clothes, then back to his eyes. He wasn't like the other two. For one, he wore a uniform. Camouflaged, like the army. For another, he looked genuinely concerned. "Are you in the army?"

"I was," Leroy said. He thought for a second. "Actually, I guess I still am, sort of."

"Are there more of you?"

"Nope," Leroy said. "Just me. I can explain if you'll give me your name."

"Cindy Wilson."

Leroy stuck out his hand. "Hello, Cindy Wilson, I'm Leroy."

Hesitantly, Cindy took Leroy's hand. "How did I get here?"

"Don't know. I found you in a heap at the bottom of the creek bed. You were out cold, with a nasty bruise on your forehead."

"I ran into a tree," Cindy said, as she tried to sit upright. She winced, massaged her temple, and caught the wet cloth as it dropped from her head. She continued until she was sitting straight. She looked around and realized she was sitting on a brown tarp.

"Why did you run into a tree?"

"I was running from two men." Her eyes went wide as she remembered her mother's predicament. "They have my mother," she said in a raised voice.

"Where?"

"In town. Sayre." She pointed to the northeast. "That way, less than two miles." She tried to get to her feet, but pain shooting through her temples forced her back to her former sitting position on the tarp. She relaxed as she massaged her head. "I have to help her."

"You have to help yourself first," Leroy said. "You could have a concussion."

"Concussion or not, I still have to help my mother."

"What's your mother's name?"

"Laura."

"Was she okay the last time you saw her?"

"No, well yes. Yes and no."

Leroy flexed his shoulders and massaged his neck.

"The two men busted in on us. I escaped. She couldn't get away. They would have taken her into town. She's not safe there. They could be—" Cindy dropped her chin toward the ground and closed her eyes. When she opened her eyes, they were moist. "I need to go."

Leroy pulled a water bottle from the satchel on his hip, twisted the cap off, and extended the bottle toward Cindy. "You need to drink some water."

Cindy hesitated, looked into Leroy's eyes, and took the bottle. She sipped first and then took a long swig. She wiped her mouth as she handed the bottle back to Leroy.

"Are you feeling dizzy or nauseous?"

"No," Cindy said. "I'm feeling like I need to help my mother."

"Okay, I get that. Can you start at the beginning and tell me what happened?"

"Rather than talking, I need to be going," she said, as she looked around at the darkness. "How long was I out?"

"I found you a couple of hours ago, well before dark."

"I need to go."

Leroy took a seat on a nearby log. "Suit yourself," he said, as he motioned with his chin in the direction of town.

Cindy got to her feet, wobbled a bit, and reached out for a small sapling. She massaged her temple.

"Just out of curiosity, how do you plan to go about helping your mother?" Leroy asked. "How many men would be holding her in town?"

Cindy tightened her grip on the sapling. "Ten or so."

"Armed?"

Cindy nodded and took a seat back on the tarp. She stuck out her hand for the water bottle.

Leroy handed her the bottle and then raised his eyebrows, inviting her to talk.

She took another long swig and then sat the bottle beside her on the tarp. She took a deep breath and exhaled. "From the beginning? The very beginning?"

"Sure, if you want," Leroy said.

Cindy felt her forehead. She wet the cloth with some water from the bottle and held the cloth against the egg. "We lost my dad and my older brother to the plague two years ago. We lived in Los Angeles at the time. We hung around several months and were able to make do with the help of neighbors, but with all the turmoil, we decided to head east to Albuquerque. My mother had a sister living there. We had saved up gas for the car."

"How did you end up in this place?"

"We never did find my aunt. Albuquerque was just as bad as LA, so we drove east until we ran out of gas. We walked for days, until we ran out of food. We took up residence in a small building over there." She pointed. "We have been there, raiding the town at night for food and water, for the last year."

"And the people in town let you get away with that?"

"We went out only at night. We were fast and quiet. We took only what we needed. Everything was fine, until today."

"How many men did you say?"

"There's a group of about ten who are the most active. There are other people in town, but they are rather docile."

"Where in town would they have taken your mother?"

"I don't know for sure. The sheriff's office has been completely vacant. But there's still been some activity around the police department. These men seem to hang out there. That would be my guess."

"Any of the men wear a uniform?"

"No uniforms. But there's one who wears a cap with an embroidered badge. About your size, maybe a little taller."

"He's the one who took your mother?"

"No, he wasn't there," she said. "Two other men, one thin and wiry, the other was much bigger."

"Okay," Leroy said. "I don't see any problem with checking things out… from a distance."

"You're willing to help?"

"I'm willing to check things out."

Cindy nodded as she tightened her lips and exhaled. She glanced around at the dark clumps of brush and trees. "This streambed goes almost to the west side of town. Less than two miles."

"How are you feeling?"

Cindy used the sapling to pull herself up. She blinked a few times and rubbed the egg on her forehead. "Headache, but not as bad as before." She handed the cloth back to Leroy.

"You really should rest a while longer," Leroy said.

"I can't rest. There's no telling what they're doing to my mother."

Leroy nodded and stood. He rolled up the tarp, strapped it to his backpack, and kicked sand on the fire until it was out. He slung the pack over his shoulders and looked at Cindy. "Lead the way."

"Do you intend to just leave her in that cell?" Gentry asked, as he stood facing Fred in the middle of the police department lockup. The room included two cells. Laura sat on a bunk in one of them. Eight other men, including Jack, sat or stood around the room listening.

"Yeah, until I catch her daughter," Fred said in a stern voice.

"Why?" Gentry asked. "She won't be raiding the town anymore. What's the point in keeping her locked up?"

Fred glanced at Laura and then looked back to Gentry. "I caught her. I get to decide what I do with her."

Gentry rubbed his face and looked around at the other men. Of the men in the room, he felt like he could count on four of them for support when it came to dealing with Fred. Three of them would be neutral. Only one would definitely be on Fred's side if it came to blows. Gentry didn't want it to come to blows, not with Fred. He could be explosive. There was no telling what he would do, at the least little provocation. He looked back to Fred. "I say we invite her to stay if she wants, and let her go if she doesn't. She would be free to move on or stay."

"And I say it's not up to her, or to you," Fred said. "I plan to look for the daughter at first light. I'll decide what to do with them both when I find her."

"Until then, the woman stays here under my protection," Gentry said.

"Fine. Just make sure she stays here until I say otherwise."

Gentry nodded. "She'll be here for tonight."

"So will I," Gentry said. He turned to Jack. "Did you get their stuff from Simpson's place?"

"Most of it," Jack said, as he pointed to a couple of backpacks in the corner of the room. "The only stuff still there is the bed linens, some utensils, and a few cans of food."

"I said to get it all," Fred said in a gruff voice.

"It can wait til tomorrow," Gentry intervened.

Fred turned to Gentry. "I told him I wanted it all here tonight."

Gentry took a step closer to Fred. "You're not in charge here."

Fred took a long pause and stared at Gentry. "We'll see," Fred said, as he shot a look at Jack.

Jack got up and walked toward the hall.

"And if the girl's back there, don't lose her this time," Fred said.

Jack nodded as he entered the hall and disappeared into the darkness.

Fred stared at Gentry for several long seconds and then walked over to an old sofa against one wall. He reclined on the sofa and closed his eyes.

Gentry shook his head, looked around the room at the other men, and then raised his shoulders. He flicked his hands in the air.

Without saying anything, the men began to file out of the room.

Leroy stood next to Cindy in the dark shadows behind a double-trunk pine tree. The tree was next to a tan, brick, two-story house directly across the street from the Sayre, Oklahoma, police department building. It was a one-story, red brick structure with no windows. There was just a single glass door on the front of the building. Dull light flickered from inside. He watched as eight men filed out the front door and dispersed in various directions.

"I think you were right," he whispered. "This is where they have her." He glanced at Cindy and saw her nod, barely visible in the darkness. "That big man you mentioned, is he among those men?"

Cindy studied the men as they walked away. The stars provided enough light to make out the men's general size and shape. She pointed. "There's the skinny guy, out front. The big man isn't with them. And neither is the one who wears the cap and badge.

"Possibly two men left behind," Leroy whispered. He exhaled sharply. "This might be our best chance."

"Best chance for what?" Cindy asked.

"I thought you wanted your mother back," Leroy said.

"They have guns," Cindy said. "I don't want her shot."

"She's your mother," Leroy said, as he looked at Cindy. "But like I said, this might be our best chance. They're not expecting you to show up here. And they're sure as hell not expecting me."

"So we just walk in the front door?" Cindy asked.

"Maybe, but first I want to check on a back door." Leroy stepped from behind the tree, scanned up and down the street, and then motioned for Cindy to follow.

Leroy, followed closely by Cindy, sprinted across the four-lane street and slowed to a trot when he reached the right side of the building. Again, there were no windows, but two-thirds of the way down the side of the building there were two roll-up metal cargo doors with a single pedestrian door between them. Both the cargo doors and the pedestrian door included glass windows. Leroy stopped at the edge of the first roll-up door, flattened himself against the red brick wall, and carefully peered through the glass. Starlight glinted off the bumper of a truck parked in the bay behind the door, but otherwise, the area was dark. He guessed the area behind the doors amounted to a garage for two vehicles. The garage would be situated behind the office and reception areas of the police department.

Leroy pulled his head back from the glass and glanced at Cindy, who was next to him and also flat against the wall. Leroy then ducked under the glass windows of the metal door and tiptoed to the center pedestrian door. He twisted the knob and pulled slightly, enough to tell that the door was not locked. He turned his head toward Cindy. "Wait here. I'll be back in a flash."

He saw the outline of Cindy's chin nod up and down in the dark.

Leroy pulled the door open and stepped inside the garage between two vehicles, a pickup truck on the left and a car, behind the second bay door, on the right. He stepped quietly to the rear of the two vehicles and turned toward the office part of the building. On the west side of the garage he found a single pedestrian door. He twisted the knob and pulled the door open a hair, confirming that it, too, was not locked.

Leroy returned to the outer door, stepped outside, and motioned Cindy toward the front of the building. He stopped in the center of the wall and turned back, face to face with Cindy. "I want you to turn yourself in," he whispered.

"What?"

"You go in the front door and back to wherever they are," Leroy said. "Keep their attention on you. I'll come in from the rear."

"And then what?"

"We get your mother and leave."

"They'll just let us walk out?"

"I'll figure something out," Leroy said. "This is your best chance, but I'll leave it up to you."

Cindy paused for a moment and then looked at Leroy. "If you change your mind, or somehow get tripped up, I'll be stuck."

"True," Leroy said. "There's a risk. There's always a risk. But I won't change my mind. I'll do my best to do what I say I'll do."

Cindy nodded. "Okay."

"Count to sixty and then walk in like you intend to surrender. That should give me enough time to get in position."

"Okay," she said. She then turned and headed toward the front of the building.

Leroy returned to the pedestrian door and entered.

◆◆◆

Cindy reached the front door and stopped. *What am I doing? I don't even know this guy.* But then, what choice did she have? There was no way she could take on even one man, much less ten men. She had no food, water, or even clothes, and she had nowhere to go. Even if she did have a place to go, her mother would be left to the mercy of these men. She could already be in dire straits. She had only one option. She had to trust Leroy. Trust that he wouldn't change his mind, and trust that he knew what he was doing.

Cindy pulled on the glass door and stepped into the practically pitch dark that turned out to be a reception area. A dull light flickered from down a hallway that apparently led back to the offices, and hopefully, her mother. Cindy had forgotten to count to sixty, but she figured it had been about two minutes. She crept to the hallway entrance and stopped. It was then she realized she was breathing hard and her hands were shaking. She took a deep breath and, as quietly as possible, exhaled. She closed her eyes and tried to focus. In her mind's eye she saw herself entering the back area and seeing the two men. She saw them see her. She tried to imagine their reaction, but came up empty. She had no idea what was about to happen. She just hoped her mother was here and Leroy was in position.

She could see a little more light, flickering, from what appeared to be a room at the end of the ten-foot-long hall. There was one door, presumably to an office, on each side of the hall, about midway. Both doors were closed.

Using just the balls of her feet, she kept her approach down the hall completely silent. She didn't want a heel strike to give them advance warning. Her mother would be proud of her stealth. About four feet from the end of the hall she heard a snore and then steady breathing, as though someone was asleep. Then she heard the creak of a chair. At the end of the hall she was able to survey the room. There were two cells composed of metal bars occupying one end of the room. From her angle she could only see the entire inside of one of the cells, the one on the right. It was empty. The other end of the room included a sofa, several chairs, and a desk. A man sat at the desk with his back to her. A candle on the desk flickered. A second man appeared to be asleep on the sofa. Between the cells and the two men was the entrance to another hall, completely dark. There was no sign of Leroy.

Cindy took one more step, leaned her head just past the corner, and peered to the left. Her mother lay flat on her back on a bunk inside the left cell. Cindy couldn't tell if she was asleep, but she doubted it. Her mother had trouble sleeping in the best of circumstances.

It was just as they had hoped: her mother guarded by only two men. The best situation possible, given the circumstances. That could all change if anyone else came in the front door. Cindy wondered about the eight men she saw leaving. Where were they going? Would any of them be coming back tonight? It was then Cindy decided she had to go all in.

CHAPTER 8

Cindy took another step, which put her completely inside the room. She glanced from her mother in the cell, to the two men at the other end of the room. There was no reaction from any of them. The one man was still asleep on the sofa, and the other was fiddling with something at his desk. She looked down the hall on the far wall, into the darkness, but could not make out any sign of Leroy.

Cindy took in a deep breath, and as loud as she could she yelled, "Hey!"

The sudden noise got a definite reaction. The man in the chair shot up about three inches. The man on the sofa practically choked on his tongue. And her mother bolted up, obviously surprised to hear her daughter's voice.

The man in the chair was the first to get to his feet. He spun around. His hand stopped at the butt of his pistol in the holster on his hip when he saw Cindy.

The man on the sofa snorted a couple of times and cocked his head to the side. He slowly got to a sitting position.

"What are you doing here?" Laura asked in a high-pitched voice.

Cindy took several steps toward the cell. "I want my mother," she said in a stern voice.

The two men did just as she had hoped. The man on the sofa got to his feet, and they both took several steps toward Cindy.

"I'm wondering the same thing," the man wearing the ball cap with the gold badge, said.

Cindy backed closer to the cell holding her mother. As she did so, she noticed a black rifle leaning against the corner at the end of the sofa. With a girl such as Cindy, unarmed, the big man who took her mother obviously saw no need for the rifle.

"Like I said, I came for my mother," Cindy said in a calm voice, as she backed completely to the cell. She pulled on the door, but found it locked. "Which one of you assholes has the key?"

Both men looked at each other and then took several more steps. They stopped just past the entrance to the dark hallway.

"You saved me a lot of trouble by coming here," the big man said. He took two more steps forward.

Cindy saw Leroy step from the hallway and take a position behind the men. The man with the cap pivoted, apparently catching or hearing the movement.

Then the bigger man spun around and froze.

Leroy pointed a large black pistol at the two men. He motioned the barrel toward the man with the ball cap. "Two fingers," Leroy said. "Remove it slowly, place it on the floor, and slide it with your foot toward me."

"I'm the police chief of this town," the man with the ball cap said. "Chief Gentry. This is Fred Baker, one of my officers."

Leroy motioned the barrel of his pistol toward the man's holstered gun. "I won't ask again."

"You're committing a crime," Gentry said.

Leroy focused on the man's eyes and extended the pistol slightly.

Gentry reached with his thumb and index finger, removed the gun by the handle, a Glock 17 just like Leroy's, and bent down as he placed it on the ceramic tile floor. With his foot, he slid it toward Leroy.

"Like the lady said, who has the key?" Leroy asked.

"We have more men due back here any minute," Fred said. "Lower your weapon and we'll discuss this in a civilized manner."

"Nothing to discuss," Leroy said. "You have her mother locked up. We want her. If you don't produce the key in about ten seconds, I'll shoot you both and look for the key on my own."

"What about our men," Fred said. "They should be walking in the door right about now."

Leroy glanced at the rifle in the corner and then looked back at Gentry and Fred. "Eight men not expecting me here with your rifle."

Fred looked at Gentry.

Gentry looked at Fred, pursed his lips, and nodded. "The key is in that desk. Center drawer."

"Get it," Leroy said, as he motioned with his gun.

Gentry put both hands in the air, shoulder height, as he walked past Leroy.

Leroy backed away a few steps so he could cover Gentry and Fred.

Gentry opened the drawer, removed a key, and extended it toward Leroy.

Leroy lowered his chin and raised an eyebrow at Gentry.

Gentry nodded, raised both hands again, shuffled to the cell, and unlocked the door. He swung the metal-barred door open.

Cindy hugged her mother as she stepped from the cell. "This is Leroy," she whispered.

Laura separated from Cindy, smiled at Leroy, and walked toward him, past Gentry and Fred. She went straight for Gentry's pistol and picked it up from the floor. She glanced at the slide as she backed away from Leroy, toward the sofa. She then raised the pistol and pointed it at Leroy.

Leroy glanced back at Laura and saw her pointing the gun at him. He inhaled and exhaled deeply.

"Mom!" Cindy screamed. "What are you doing? He's helping us."

"We don't know him," Laura said, "and we don't know if he's helping us or helping himself." She motioned her pistol toward Leroy. "Place the gun on the desk."

"You're doing the right thing," Fred said, as he took a step toward Leroy.

Laura pivoted, took a second handhold on her pistol, raised the barrel, and took aim at Fred. "Stay exactly where you are. Better yet, you and Chief Gentry step into that open cell."

Fred hesitated, glanced at Gentry, and then back to Laura.

Laura motioned with the gun. "Now," she said, as she cocked her head slightly to one side.

Fred shrugged his shoulders and followed Gentry into the cell.

"Cindy, close and lock the cell," Laura said, as she swung the gun back to Leroy.

Cindy did as she was told. She kept the key in her hand.

"You look like you know what you're doing with that thing," Leroy said, as he sauntered to the desk. He laid the gun down and then turned back to Laura. "Now what?"

Cindy ran to her mother. "Mom, he helped us. If he had intended anything else, he could have had me back in the trees. He didn't have to risk himself to get you out of jail."

Laura kept her eyes, and the gun, trained on Leroy. "You just happened to come along?"

"Yep," Leroy said.

Laura looked up and down at his uniform. "Are you in the military?"

"He explained all that to me on the way here," Cindy said. "He was stationed in California. He lost his wife and two kids to the plague. He was headed east when he came upon me. I was out cold. A tree got in my way. He helped me, and agreed to help you."

"Where are you from?" Laura asked Leroy.

"Mom!"

"It's okay," Leroy said. "She's just trying to protect you." He looked at Laura. "Originally? I was born in Ohio, but I've lived all over, including St. Louis and California."

Laura stared at Leroy for several long seconds and then at her daughter.

"I think he's okay, Mom," Cindy pleaded.

"I wouldn't trust him in these times," Fred said from the jail cell. "He could have killed a real soldier and took his uniform."

"That's true," Leroy said in a calm voice. "But I didn't. I have a military ID to prove it."

"Let me see," Laura said.

Leroy reached into a back pocket, produced a leather wallet, and flipped it open to reveal a US Army military ID card. He extended the wallet to Cindy, who handed it to her mother.

Laura read the card. *SGM Tubbs, Leroy L.* "What does SGM stand for?"

"Sergeant Major. I joined when I was twenty-two."

Laura took the card out and flipped it over. "According to this, you're forty-eight."

Leroy nodded. "About time for me to retire," he said, as he removed his boonie hat and smoothed his still-thick brown hair.

Laura replaced the card and then flipped the middle section of the trifold over. The other side, behind clear plastic, revealed a photo of a woman and two girls, both about Cindy's age. She closed the wallet and handed it back to Leroy as she lowered the pistol. "Sorry."

"No need to apologize," Leroy said. "Like the man said, these are rough times."

"We need to get out of here," Cindy said.

Laura looked at the two backpacks on the floor next to the desk and a small pile of clothes and a few cans of food. She stepped to the packs. "Let's get this stuff packed," she said, as she knelt. She put Gentry's pistol on the desk.

Cindy joined her and placed the key to the cell on the desk. They knelt and began stuffing items into the packs.

Leroy retrieved his pistol and walked over to the cell holding Fred and Gentry. He pointed the gun toward Gentry. "Remove the holster."

"I'm not going to do that," Gentry said. "I don't believe you'll kill a man over a holster."

"We're taking the pistol," Leroy said. "You don't need the holster."

"I can get another Glock," Gentry said. "I can't get another holster."

Leroy nodded. "Fair enough," he said, as he holstered his own gun, turned, and walked to the other end of the room. He picked up the rifle from the corner and turned the rifle in his hand, examining the action and components. *Daniel Defense AR15 M4 with quad rails and iron sights.* "Nice rifle." He removed the thirty-two-round magazine, pressed on the top of the cartridges, and then reinserted the mag into the magazine well until it clicked. "I'm taking the rifle."

"That's my rifle," Fred said in a raised voice.

"Uh-huh, and I don't have to shoot you to take it," Leroy said. "You should be happy about that." The corners of his mouth turned up slightly.

Fred gripped the bars of the cell with both hands. His knuckles turned white.

Leroy then went to the desk and opened all the drawers. He found several boxes of ammunition. "I'm taking the 9mm and the 5.56, as well."

Gentry shook his head and took a seat on the bunk.

Just as Laura and Cindy lifted their packs, the sound of the front door closing and footsteps echoed from down the hall.

"That will be my men returning," Gentry said with a smile.

Leroy flipped the safety on the rifle and motioned for Laura and Cindy to move away from the hallway opening. Leroy stepped to one side.

The footsteps grew closer.

"There's a man in here with a gun," Fred yelled.

At that same moment, a slender man with both arms full of blankets and tarps stepped from the hall and into the light. He froze when he saw Leroy and then dropped the bundle on the floor. He moved his hand toward the revolver in its holster on his hip.

Leroy pointed the rifle barrel at the man's face. "Don't."

The slender man raised both hands as he glanced around the room.

"Thumb and index, remove the pistol and place it on the floor," Leroy said, as he motioned with the rifle.

"Jack, you dumbass," Fred yelled.

Jack dropped his chin, removed the revolver, and placed it on the floor.

Leroy motioned toward the cells with the rifle. "Join your friends."

Jack started moving in that direction.

"Anyone behind you, Jack?" Leroy asked.

"No," Jack said.

"Dammit, Jack!" Fred yelled from the cell.

Leroy grabbed the key from the desk and glanced at Laura as he followed Jack. "Keep them covered while I open the door. If anyone comes out before he goes in, shoot them."

Laura picked up the Glock from the desk, assumed a shooting position with both hands, and stepped toward the cell.

Leroy unlocked the door, pushed Jack inside, and closed and locked the door. He returned the key to the desk. He glanced at the pile on the floor as he retrieved the revolver. "Do you need any of this stuff?"

"The tarps and blankets," Laura said. She motioned to Cindy.

They each rolled two blankets inside of a blue tarp and strapped the bundle to the bottom of each of their packs.

Leroy stuffed the revolver inside his waist band, picked up the six cans of food from the floor, and held them with one arm against his abdomen. He stood up with the food in one arm and the rifle in the other hand. He sat the food on the desk. He looked at Laura and Cindy. "If you still have room, let's take the food."

Leroy opened the cylinder of the revolver and examined the five rounds it contained. "Any more ammo?" he asked, as he looked at Jack inside the cell.

"No," Jack replied.

Gentry shoved Jack on the shoulder, pushing him into the bars. "Who carries a five-shot thirty-eight with no extra ammo?"

Leroy looked at Cindy. "Ever use one of these?"

"I know how to shoot," Cindy said, as she took the revolver from his hand. She tossed the revolver inside her pack and hefted the pack over her shoulders. She pulled at the shoulder straps and jumped up to position the weight.

"Are you alright with all that?" Leroy asked.

"I'll manage," she said.

Laura lifted her backpack over her shoulders and went through the same routine to position the weight. "I think we're ready," she said, as she headed for the front hallway.

"This way," Leroy said, as he stepped toward the back hallway. He grabbed the key to the cells and two one-gallon jugs of water from the desk as he passed by.

Cindy and Laura fell in behind Leroy as he headed toward the garage.

Leroy glanced a final time at Jack, Gentry, and Fred, all three with both hands on the bars, staring at him.

Leroy hurried through the open door leading into the garage, maneuvered around various items of equipment, and stopped between the two vehicles. He threw the key into the darkness of the far corner and heard it hit the wall, then clang to the floor. He placed the rifle and the jugs of water on the hood of the car and retrieved his pack from the concrete floor. "I wonder if one of these runs?" he asked as he hefted the pack to his back. He opened the door to the sedan and felt in the dark for keys in the ignition. There were none. He then opened the passenger door of the pickup truck, reached over, and felt for the ignition. "Bingo," he said. He turned the key.

The engine turned over several times and then fired to a rough idle.

"Damn," he said, as he swung the pack off and threw it in the back of the truck. "Ladies, I believe we have a ride."

As Laura and Cindy removed their packs and put them in the truck's bed, Leroy darted to the bay door and searched for the chain usually on most of those type doors for opening and closing. He wrapped his hands around the chain dangling to one side and pulled.

The door went up a few inches.

He pulled hand over hand until the door was completely up. He then retrieved the rifle and jugs of water, walked around the front of the truck, opened the door, and slid behind the wheel. Laura and Cindy got in on the passenger's side. He put the water on the passenger side floor and leaned the rifle against the seat, barrel pointed at the floor. He put the truck in drive and pulled out, without turning the lights on. He let the truck roll the few feet to the road. "Which way?"

"Left," Laura said. "At the third intersection, turn right. Follow that to Main Street and then left out to the Interstate. Presuming you're still headed east."

"I am," he said, as he turned the wheel and accelerated.

"How is this truck still running when so many others are not?" Cindy asked.

"They must have treated their gasoline with an extender, but even with that, I'm surprised it runs after this much time," Leroy said. "By the way, I presume you two are headed east, as well?"

Laura leaned forward from the right side of the bench seat and looked past Cindy in the middle. "We are."

When the truck turned on the Interstate and they were heading east, Leroy glanced through the rear window behind him. He saw no one on his tail. He increased his speed, cruised several miles in the dark, and then switched on the lights. The dash lit up and he read the gas gauge. "We have a hair more than three quarters of a tank," he said. "That should get us well past Oklahoma City. Couple of hours."

"Should we look for more gas?"

"I think the chance of finding gas that still works is about slim and none," Leroy said. "I say we drive as far as possible on what we have. We'll have to walk from there."

"I agree," Laura said, as she placed her head back against the head rest. "I'm just glad to be out of that cell." She raised her head and looked at Cindy and then Leroy. "Thank you both."

"Your daughter refused to let you remain there even one night," Leroy said. "Determined."

Laura returned her head to the head rest. "Don't I know it."

CHAPTER 9

"I think we should stop for the night," Leroy said. "None of us have eaten."

The sudden sound of Leroy's voice brought Laura to consciousness, sure she had only just closed her eyes. She lifted her head from the headrest and looked at Leroy behind the wheel. "How long was I out?"

"Probably over two hours," Cindy said, as she shifted in the seat between Leroy and Laura.

"We're through Oklahoma City?" Laura asked.

"Fifteen minutes ago," Leroy said. "No problems. The interstate was empty."

"Can we make it through Shawnee?" Cindy asked, as she studied Leroy's partially unfolded roadmap with the help of the overhead dome light.

Leroy glanced at Cindy's finger on the map and then at the dash. "Sure."

"Past the North Canadian River, the other side of Shawnee, it's fairly open," Cindy said.

"The bridge should be coming up," Leroy said.

Laura and Cindy looked out the side windows as they approached and crossed the bridge. There wasn't much to see in the dark.

Cindy returned her attention to the map. "There's an exit two miles up."

Leroy nodded. Five minutes later, he exited down the ramp and stopped at the crossroad.

"The truck stop," Laura said, as she pointed at the dark facility in front of them, on the right. "Looks deserted."

Leroy turned his head in every direction and studied the shadows and glints of the truck stop. He examined every detail of the two tractor-trailer rigs and several cars in the large parking lot. And he paid particular attention to the main building, its dark windows and doors.

"I would be surprised if anyone was here," Laura said. "This is so far away from everything." She swiveled her head to look in all directions. "There are no other facilities around."

Leroy stepped on the gas and let the truck roll across the road and into the lot. He let the truck creep along in a wide circle that took them past the trucks, cars, and the building. "Like the lady said, looks deserted." He pulled the pickup behind one of the tractor-trailer rigs so they would be blocked from view from every direction except the trees and brush behind the main building. He cut the engine and listened to the quiet. Soon, he perceived the night noises around the area, mostly crickets. He opened the door and stepped out.

Laura and Cindy slid from the seat, out the passenger door, and joined Leroy in front of the truck.

"This world sure seems much lonelier now," Laura said, as she stared into the darkness across the parking lot.

"Except for a few conveniences," Leroy said, "we've returned to the way it was hundreds of years ago, when there were a lot fewer people."

"We need to eat," Cindy said, as she stepped off toward the back of the truck.

"Let's skip a fire," Leroy said, as he fell in behind her. "I have a small backpack stove."

A half hour later the three of them sat in the dark, reclined in the bed of the truck. Each held a small aluminum camp plate topped with a black-eyed pea and canned tuna concoction, which they were spooning into their respective mouths.

Laura chewed and swallowed a mouthful and took a swig of water from a plastic bottle. "Why were you traveling east?" Laura asked Leroy.

"Before I left California, months ago, there was a rumor of efforts back east to reestablish some level of government. If true, I figured the military would be part of the effort and I might be able to help. There was nothing keeping me in California, so I headed east."

"Where?"

"The rumor didn't say. But I do know that the fall back position for the executive branch is Mount Weather, in Virginia. For the Joint Chiefs of Staff, it's Raven Rock in Pennsylvania. Both are underground facilities."

"The president died early from the plague," Cindy said.

"True," Leroy said. "But there's a line of succession starting with the VP, the speaker, president pro tem of the senate, and the cabinet officers."

"And if all of those people are dead?" Laura asked.

"The military had the guns," Leroy said. "There must be a general, colonel, or second lieutenant still alive somewhere."

"So you're headed for Virginia then?" Cindy asked.

Leroy took a bite, chewed, and swallowed. "Generally, I guess. I was hoping to get better information as I moved east."

"That could take months," Laura said.

"Yeah." Leroy nodded. "I don't have anything better to do. What about you guys?"

Laura placed her empty plate on the truck bed next to her outstretched bare legs. "We were just trying to get away from the big city. There was nothing to stop for in the desert, so we kept moving until we found that place in Sayre."

"What do you plan to do now?" Leroy asked.

"I recommend we hang together," Cindy said. She looked at Leroy. "If you don't mind."

Laura looked at Leroy without saying anything. His features were barely visible in the dark, but she could make out his eyes. They were looking at her.

After an awkward pause of a few seconds, Leroy shifted his eyes to Cindy. "I don't have a problem with that."

"How much fuel is left in the tank?" Laura asked.

"Between a quarter and half," Leroy said. "Another hundred miles or so. We walk after that."

"Stay on the interstate?" Cindy asked.

"I've found it safer to walk a half mile or so off the road." Leroy said.

"Slower that way," Laura said.

"But safer," Leroy countered.

Laura nodded as she picked up her plate. "We need to organize our packs in the morning," she said to Cindy. "They need to be as light as possible."

Cindy stood, holding her plate and jumped over the side of the truck to the ground. "Where are we sleeping?"

Laura swiveled her head, peering into the dark.

"I recommend the back of this truck," Leroy said. "I have a tent I can set up over there in the grass."

"That works," Laura said, as she stood up.

◆◆◆

The next morning, Laura and Cindy sorted through the items dumped from their packs and were prioritizing what they needed and what they could do without.

Laura laid out a couple of t-shirts, two pair of shorts, and two pair of jeans, one black and one blue, along with underwear, socks, two sports tops, and the puffy jacket. She placed her cap on top of the pile. "Some clothes, but mostly food and water," she said.

Cindy set aside similar clothes and began sorting the cans of food and water, dividing the weight up evenly. She glanced at Laura. "So what do you think of Leroy?"

Laura glanced at Leroy in the distance, folding his tent. "Seems capable."

"That's it?" Cindy asked. "He basically saved our lives."

"Too early to tell," Laura said. "Seems okay. We'll see."

"He reminds me of Dad," Cindy said.

Laura glanced at Leroy again. "He's nothing like your father. Your father was much younger."

"Leroy's not that much older than you," Cindy said. She glanced at Leroy. "I like him."

"He's way too old for you," Laura said.

"Not that way," Cindy said. "I'm just glad I ran into him."

"As I understand it, you ran into a tree," Laura said. "He found you."

"Okay, whatever. I'm glad he's here."

Laura looked at Leroy again and watched as he attached the tent to the bottom of his pack. "Wish we had a tent like that, mosquitoes kept me awake a lot of the night."

"There's room for two in there," Cindy said with a smile.

"Uh-huh," Laura said, as she started stuffing items into her pack.

"How's it coming?" Leroy asked, as he approached the truck. He lifted his backpack and placed it in the truck's bed.

"Almost done," Laura said. "We don't have enough food to get very far."

"We'll scavenge along the way," Leroy said. "Hunt, if we have to."

Cindy picked up the road map, unfolded it, and spread it out on the truck bed. "We're about out of map. It only goes to the east side of Oklahoma. Fort Smith, Arkansas is right on the edge."

"How far is Fort Smith?" Leroy asked.

Cindy studied the map a few moments. "Looks like just over a hundred miles or so."

"We should be able to make it that far with the truck," he said. "The interstate skirts the northern edge of the city. There are plenty of communities and houses up that way. We can hole up a couple of days while we re-provision."

With all essentials in her pack, except for Gentry's Glock, Laura zipped the pack closed and jumped out of the truck with the pistol in her hand.

"Wish I could have gotten that holster for you," Leroy said.

"Gentry was right, it wasn't worth killing for," Laura said. "I'll manage." She looked at Cindy. "Where's the revolver?"

"In my pack," Cindy said. "I can get to it if needed."

Laura nodded and looked at Leroy. "We're ready."

The three of them hopped in the cab in the same configuration as before with Leroy driving, Laura on the passenger side, and Cindy in the middle. She wrapped her legs around the rifle, which was again barrel down.

Leroy started the truck, pulled out, and accelerated up the on-ramp to the highway.

As they cruised along the empty highway, with only a few stalled cars along the side, no people, Laura gazed out the side window. She was amazed how, in only a few miles, the landscape had turned from mostly brown low scrub to much greener brush and trees. She examined the terrain, the hills and gulley that would eventually turn to mountains and valleys as they continued east. She wondered how the three of them would ever be able to walk to Virginia. And to make matters worse, soon summer would be over; fall and winter would be cold. There would be snow, especially in the mountains of Tennessee and Virginia. She glanced at her brown, mostly nylon, mesh hiking boots and wondered how they would fare in the ice and snow. She thought of her single puffy jacket. Maybe they should just find a place and hole up for the cold months. Maybe they should head for Florida instead of Virginia. How would that sit with Leroy? Her mind turned to Leroy. Two women alone with a strange man. He seemed nice enough. And she liked the way he handled himself in Sayre. He was strong and determined, but he had a heart. The fact that he had lasted twenty-six years in the army, promoted along the way, said a lot about his character. He was different from her late husband. Dave was smart, more the office type. Sophisticated. He was a good provider, and he made her laugh. She wasn't sure he could ever be replaced. Plus, he was Cindy's father. She thought back to Cindy's suggestion that the tent was big enough for two. Had she gotten over her father's death after less than two years? They had been inseparable. How would she feel if her mother hooked up with another man? The question had not even entered her mind until now. Until Leroy. He was certainly handsome enough. Athletic. He displayed some patience. Cindy was obviously infatuated. Laura brought her mind back to reality. She watched the trees and hills pass by as she gazed out the window. They needed to get to where they were going without starving or getting killed by marauders. But she had to admit, she felt a little safer with Leroy around.

"What did you do in the army?" Laura asked.

"A little of everything, from ranger to first sergeant."

"First sergeant?" Cindy asked.

"Mostly admin, keeping the troops organized and on task," Leroy said. "What about you guys?"

"I graduated from high school, worked a small job, and was thinking about college when the plague hit," Cindy said. "Dad got sick and here we are."

"Laura?" Leroy asked.

"Personal trainer."

"Mom was on television," Cindy said. "She competed in the American Ninja competition. She slipped in the final round."

"I'm impressed," Leroy said.

"That was ten years ago. I was in better shape then."

"Uh-huh," Leroy said.

"She's being modest," Cindy said. "She could probably kick your butt."

"No doubt," Leroy said.

"Where did you learn to shoot?"

"My dad," Laura said. "He had a ton of guns. He started taking me to the range when I was in my early teens."

"Where was that?"

"Texas, near Dallas," Laura said. "We moved to California when I finished high school. Went to college in LA. I started out in nursing, but switched to health fitness. I met my husband there."

They entered the outskirts of Fort Smith and continued along the interstate around the north side.

Leroy glanced at the gas gauge and began looking for a good place to stop. He saw a number of commercial buildings and some residential communities. There were very few people. Those few he did see, gawked at the truck as though they had never seen one.

With the gas needle on empty he figured there couldn't be more than a gallon of gas left in the tank, probably less. He decided to turn off and find a place to hole up before the truck ran completely out.

He scanned the road ahead until his eyes locked on two hotel buildings, two different well-known chains, in a relatively open area. There was a school on one side and a group of mini-storage structures on the other. The entire area looked deserted. Leroy pointed out the windshield. "How about we check out those hotels?"

"How are we on gas?" Laura asked.

"Almost out," he replied.

"Let's try the hotels," she said.

When they came up even with the hotels, he turned the wheel, drove across the grass verge and into some low scrub. He pushed through the barrier fence and drove up into the first hotel's parking lot. He stopped in the middle of the lot and looked in all directions. With no one in sight, he pulled up to the main doors and clicked the engine off.

"Let's check it out," he said, as he opened the door and stepped to the pavement.

Cindy handed the rifle to Leroy and then she and Laura slid out the passenger's side. Laura held the Glock in her hand.

Leroy approached the double glass automatic sliding doors, both smashed, and stepped through the metal frames into the reception area. The floor was littered with glass, trash, and debris, along with obvious indications of animal habitation. The interior also smelled like rotting flesh. "Let's try the other hotel," he said, as Laura and Cindy walked up and stood beside him.

The three of them turned, exited the building, and walked across the hotel's front parking lot, which faced the back of the other hotel. They walked through what was once a manicured grassy area, but now overgrown with weeds and dotted with bare spots. They crossed the rear parking lot of the adjacent building and walked around to the other side. They stood for a moment, facing the front entrance.

"It was once the nicer of the two hotels," Laura said.

Leroy started off toward the front entrance. "It still is; the glass doors are intact."

"How is that even possible," Cindy said, as she and Laura fell in behind Leroy.

Leroy leaned his rifle against the adjacent wall and pushed and pulled on the doors with both hands. When they didn't open, he put the finger tips of both hands in the small gap between the doors and pulled with increasing amounts of strength until he reached the extent of his muscle power. The doors did not open. "I need something to pry with," he said, as he looked around.

"I still have a small pry bar in my pack," Laura said.

Leroy threw Cindy the truck keys. "Just bring the truck over here."

Cindy darted off in the direction of the truck.

With Cindy out of ear shot, Leroy turned to Laura. "She can drive, right?"

"She can drive," Laura said.

Leroy nodded and looked back at the hotel doors.

"Do you really think we can walk to Virginia?" Laura asked. "It will be winter soon." She glanced at her boots. "These boots weren't made for snow."

Leroy looked at her bare legs leading down to the nylon mesh, high-top boots. He took a deep breath and then exhaled. "We can look for more gas, but I doubt there's any left that will still fire an engine. Plus, it will take time and we'll risk coming into contact with who knows what kind of people around here."

"We should at least try to find better gear," Laura said. She turned in the direction of the truck approaching and then looked back at Leroy.

"There were some businesses on both sides of the highway at the last exit," Leroy said. "A mile back. We can check there."

Laura smiled and walked to the rear of the truck as Cindy brought it to a stop under the hotel's portico. She opened her pack and rummaged. Her hand came out with the pry bar. She walked over and handed it to Leroy.

He walked to the hotel doors, inserted the wedged end of the bar in the gap between the doors, and pushed.

The doors slid apart an inch, but then slammed back closed when he removed the pry bar.

Leroy handed the pry bar to Cindy. "You pry; your mother and I will pull."

Cindy took the bar, inserted the pry end, and pushed.

The door opened an inch.

Leroy from one side and Laura from the other wrapped their fingers from both hands and pulled.

"Don't let go of that bar while our fingers are inside," Leroy said.

Cindy nodded.

Leroy and Laura pulled as hard as they could until, finally, the doors slid apart a foot.

Leroy looked at Laura. "Remove your hands while I hold on."

Laura let go of her edge of the door. The door stayed in place. Leroy let go. The one foot gap remained.

Leroy squeezed into the opening and placed his back against the edge of one door and both hands against the edge of the opposite door. He pushed until the door was open another foot. He then stepped inside, followed by Laura and Cindy.

"Much better condition," Leroy said, as he looked around at the front desk and the reception area. "Dust on the floor, but otherwise the place is relatively untouched."

"Unbelievable," Cindy said, as she stepped forward and did a three-sixty. "We actually get to sleep in a real bed."

Laura stepped forward and then looked back at Leroy.

"Let's check out the businesses back at the last exit," Leroy said, "see if there's anything we can use."

"Drive or walk?" Cindy asked.

"We probably have a gallon of gas left, I say we drive," Leroy said.

CHAPTER 10

"Bingo," Leroy said, as he turned the wheel and pulled to a stop in front of a line of strip mall stores. "Who would have thought?" He gestured toward the store directly in front of the truck.

"An outdoor outfitter," Cindy said.

"The door's busted," Laura said. "I wonder what's left."

"Let's find out," Leroy said, as he opened his door and stepped out.

With rifle in hand, he approached the front of the store, stepping carefully on the broken glass. "Someone wanted in awful bad," he said.

"Did they really need to break the plate glass and the doors?" Laura asked.

Leroy ducked as he stepped through the door's metal frame. He scanned the interior. Except for a few miscellaneous items littering the floor, obviously not wanted, the shelves and the displays were all bare.

"Stripped," Laura said, as she walked to the cashier's counter and palmed the little silver bell next to the register. The bell clanged. "As usual, no help when you need it."

"Let's check the back," Cindy said, as she darted to a door in the rear of the store. She opened the door and stepped through, followed closely by Leroy and Laura.

The large room was lined with shelves made of two-by-fours and plywood. Except for a layer of dust, all the shelves were empty.

"I think we're about two years too late," Laura said.

Leroy pointed to a wood door off to the side. "Let's check behind door number three," he said, as he stepped off in that direction.

He turned the knob and pulled. The inside of the small closet contained a few cleaning supplies—mops, buckets, and such. Leroy picked up two one gallon buckets, one yellow and one blue. "These might come in handy."

"We can check the other stores," Cindy said.

Leroy led Laura and Cindy out of the closet, through the store room, back into the main part of the store, and then outside. Leroy threw the plastic buckets into the rear of the truck as he walked out to the edge of the road. He looked up and down a few seconds and then walked back to Laura and Cindy, still standing in front of the store. "There's a sign for a home improvement store a couple of blocks up, let's check that out," he said, as he opened the driver's side door. "Everything else in this plaza would be useless to us. Tattoo parlor, pizza shop, that sort of thing."

Laura and Cindy slid to their respective spots.

"What are you looking for at the home improvement store?" Laura asked.

"Not that many people here. I'm thinking we should hang around a few days; we can scavenge food and equipment. There might be some tools left in the store."

"I don't see anyone around," Cindy said.

"There's bound to be some people, somewhere," Leroy said, as he started the truck and pulled out. He drove up the road and parked in front of the store's main entrance. Like most other establishments in the area, the glass in the double doors was shattered.

The three of them got out, Leroy with the rifle, Laura with the pistol, and walked into the dimly lit interior. The first thing Leroy noticed was the inventory still on the shelves. Not much, but some.

"Tools are usually to the left," he said, as he started off that way, followed by Cindy.

"I'm going to check on storage containers," Laura said.

Leroy stopped and turned. "Storage containers?"

"If it rains while we're here, we can catch the water," Laura said.

Leroy nodded, smiled, and continued toward the tools.

Cindy trailed behind Leroy. "I still think we should try to find some gas," she said.

Leroy glanced in her direction.

"If we're going to be here a few days, why not?" she asked.

Leroy cocked his head. "Okay. Doesn't hurt to look."

"Where should we look?" she asked.

"Some place that stores their own fuel," he said. "Maybe a fire department. Police department motor pool. Something like that."

Cindy smiled. "So you plan to stay at that hotel?"

"Yeah, looked clean enough. We can check out the rooms and see if anything was left behind. I also want to check out that mini-storage."

Leroy reached the tool section and walked to the back wall like he knew where he was going. He walked along in front of various tools, surprisingly still hanging on their displays. He picked up a heavy hammer, a large chisel, and a big pry bar. "These should open most doors."

"Why is all this stuff still here?" Cindy asked.

"I guess there's just not that many people around, and the ones that are still here must not need tools. They would be heavy to carry."

Cindy nodded.

"Let's find your mother," Leroy said, as he headed back to the front of the store.

Cindy fell in beside him. "So, what do you think of Mom?"

Leroy glanced at Cindy. *Typical daughter*, he thought. He couldn't help but admire Laura's muscular frame and pretty face. She seemed bright and capable. He understood why she and Cindy had been able to survive all those months on their own. She was nothing like his wife, Jill. Jill was a typical military wife, ready to pick up and move when necessary, but also much more demure and shy. Leroy couldn't imagine his wife holding a pistol and barking orders the way Laura did. One wasn't better than the other, just different. He liked both types. "She's okay," he said with a cock of his head.

At that moment, they nearly ran into Laura as the three of them reached the same end cap, Laura coming up one of the aisles. She carried a plastic twenty-gallon container. "Last one," she said, as she held it up. "Who's okay?"

"What?" Leroy asked.

"You were saying she's okay," Laura said. "Who's okay?"

Leroy felt his face turn red as he glanced at Cindy.

Cindy tightened her lips and just looked away.

"Uh—"

Cindy turned back to face her mom. "He was talking about the hotel."

Leroy raised his hand holding the tools. "Found some tools."

Laura gazed for several seconds at Cindy, then at Leroy, and then stepped off toward the front of the store. "Do we have all we need for now?"

Leroy glanced at Cindy and winked. "I think so," he said, as he and Cindy caught up.

Leroy raised the hammer above his head and swung it down against the padlock with a loud *bang*. The lock broke into two pieces and clanged to the pavement in front of the metal door. He slid the hasp back, reached down, and raised the door.

Laura and Cindy stepped forward, into the unit, and looked around at various pieces of furniture, some broken, all of them well-used. "Next," Laura said.

Leroy shifted to the next storage unit and repeated the process. The second lock took three hits before it popped open. Leroy removed the lock and opened the door. Inside were a child's swing set and other miscellaneous outdoor toys.

The process continued until they had opened ten units, all the units on one side of the first of the four separate buildings. None of the units contained anything of particular use, mostly just junk.

"What, exactly, are we looking for?" Laura asked, as the three of them stood staring into the tenth unit, at eight used car tires and two cases of engine oil.

"I don't know," Leroy said. "Maybe it was a bad idea."

"It didn't take that long," Cindy said. "I suggest we keep going."

Leroy tightened his lips and looked at Laura.

Laura shrugged her shoulders and walked off toward the other side of the building.

Cindy picked up Leroy's rifle that had been leaning against the wall between the metal doors of the ninth and tenth units and followed Leroy and Laura around the building.

Leroy slammed the hammer against the next padlock, watched it clang, broken, to the pavement and raised door. He then stepped inside the unit and looked around at the numerous cardboard boxes, all marked with their contents. "Kitchen," he said out loud as he read the side of one of the boxes, and then looked at other boxes, "bathroom, garage, hey this one sounds promising."

Laura joined him next to the box. "Winter clothes," she said, as she raised an eyebrow. She picked up the box from the top of another box and dropped the clothes box in the open center section of the unit. She opened the top leaves and started sifting through the contents.

Cindy joined her and the two of them began pulling out various articles of clothing and letting them drop to the concrete floor. Finally, Laura stood back with a black parka in her hands and held it against Cindy's back. "This should fit." She threw the jacket toward the open door, starting a pile of useful items.

Leroy continued looking through the other boxes until he saw one marked *camping*. He dragged the box in the open and flipped it over, spilling the contents onto the floor. His eyes lit up when he saw a compact pop-up tent and four compactable sleeping bags. "These will definitely come in handy."

Cindy turned to Leroy and the items he was separating from the rest of the stuff in the box. She picked up one of the sleeping bags and tossed it up and caught it. "It's light," she said. "Lighter than the blankets and tarps we're carrying now."

When Laura reached the bottom of the box, she turned toward the pile of clothes that had formed near the door. "Two parkas, some sweaters, and a few sweatshirts," she said, as she turned toward Leroy and Cindy. "Is there anything marked winter boots?"

"No, just children's clothes, pots and pans," Leroy said. "Other than the tent and sleeping bags, there's nothing else we could really use. At least not useful enough to justify the carry weight." He looked around the unit and focused on a pair of rod and reels leaning together in a corner. "These might come in handy," he said, as he stepped over and grabbed the two rods. He bent down and picked up a small tackle box. "Taking this stuff would only make sense if we end up with transportation. But we'll take them for now."

"What about those aluminum pots?" Cindy asked, as she pointed to the camping gear.

Leroy bent down and picked up one of the pots and examined the bottom. "Two quarts."

"There's three of us," Laura said. "We will need the extra capacity. Take them both."

"And the mugs," Cindy said, as she picked one up from the floor. "They're pretty light. We can eat and drink out of these."

Leroy picked up the second pot and the three other mugs. He dropped everything except the rod and reels into a nylon laundry bag and slung it over his shoulder. "Anything else?"

"I think that's it," Laura said, as she glanced around. "Wait, take these," she said, as she bent down and scooped up two thick candles from the pile of camping gear.

Leroy opened the nylon bag so Laura could drop them in. He stepped outside the unit and looked up at the sky. "It's getting late. What do you say we find our rooms and prepare something to eat?"

Laura nodded, retrieved her pistol from the top of a nearby box, and scooped the pile of clothes into her arms. She and Cindy followed Leroy, carrying the camping equipment, as he headed back to the truck still parked on the other side of the building.

As they rounded the front corner, Leroy saw two men standing at the driver's door, peering inside. He stopped, bent down and placed the hammer, camping equipment, and rods on the pavement and took the rifle from Cindy's hands. He flipped the safety lever and held the rifle at the ready position in both hands as he approached the two men. "Can we help you gents?"

Both had beards and long hair, and wore stained and wrinkled shirts and pants, along with sneakers that should have been discarded months earlier. They were both slender. They looked like pretty much everyone still walking around these days, like street people.

The taller of the two pushed back from the truck, turned toward the sound of Leroy's voice, and immediately raised his hands. "Meant no harm."

The shorter of the men raised his hands, but much slower.

Laura and Cindy stood behind Leroy. Laura scanned the surrounding area for anyone else that might be around.

"We heard the banging," the shorter man said. "I'm Jason; this is Art. We live near here."

"We're not armed," Art said. "Can we put our arms down?"

Leroy nodded. "You say you live around here, what's it like?" He lowered the barrel.

Jason and Art lowered their arms. "It's rough. Not much food left. There're a couple of bullies left in town we steer clear of."

"Anyone, besides you, that might have heard the banging?" Leroy asked.

"Maybe, it was pretty loud," Jason said. He looked at Art.

Art nodded.

Laura continued past Leroy, around to the other side of the truck, and dropped the pile of clothes in the back. She kept the pistol in her hand and rejoined Leroy and Cindy.

"I haven't seen a running vehicle in weeks," Jason said, as he patted the truck's hood. "What are you using for gas?"

"It's about out of gas," Leroy said. "You wouldn't happen to know of any gasoline stored that might still work?"

Jason gestured to a group of houses in the distance. "The fire station on the other side of those houses had a large tank, but not sure anything in it would still work," Jason said.

"Where are you guys living?" Art asked.

"We're on the move," Leroy replied. "Just passing through."

"On the move to where?" Jason asked.

"East," Leroy said. "There's a rumor of a government forming."

"And you think the army might be part of that effort," Jason said.

Leroy shifted the rifle to one hand. "That's right."

Jason nodded and then smacked Art on the shoulder. "I guess we'll move along, if that's okay with you," he said, looking at Leroy.

"No problem," Leroy said. "Like I said, we're just passing through."

Jason pushed Art toward the southwest, toward the housing community in the distance across a field of low scrub.

When they were out of earshot, Leroy handed the rifle to Cindy and picked up the hammer and camping equipment. "We should get this stuff organized and be ready to move quickly," he said, as he stood up. He dumped the contents of his arms into the back of the truck, walked around to the driver's side, and got in as Laura and Cindy were getting in from the other side.

"Should we continue with the storage units tomorrow?" Laura asked.

"I'd like to," Leroy said. "Let's see how it goes tonight."

"Do you think they will come back with their friends?" Cindy asked.

"Yeah, I do," Leroy said, as he started the truck and put it in gear.

"I wonder why the people around here didn't already break into the storage units." Cindy asked.

"At this point, they need food," Leroy said. "Unlikely the units would contain any food. That would be my guess."

Leroy turned the wheel and steered the truck west, across an open field, toward the two hotels in the distance.

CHAPTER 11

Seventy-five yards from the hotel, just as the front wheels popped up on the hotel's outer parking lot, the truck started spitting and jerking as the engine gulped for fuel. It made it almost to the front door when it finally coughed one final time and died.

"I guess that's it," Leroy said, as he turned the key off.

"They might have been lying about the lack of gas around here," Cindy said.

"Maybe," Leroy said. "Let's see how it goes tonight before we decide whether it's a good idea to check out that fire station."

It took two trips to get everything up to the second floor. They selected two adjacent rooms, near the stairs, in the middle of the building.

Leroy dropped his pack off in one of the rooms and then helped Laura and Cindy with moving the rest of the gear into the second room. Both rooms were a little dusty, but otherwise, were ready for guests. There was a slight odor in the lobby and on the second floor, but nothing too overwhelming. Leroy thought it probably emanated from one of the upper floors.

"If you guys want to start getting this stuff organized, I'll go next door and warm up something to eat." When Laura and Cindy agreed, Leroy went next door and retrieved the gas backpacking stove from his pack, hooked up the gas bottle, and started pulling various cans of food from his pack. He still had gas for the stove because he rarely used it, preferring an open fire while he traveled.

He slid one of the windows open for ventilation, opened a couple of cans of soup, two packs of Ramen noodles, and mixed it all together in the largest aluminum pot he had. He burned just enough gas to heat the soup and soften the noodles and then called out to let Laura and Cindy know it was ready.

They entered the room a few seconds later and took a seat on the single king size bed.

Leroy spooned some soup into two aluminum mugs and handed each to Laura and Cindy. He kept a third of the soup and ate directly from the pot, after taking a seat in the only chair in the room.

"I just don't see how we're going to walk to Virginia," Laura said. "We don't have much food left."

"A few cans," Cindy said.

Leroy spooned some soup into his mouth, chewed, and swallowed. "We need to start hitting some of those houses tomorrow."

"Maybe we should split up," Cindy said. "We could cover a lot more ground."

"I suppose you can do that if you want, but if we're going to travel together, I recommend we stay together. Better security that way. We can watch each other's backs."

"This is a new area," Laura said. "We have no idea of the risks." She looked at Leroy. "I think we should stay together, work as a team."

Leroy nodded.

Cindy sat her empty mug on the night table beside the bed, filled it half full of water from one of the plastic jugs, swirled it around, and drank the contents. The process pretty much cleaned the inside of the mug of soup residue.

After watching Cindy, Laura and Leroy did the same thing. "Good idea," Leroy said, as he placed the clean pot on the table beside him. He glanced out the window. "It's getting dark."

"We'll finish getting organized," Laura said, "and then turn in."

"I'm going to sleep in the lobby," Leroy said. "There are several entrances, but only one set of stairs. I'll find a place to keep watch."

Laura raised an eyebrow and smiled. "Thank you."

"I'll see you two in the morning," Leroy said, "provided we don't have visitors tonight."

Everyone stood up and meandered to the door. Cindy placed a hand on Leroy's arm. "Is there anything we can do to help?"

Leroy pursed his lips into a slight smile as he raised his chin. "You two just get some sleep. We'll likely be busy tomorrow."

Leroy grabbed the rifle, touched the butt of the Glock in his holster, and followed Laura and Cindy out the door. "I'll be downstairs if you need anything," he said, as he walked past their door.

"We'll be ready early," Laura said, as she and Cindy entered their room.

Leroy took his time down the carpeted stairs and entered the dimly lit lobby. He walked out the open front glass doors, and stood off to the side, out from under the portico. He unzipped his pants and urinated while he gazed at the stars. Finished, he took a look around the area for any movement. Seeing none, he walked back into the lobby. From the sofa and chairs around the room, he removed several cushions and arranged them in a corner that gave him a view of the front entrance and the stairs. He rolled to his back and placed the rifle on the floor next to him.

He tried to imagine what he would do if he were Jason or Art. They would be wondering if the truck was, indeed, almost out of gas, so they might go for the truck. Or they might be wondering how much gear and food was tucked away in the backpacks clearly visible in the bed of the truck. Would they take a chance on confronting three armed individuals, especially when there were empty houses out there with food still to be had? Leroy guessed that would depend on how much firepower they had, and how much they wanted the truck or the gear. Actually, it probably had more to do with their personalities and how protective they were of their turf. At the time of their encounter, they didn't have any firepower. But their friends surely did. Telling their friends of the strangers breaking into the storage units would be the first thing they would do. Alone, they didn't seem to be the type to take a chance. But their friends could be another story. Leroy fully expected a visit. They would know the building, because of the truck out front, but they wouldn't know which room. And they might not expect Leroy in the lobby.

Leroy shifted, trying to get comfortable on the thin cushions. His thoughts turned to Laura and Cindy. What were the chances he would run into such a duo, two extremely attractive women who had survived the plague, survived two years after the plague, and were basically traveling along the same route as Leroy? In this post apocalyptic world, Leroy hadn't even thought about meeting a replacement for his wife. He was too busy just trying to survive the elements. Running up on Laura and her daughter, and them willing to travel with him, was both a blessing and a curse. What man wouldn't be attracted to Laura? But having the two of them around, also meant he had two other people to worry about. And having such an attractive couple of women around him made him a target for other men who might desire the company of a beautiful woman.

Leroy tried to clear his mind as he shifted to his side and brought his knees up into a fetal position. He always slept on his side. With his eyes shut, he focused on the black void, empty of any thoughts. Each time a thought tried to enter from the edge, he refocused on the blackness, the emptiness. Soon his breathing became rhythmic, and he snored lightly.

Leroy blinked his eyes open and glanced around the still-dark lobby. He peered at the front glass doors, the brightest part of the room. He was accustomed to waking up at night, but there was usually a reason. He lay still and listened.

At first he heard only the normal night noises. But then he heard a low-pitched squeak. Like a door being opened. Like a truck door being opened, slowly, to minimize the squeaky hinges.

Leroy rolled to his feet in one fluid motion, grabbing his rifle on the way up. Stepping on the balls of his feet, he quietly moved to the glass doors, and flattened himself against the wall next to the glass. He leaned his head out, peered through the glass, and focused on the dark hulk of the pickup. He saw movement, the silhouette of four people standing next to the driver's side. He watched as one slid behind the wheel.

Even though he left the key in the ignition, there was no way it would start. Leroy saw no reason to confront four men, probably armed, over a truck that wasn't going anywhere. So he stayed put and watched, wondering what the men would do when the truck didn't start.

A few seconds later, the sound of the engine turning over drowned out the nighttime quiet. Leroy wondered if Laura and Cindy could hear it from their room. Probably.

The man behind the wheel tried several times to start the truck, but to no avail. He finally gave up and climbed out of the cab.

Leroy could hear whispers but couldn't make out the words. He didn't have to hear the words to know what they were discussing. Should they enter the hotel? And if so, how would they find the right room? Look for the broken door. That's what Leroy would do. And that's apparently what the four men decided to do.

Huddled in a group, the four men moved toward the front doors.

Leroy searched the men's outlines for any sign of weapons. He saw what appeared to be two rifles. Leroy didn't really blame the men for what they were about to attempt. It was their town, after all. But how far were they willing to go? The answer was equally obvious. They wouldn't attempt such an operation unless they were willing to go all the way. That alone gave Leroy the authority to take extreme action, without warning. Leroy quietly shifted the safety lever on his rifle and pressed his back closer to the wall.

The four men stepped through the opening in the doors and immediately spread out. They walked right past Leroy as they continued farther into the lobby. What little light there was from outside illuminated the four men much more than it did Leroy. That gave Leroy two advantages: concealment and surprise.

The smart move would be to simply take out all four men before they even knew what was happening. Leroy's semi-automatic rifle was more than capable. But Leroy couldn't bring himself to shoot four men in the back. That only left one option.

Leroy brought the barrel of his rifle level as he slowly turned and shouldered the weapon. He aimed at the man closest to the stairs.

"Freeze!" Leroy yelled, as he took several steps backward, along the wall, and into the deeper darkness toward the corner of the room. "Drop the weapons or I will shoot."

The two men with rifles stopped midway in their pivot, frozen, but they didn't drop their weapons. The other two men, probably Jason and Art, froze and remained facing the way they had been walking.

"He said, drop the weapons." Laura's voice came from the darkness beyond the four men. Leroy guessed she was probably at the foot of the stairs and had no doubt she had the Glock pointed at the four men.

The two armed men raised their rifles in the air, and then bent at the waist.

Leroy heard both rifles being placed on the floor. "All of you step this way four paces and go face down on the floor. Do it now."

The four men stepped backwards as instructed and went prone.

"Stretch your arms out in front of your head, palms up," Leroy said.

When the four men complied, Leroy stepped forward with his rifle aimed. He saw Laura's silhouette step into the lobby from the stairs and take a few steps toward the four men. "Keep them covered," Leroy said. "If anyone moves, shoot them."

"Not a problem," Laura said. Her voice was nervous, but strong.

Leroy released his left hand from the rifle, stepped to the first man, did a quick pat down, and then moved down the line. He found no other guns.

"We obviously made a really bad decision," one of the men said.

Leroy recognized Art's voice. "That you did."

"What are you going to do with us?" Art asked.

"I guess you didn't believe me about the truck being out of gas," Leroy said.

"I guess not," Art said.

"Well, believe this, I will shoot first next time."

"We can go?" Art asked.

"You can. Get to your feet and skedaddle."

The four men stood. Jason and Art started for the door; the other two started for the two rifles still on the floor.

"Leave em," Leroy said.

The two men stopped in their tracks. "We need our guns," one of them said.

"That's the risk you took," Leroy said. "You can leave without them, or you won't leave at all."

The two men hesitated, then pivoted, and followed Art and Jason out the doors.

"Oh, and you can have the truck," Leroy said, as the last of them passed through the doors.

Laura picked the two rifles up from the floor and stepped closer to Leroy. "Do we have to worry about them coming back, maybe with even more friends?"

"Probably not," Leroy said. "But just in case, I'll remain down here."

"What about the rifles?"

"Take them up to the room," Leroy said, barely able to make out Laura's features in the dark.

"Okay," she said. "See you in the morning, if not before." She turned and started off toward the stairs.

"Laura."

She stopped and looked back.

"Thank you."

"No prob," she said, as she turned and continued toward the stairs.

Leroy stood in the middle of the lobby and watched her dark form walk away.

"I think we should scavenge the nearby homes for food first thing," Laura said, as she stood in the middle of the hotel room with Leroy and Cindy.

"Leave our gear here, or lug it with us?" Cindy asked.

"We'll have to leave it here," Leroy said, "which I don't like all that much."

"I don't like it, either," Laura said. "Unguarded, it would be easy pickings for the guys from last night, or anybody."

Leroy rubbed his bristled face with both hands. "We don't really have a choice. Dump everything, take the empty packs, and push everything else under the beds. I really don't want to leave one of you behind, given the events of last night. Plus, we need to load up with as much as possible. Three people will be better than two."

"I agree," Laura said, as she picked up her pack from the bed and dumped the contents on the floor. "And I just got it organized."

"It's still organized," Cindy said. "It's just not together." She picked up her pack and dumped the contents.

The two of them then got down on all fours and pushed the various items under the bed.

"Maybe they won't look," Laura said.

"Hopefully, they won't return," Leroy said, as he headed for the door. "Be right back."

"What about the rifles?" Cindy asked.

Laura picked up both of the rifles, one a lever action Winchester and the other an assault style rifle, similar to the one Leroy carried. She handed the AR rifle to Cindy. "Carry this one," Laura said. "It's lighter."

Cindy took the gun, turned it in her hands several times as she examined the various components, and pushed the magazine release. The magazine popped free. She pushed on the top cartridge and then pushed the magazine back in the well.

"It has all the same bells and whistles as the one you shot with your dad," Laura said.

Cindy shouldered the weapon and aimed at the open window. She then lowered the rifle. "We should close the window. It's a dead giveaway."

"Right," Laura said, as she stepped to the window and closed the glass. She peered out for a few seconds to ensure she wasn't already being observed.

At that moment Leroy bounded through the door holding his mostly empty backpack. "We ready?"

Laura and Cindy picked up their packs and followed Leroy out the door, down the stairs, and out the front entrance.

Leroy pointed toward houses due south, across a field of scrub, in the distance.

They shouldered their packs and started walking. They crossed the field, climbed over a fence, and entered the community of middle income houses lined up along parallel streets. They walked single file.

Laura looked from one house to the next as they strolled along. She looked for houses with front doors not already bashed in. So far, halfway down the street, there were none. Every house had broken windows and broken doors. Scavengers had already hit this street. "Let's try the next street over," she said, as she veered onto the overgrown yard of the next house.

Leroy and Cindy followed without comment until they got to the next street and were facing a white house.

"This place is a ghost town," Cindy said. "Not one person."

Just as the words left her mouth, Laura spotted two men exit the front door of the white house. They were both in their twenties. A holstered pistol occupied each of their right hips.

CHAPTER 12

The two men froze when they saw Leroy, Laura, and Cindy. In unison, both men palmed the grip of their pistols, but they didn't draw. They simply stood still, staring, mostly at Laura and Cindy.

Leroy shouldered his rifle but kept it pointed down.

"We don't want no trouble mister," one of the men said. He had long red hair and some facial scrub, but not quite a beard. He was as tall as Leroy, but thicker in the middle, not fat.

The other man was leaner, shorter, more muscular, with brown hair. He didn't say anything. Both wore a backpack.

"Your hands," Leroy said, as he motioned with the barrel of his rifle.

Both men looked down at their hands still resting on their weapons. They jerked their hands away like the metal had suddenly turned red-hot.

"Like I said, we don't want any trouble," red said.

Leroy lowered his barrel a little more and took several steps closer to the men. "Scavenging?"

"Yeah," red said. "My name is Lincoln. This is Damon."

"Lincoln, are you from here?" Leroy asked.

Laura and Cindy stepped up next to Leroy.

Lincoln stared at Cindy for several long seconds before he answered. "Oh, yeah, we're both from here."

Leroy turned to Damon. "The houses look like they might be played out."

Damon looked at Lincoln and back at Leroy. "Pretty much," Damon said.

Leroy shifted his rifle to his left hand. "I'm Leroy. This is Laura and Cindy."

Cindy smiled.

Jason and Damon both smiled back.

"So what's the story around here?" Leroy asked.

"Apparently the same as everywhere," Damon said. "Plague, we lost most of the population, what few are left have been scavenging, hunting, and fishing."

Leroy nodded and glanced at Laura.

"So every house in this community has been emptied," Laura said.

"I think so," Lincoln said.

"What about other areas?" Cindy asked.

Damon looked at Cindy. "Probably not every community, but the best ones have."

"We ran into a couple of locals yesterday," Leroy said. "Art and Jason."

"They're derelicts, but fairly harmless," Lincoln said.

"They hang out with a rougher crowd, though," Damon said.

"We met their homeboys, too," Laura said. She shifted her rifle to the other hand.

"What about gas?" Cindy asked. "Is there any still around?"

Damon chuckled. "Gas? That ran out months ago. Did you guys drive here?"

"We did," Leroy said.

"I'm surprised anything still runs," Lincoln said.

Leroy glanced up and down the street and back at Lincoln. "If the gas was treated with an extender, it might still work."

"Art and Jason said something about a fire station nearby," Laura said.

Damon pointed to the south. "Yeah, not far. But I don't know of any gas there."

"Sometimes fire and police services maintain a small amount of fuel," Leroy said. "It's a long shot."

"We can show you," Lincoln said.

Leroy perked up. "Okay." He glanced at Laura and Cindy. "Lead the way."

Lincoln nodded, motioned, and then he and Damon started walking south down the road.

The five of them chatted as they walked, passing house after house until they exited the community and stepped out on a sidewalk. Directly across the street stood a neighborhood fire station composed of a single bay. The overhead bay door was up. Two fire trucks occupied the bay, end to end.

Leroy led everyone around to the back of the building and then marched directly to a large white cylindrical tank at the edge of the property. He knocked at several spots up and down the tank and listened to the different pitches. "I think there's fuel in here," Leroy said.

Damon stepped up and knocked on the tank. "Yeah, but it's probably diesel."

"If the diesel in the tank is any good, wouldn't the fire trucks start up?" Laura asked.

"We can find out," Leroy said. "But they would have filled the fire trucks from a pump, like at a regular gas station." He knocked on the white tank again. "This was meant for storage, for emergencies when the pumps didn't work."

Everyone followed Leroy into the bay and watched as he climbed into the cab of the first truck.

He searched around until he found the key, already in the ignition, and went through the process to start a diesel engine. When he pushed the start button nothing happened. "Battery," he said, as he stepped down from the cab. "We need to find a vehicle that burns diesel and has a good battery," Leroy said. He looked at Damon. "Know of any?"

When Damon realized Leroy was looking at him, he twisted his lips around while he thought. "I don't know, maybe," he said. "Almost everyone around here owns, or owned, a pickup. A lot of them burn diesel."

"That stuff is pretty old," Lincoln said. "You think it will fire an engine?"

"It's a long shot," Leroy said. He then studied Damon's face for several seconds. "What do you say we team up?"

"What do you mean?"

"We work together to find food and maybe a truck, and we divide up the proceeds," Leroy said.

Damon looked at Lincoln.

"I'd like to concentrate on north of the river," Leroy said.

Lincoln gestured with both hands. "Sure, why not?"

"I don't have a problem with that," Damon said.

"Where are you guys living?" Laura asked.

Damon pointed. "About a mile west of here. It was my parent's house."

"Plague?" Cindy asked.

Damon and Lincoln both nodded.

"We were working our way east from there when we saw you," Lincoln said. "We found a few things left behind yesterday, not much."

"What's east of here?" Cindy asked.

"About half a mile there's a golf course," Damon said. "There're houses on the other side of that."

"Okay," Leroy said. "We head east and keep an eye open for any possible vehicles along the way."

Everyone nodded and started walking east. Damon and Lincoln led the way. Everyone chatted, except Leroy. He kept his head on a swivel as he walked.

They checked several houses along the way. The front doors were intact, but the food and anything else that might have been useful was gone. Several of the houses still had human remains. Apparently the owners didn't lock the door when they collapsed or lay down for the last time. Soon, they entered what was once a nice golf course. Weeds sprouted from the fairways and greens. They crossed over several fairways arranged in parallel and entered a narrow strip of thick woods. On the other side they stepped into the backyard of an upper middle-class house.

"Might as well start with this one," Laura said, as she opened the door to the screen enclosed patio and stepped up to double glass doors. She knocked on the glass.

"Expecting someone to be home?" Cindy asked.

"Not everyone died from the plague," Laura said. "Those left are staying somewhere."

Cindy cupped her hands against the glass and peered inside. "Don't see anyone."

Laura pulled on the handle and slid the glass door open. She stepped inside, followed by everyone else.

With his rifle at the ready, Leroy walked through the kitchen and checked each room. Finding the house empty, he returned to the kitchen to find everyone going through the cabinets and drawers. Leroy looked at the pantry door he was standing beside and pulled the door open. He stepped into the pantry and looked around at the shelves stacked with various items of food. He shifted several boxes and found that anything made of grain, such as pasta and rice, was inundated with weevils. Holding his rifle in one hand, he scooped an armful of cans from one shelf, moved to the counter next to the sink, and dropped the cans. "There's stuff in the pantry."

Laura and Lincoln continued removing items from the cabinets while Damon and Cindy disappeared into the pantry.

As Leroy helped empty the cabinets, he heard Damon and Cindy mumbling inside the pantry, but could only make out intermittent words. It sounded like chitchat, mostly. Damon's attraction to Cindy was obvious. Whether there was any attraction to Damon on Cindy's part was much less apparent. Leroy wondered what would happen if she, or Laura for that matter, met someone of interest in Fort Smith, or anywhere along the way. Would such an encounter derail their willingness to travel east? Leroy quickly realized it was pointless to contemplate such developments. He simply needed to take one day at a time. Provision with the resources he could find and move on. Move on until he found a reason not to move on. Laura popped into his mind.

Leroy heard Laura's voice and realized she said something. "I'm sorry, what?"

She held up a can of tuna. "Tuna," she said. "These people apparently liked tuna."

Leroy studied her face. She really was quite attractive. Blue eyes, shoulder-length blond hair, high cheek bones. Leroy didn't know her age, but it had to be something in the early forties, given her daughter's age. She didn't look it. He thought about the life she must have had before. He wondered what kind of man she was married to and how long she was married. He thought about how devastated she must have been when he succumbed to the plague, along with pretty much everyone she knew. She was lucky to still have her daughter. Suddenly, he realized that his pause in responding was becoming awkwardness. "I'm sorry, tuna is a great find." He smiled at her and then turned back to his cabinet.

Twenty minutes later the five of them were loaded with everything of value the house had to offer. But their packs were still far from full.

"We need to check some other houses," Laura said, as she headed for the front door. She pulled the door open, took a step out to the portico, and immediately began back peddling. She pushed Lincoln, immediately behind her, back into the room.

"What is it?" Leroy asked.

With herself and Lincoln back inside, she closed the door. "Men, five of them, armed, walking up the street this way," she said, as she dashed to the adjacent window and separated the blinds with her thumb and index finger.

"Did they see you?" Leroy asked.

"Yep," she said. "They're now headed directly for this house."

Leroy stepped next to Laura and parted the blinds. She was right. Five men, headed for the house, with rifles shouldered and pistols in hand. Leroy counted two rifles and three handguns. Three of the men were middle aged; the other two were younger, in their twenties. The two younger men wore backpacks. They all looked a little rough for wear.

Laura dropped her hand, letting the blinds close. She looked at Leroy. "Do we confront, or make a hasty retreat out the back?"

Leroy searched Laura's face for any indication of which she desired. Her glance at Cindy made up his mind. "We retreat," he said, as he turned and fast walked toward the back doors. "We need to get out before they surround the house."

The others fell in behind. The fast walk quickly turned into a trot.

Leroy stopped at the glass doors, took a quick peek outside, and pulled the door open. "Mad dash for the trees," he whispered. "Don't stop until you are twenty yards in. Go," he said, as he gave Damon, Laura, Cindy, and Lincoln a light shove.

They ran in single file, with Leroy bringing up the rear. He looked over both shoulders as he jogged. Everyone was well inside the tree-line when Leroy took his final look. Through the trees and light brush he saw two men emerge into the backyard from around the corner of the house. If he saw them, there was a good chance they saw him. "We need to form a defensive line," he said just loud enough for Damon, still in front, to hear.

Damon glanced back and then slowed as he looked for cover. Everyone bunched up around him.

Leroy immediately began pointing at each person in his group and at the respective cover he recommended—all thick trees. With everyone behind a tree, Leroy low trotted over to Damon, who was farthest to the right, while facing the way they had come. "Watch your flank," he said. When Damon nodded, Leroy trotted to the left, paused next to Lincoln, and checked his cover and line of sight. He then trotted over to Laura and Cindy, both behind the same large tree trunk. "You two okay? Any questions about the rifle?"

Cindy flipped the safety lever and shouldered the weapon. "I'm okay."

"That's a thirty-round magazine, make them count," he said.

Cindy nodded.

Leroy glanced at Laura, holding her Glock to her side. He gave her a quick smile and a nod and then low trotted to a fat tree several yards to the left. He shouldered his rifle and flipped the safety lever in one fluid motion. He scanned the trees and brush in front of and to the left of his position, looking for movement.

One of the two men he saw rounding the corner of the house wore a red t-shirt. The other wore something in green. He watched for both colors and listened for any indication the men had entered the trees. He detected no sounds, outside of the normal birds and insects. He heard a squirrel barking in the distance, off to the left. He switched his attention in the direction of the squirrel.

As he watched and listened, he found himself uncharacteristically worried about his comrades, especially Laura and Cindy. The image of one or both of them shot flashed through his mind. He wondered if taking a stand had been the right move. Should they have kept running? Against only five men, taking a defensive position was probably the right move, especially if his side were all armed and trained. Armed, yes; trained, not so much. But he also didn't want to be overrun from behind while advancing to the rear. He would be hampered by the slowest person in his group, which might be himself for all he knew. Only the outcome would determine which option was better.

With no sight or sound of movement for over three minutes, Leroy began to wonder if the five men had decided not to chance it. It was also possible two or three were waiting until the others could work their way around. Leroy thought about whether the five men, from the back yard of the house, could have heard Leroy and his gang stop. Maybe. Probably.

Were they at this very moment set to move in from the front and either or both sides, simultaneously? An attack from the rear was even conceivable. Leroy didn't have the firepower or the ammunition for a prolonged encounter. He had two extra 9mm magazines in his backpack, but he and Cindy had only the one 5.56 magazine for each rifle. He had no idea how much extra ammo Lincoln and Damon carried.

Leroy looked to his rear. The openness of the golf course, only thirty yards away, was visible through the trees. He realized that stopping to form a defensive line had been the best tactical move. They would have all been easy targets sprinting across the open golf course with potentially the five men behind them with trees for cover. But that was then, when he thought the five men might give chase. Over five minutes had passed with no sign of pursuers. Was remaining here still the best course of action?

Leroy used one hand to remove his hat and scratch his head. He replaced the hat and then swiveled his head in all directions. He looked at Laura, Cindy, Lincoln, and Damon all still behind their trees, waiting. He then ducked low and side stepped until he was standing behind Laura and Cindy. "I think we should continue our retreat. Either they decided not to pursue, or they're working their way around us."

"Or they're gathering more men," Cindy said, without lifting her cheek from the rifle's butt as she continued her aim.

"Or that," Leroy agreed.

CHAPTER 13

Laura looked in all directions. "Back across the golf course?"

"We should probably take the long route, around the golf course," Leroy said.

Laura nodded.

Leroy motioned to Lincoln and Damon to follow, ducked low, and stepped off toward the open fields, with Laura and Cindy close behind.

Lincoln fell in next to Cindy.

Damon trotted up next to Leroy and assumed his pace. "What do you think?" he whispered.

"Don't have a clue," Leroy said. "But I think staying where we were any longer would be a mistake. Those guys may have friends. Eventually we would be surrounded.

"We should go around the golf course," Damon said.

"Agreed," Leroy said, as he stopped at the tree-line with the golf course and took a knee.

Damon knelt beside him. "There's a line of trees up there," he said, as he pointed to the north.

Leroy looked at the line of trees that stretched across the north end of the golf course. The trees backed to at least five of the parallel fairways. If the five men had set up an ambush, that's where they would be. They would have firing angles across the entire golf course, and plenty of cover should anyone approach the trees directly.

Leroy looked to the south, at a group of buildings on the far end of the course. "Pro-shop?" Leroy asked, as he pointed at the buildings.

"And maintenance buildings," Damon said.

Leroy studied the buildings for several moments. The buildings would likewise provide good cover against anyone crossing the golf course. Leroy suddenly had a bad feeling.

"I don't like it," he said. "What's to the south, along this tree-line?"

"A pond, not that big, we could travel south the length of the pond and then west. We'd be in more housing areas."

"And to the north?"

"These trees go almost all the way to the interstate," Damon said. "We'd come out behind the mini-storage buildings. About half a mile."

"North it is," Leroy said, as he raised to a crouch and joined Laura, Cindy, and Lincoln bunched ten yards back. He motioned with a finger to the north. "Let's move through these trees to the north. We'll come out behind the mini-storage."

"Lead the way," Laura said, as she stood up.

Leroy led everyone through the brush, stopping frequently to watch and listen. He paid particular attention to the clump of trees at the north end of the golf course. The trees stretched west in a narrow band. To their north was another fairway running perpendicular to the others. Leroy continued in his line of trees until they ended forty yards or so beyond the northern-most fairway. Leroy paused behind a tree and scanned in all directions for a full minute. The white buildings of the mini-storage facility stood in the distance. He then looked back. Seeing that everyone was waiting for him, he turned back to the front and dashed off.

The others followed.

Leroy stopped when he reached the first mini-storage building and waited for everyone to catch up.

"I think we're okay," he said, as he visibly relaxed.

"Now what?" Cindy asked.

Leroy looked at the hotels to the west and at the interstate to the north. He pictured the position of the housing area they had just left in relation to the interstate. He looked at Damon. "What's on the east side of that housing area?"

"More houses," Damon said. "They stretch all the way to Five-Forty, which runs into Interstate Forty. There're probably a thousand houses between here and there."

Leroy looked at the sky to judge the time. Close to noon. He looked at Laura, Cindy, Damon, and Lincoln in turn. "I'm going to load up with more ammo and head back."

"Back where?" Laura asked. She raised an eyebrow.

"The houses we just left. It would be the last thing they would expect, especially if I come in from the north."

"We need the food," Damon said. "Count me and Lincoln in."

Lincoln nodded.

Laura looked at Cindy and tightened her lips.

Leroy knew what she was thinking. Should she subject Cindy to such risks? He tried to put himself in her place with his own daughters. Probably not. But then, leaving her behind wasn't all that ideal either. He looked at Laura.

She looked at Leroy. "We're coming."

"Are you sure?"

"Yes," Laura said. "I can hang back with Cindy if it starts to look too risky."

In a group they walked to the hotel, dumped the contents of their packs, and opened a couple of cans for lunch. Leroy grabbed three extra boxes of 5.56 and threw them in his pack, along with an extra box of 9mm. The group then walked parallel to, but well away from, the interstate until they were on the north side of the housing community.

Leroy led the group between the houses to the fronting street. He looked up and down each street in his view. He saw two separate people in the distance. Neither appeared to be armed. He faced the house he had just walked alongside. Like every other house on the street, it was a single story with walls of red brick, sitting on an overgrown lot. Leroy imagined that the yard had once consisted of manicured grass and neatly trimmed bushes. "Might as well start here."

Everyone signaled their agreement by falling in behind Leroy as he stepped up on the porch. Like at the house earlier in the day, he knocked. After several moments of no response, he retrieved the pry bar from his pack, jammed it into the crevice next to the door knob, and wrenched the door until it opened. Leroy checked each room, while the others went straight for the kitchen. Leroy joined them and helped go through every cabinet, drawer, and closet. The dry goods had all succumbed to an invasion of weevils, just like before. The remains of flour, rice, and oats had all been reduced to a fine light powder intermingled with specks of black. Granola bars, rice cakes, chips, and crackers had all been ravaged by roaches or rodents. The only items of food to survive were cans and jars.

The team loaded up with everything still edible and practical to carry. A large jar of pickles was deemed too heavy.

They worked their way down the line until they had searched four houses on the same street. Only the first house provided anything of significant value.

Leroy stood with the others at his side on the street in front of the fourth house. "I guess we keep looking until we find more."

"It's getting a little late," Laura said. "I'm starting to worry about all the stuff we left at the hotel."

Leroy looked at the sky and rubbed his whiskered face. "One more house and we head back."

Laura nodded.

Same as before, Leroy forced the door and pushed it open. He was immediately hit with a foul odor. He stepped back onto the portico.

The others turned away and pinched their noses.

"I say we skip this one," Cindy said.

"The occupants died here, which means they didn't leave with anything," Leroy said. "I say we check it out."

"I'll wait out here," Cindy said.

Leroy turned back to the open door. He covered his nose and mouth with his sleeved bicep and stepped through the opening. He glanced back to see that Laura, Damon, and Lincoln followed.

"Check the kitchen," Leroy said, as he peeled off down a hall. "I'll check the other rooms."

Leroy's part of the house included four bedrooms and a hall bath. As he passed each room, he used the barrel of his rifle to push the door open. The remains of a single corpse occupied the bed of each of the three bedrooms. The size of each corpse ranged between what appeared to be a boy under ten and two teenagers.

He did a cursory inspection of each room but didn't really expect to find anything of value. He was right.

The master bedroom at the end of the hall was different in several ways. The bed held two corpses, there was a large gun cabinet in one of the corners, and there was an empty bottle of sleeping pills on the nightstand next to the woman. It was then that Leroy realized these people did not die of the plague. They died at their own hands.

Standing beside the bed, Leroy closed his eyes for several seconds as he thought about what might have motivated these people to take such drastic action. Either they wanted to circumvent the natural course of the plague, or they wanted to avoid the post-apocalyptic world devoid of ninety percent of its inhabitants.

Leroy stepped over to the gun cabinet and examined the display of shotguns and rifles, one of which was an AR similar to the one Leroy held in his hands. He pulled on the glass door but found it locked. He looked at the top of the nightstand on the man's side of the bed and opened each of the three drawers. He found a variety of items, including paperback books and magazines, but no keys. He tried pulling on the glass door again. Still locked. He flipped his rifle around, tapped the glass in the door with the butt, and stepped back as the glass shattered. He reached in and retrieved the AR. He looked back at the other guns and thought of taking them for barter, if for no other reason. But there was no way he, Laura, and Cindy could carry their packs and the weight of three shotguns and two other rifles. If they ended up finding diesel, which was doubtful, he could come back for the other weapons.

As Leroy examined the components of the extra rifle in his hand, he heard shuffling behind him. He turned to see Laura enter the room holding her nose.

"Plague?" she asked, as she walked to the woman's side of the bed.

"I think they all killed themselves to avoid the plague," Leroy said. "Or they wanted to avoid what the world would become."

Laura nodded as she picked up the pill bottle and read the label. "This would do it." She replaced the pill bottle and looked at Leroy. "Find something useful?"

He held out the extra rifle. "I have a gift for you."

Laura walked around the bed and joined Leroy at the gun cabinet. She took the rifle in her hands. "Thank you."

Leroy bent down and pulled on the single drawer under the glass door. It slid open immediately. Leroy bent closer and examined the various boxes of ammunition.

Laura bent down and scooped up two AR magazines, thirty-two rounds each. She pulled her arms out of her backpack straps and let the obviously heavy bag drop to the floor.

"Any luck with the food?"

"Lots," she said. "We'll have to make a second trip for the rest of it."

Leroy removed all the 5.56 ammunition, seven boxes, from the drawer and stacked them on the nightstand. He slipped out of his pack and dropped the ammo in the main compartment. He then held it open for Laura.

"I might as well load up these magazines," she said, as she dropped to her knees on the carpeted floor, and opened one of the boxes.

Leroy knelt beside her and opened a separate box. He started pushing the rounds into the second magazine. "So you shot a lot with your husband?"

"Not a lot, but enough to know what I'm doing," she said.

"He must have been a great loss to you."

"He was. Cindy adored her father. So did I. We expected to be married for life."

Leroy pinched his lips together and nodded.

"What about your wife and kids?"

"Same," Leroy said. "We were a team. The life of a military wife is not easy. We moved a lot. I had two remote assignments, Korea and Turkey. But we had good assignments, too. We were stationed in California twice. Once early in my career and then what would have been my last, just before the plague. I expected to retire there. I guess I did, in a way."

"But you lost your kids. Losing my husband was bad, but I can't even imagine losing Cindy."

Leroy stood up with the full magazine in his hand. "I was a wreck for a while. Drank every bit of alcohol I could find."

"You seem to have recovered," Laura said.

"Ran out of alcohol," Leroy replied. The corners of his mouth turned up into a slight smile.

Laura smiled. "I'm glad."

"Me, too," Leroy said.

They both turned to more shuffling coming down the carpeted hall.

Cindy entered the room holding her nose. "Find something?"

"Another rifle," Leroy said, as he handed the full magazine to Laura.

She placed the magazine into the well and slammed it in place with the palm of her hand. She slipped the second magazine into a pouch on her pack.

Cindy approached the gun cabinet. "What about the rest of these?"

"Too heavy for us to carry. Damon or Lincoln might want them. If not, and we find wheels, we can come back."

At that moment Damon and Lincoln entered the room. They held their noses and stared at the couple in bed for several long moments. Finally Damon shook his head and peered at the gun cabinet.

"I'll take the pump," Damon said, as he approached. "Any ammo?"

"In the drawer," Leroy said, as he pointed with his foot.

"I'll stick with my M&P," Lincoln said. "Is there any extra nine mil?"

"Yep," Leroy nodded, as he motioned toward the drawer. "Grab it all. We can divvy up later. So you like the Smith and Wesson?"

"I like it better than Damon's Glock. I can actually hit something with this," he said, as he patted the grip of his holstered pistol.

"We left a load of canned food and stuff for you to carry," Damon said to Leroy. "These people believed in long-term storage. They left a lot of stuff vacuum sealed and in glass containers. Oatmeal, powdered milk, coffee, and a bunch of other stuff, including granola bars."

Leroy took another look round the room and then poked his head into the closet. He picked up a pair of leather boots and looked inside, under the tongue. "Anyone wear a men's nine?"

"I do," Lincoln said, as he looked down at his sneakers.

Leroy handed him the boots. He bent down and picked up a second pair of leather boots. "Size six, women's."

Cindy walked over and dropped her pack on the floor. "I can wear a six." She plopped down, removed her nylon boots, and slipped the leather boots on. She stood up with them unlaced. "Yeah, I can wear these." She bent down, tightened the laces, and tied a knot. She then picked up the pack and slung it to her back.

Leroy looked at Laura. "Sorry, that's it for boots."

Laura nodded.

Cindy tied her nylon boots to her pack by their laces. "This stuff is getting heavy," she said, as she shifted the load.

Leroy led the group back to the kitchen.

A variety of cans, jars, and vacuum packs was stacked on the counter. He slipped out of his pack and began loading the items. "This will carry us for a while."

"Like I said," Laura said, "we'll have to come back for the rest."

Damon peered out the kitchen window. "It's getting dark."

"You're welcome to grab a room at the hotel," Leroy said. "There's plenty of them."

Damon looked at Lincoln. They nodded to each other.

"It will save us time in the morning," Damon said, "assuming we're going out again tomorrow."

Leroy looked at Laura and then at Damon and Lincoln. "Why not?" He slipped into his pack and led everyone to the front door. He eased the door open and scanned the outside before stepping to the portico. "Lead the way," he said to Damon.

CHAPTER 14

Following one of their better dinners, heated over an open fire in a grassy area behind the hotel, the five of them sat in the lobby, basically in a circle, as the last rays of sunlight faded and dark clouds rolled in from the north.

"We could use the rain," Laura said, as she gazed out one of the lobby windows. "I could use a shower."

"And I need to wash everything I own," Cindy said.

Laura got up and walked closer to the windows. "The plastic tub I got from the home store is in place under a down spout next to the back door." She gazed out a few moments longer and then turned back to the group. She scrutinized Lincoln and Damon, sitting across from each other, as they each tried to engage Cindy. Damon did most of the talking; Lincoln did most of the listening. Laura noted that Cindy split her attention between the two, despite Lincoln's lack of conversation. Cindy had always been attracted to the brainy silent type. Laura would have to give that check mark to Lincoln. Damon was more handsome, but also more egotistical. Laura also detected a hint of jealousy on Damon's part, toward Lincoln. Sometimes competition was a good thing, but in a world without society's constraints, probably not so much. Laura made a mental note to keep an eye on the situation.

She then turned her attention to Leroy, who was cleaning his rifle with a piece of cloth. Laura didn't know that much about the military, but based on what she imagined, Leroy definitely fit the stereotype. Organization wise, he was over the top. That was evident in the way he maintained himself, his gear, and the way he thought. Very linear. Logical. He set a goal and then set out to do whatever was necessary to get it done. At the same time, he was much more diplomatic than most men she had known. Back in the real world, she would not have been attracted to his type. But she couldn't help but admire his take-charge approach in this new world. And she especially admired the fact that he had already taken on a protective attitude toward herself and Cindy. Laura couldn't imagine Leroy ever being a threat toward either of them. That probably had a lot to do with the loss of his daughters and wife. So far, he had not made any overtures in terms of interest toward her, but she was sure he was at least concerned about her welfare. For now that was enough, perfect, in fact.

Fat rain drops hitting the glass brought her out of her reverie. She glanced back to see the sky suddenly open up with a deluge. Given the mass of clouds that preceded the storm, she expected the rain to last several hours, if not all night and into the next day.

"Cindy, let's take advantage of this rain," Laura said, as she headed toward the stairs.

Cindy rose and followed.

"Do you need me to keep watch?" Damon shouted, as Laura and Cindy started up the stairs.

"We'll be fine," Laura said. "You boys just enjoy each other's company for a while."

Laura and Cindy retrieved a bundle of clothes along with soap, shampoo, and towels from the room and one of the plastic pails from the outdoor store. They then headed back down the stairs and down the first-floor hall, away from the lobby. They exited through the rear door.

Laura propped the door open and stepped out to the concrete slab next to the water tub, already overflowing with water. The rain dropped heavily and steadily.

"Bath first, or wash first?" Cindy asked.

"Bath," Laura said, as she began stripping off her clothes. She dropped everything in a heap and used the bucket to slosh water over her head. She soaped down, washed her hair with the shampoo, and rinsed. "Your turn," she said, as she handed the bucket to Cindy.

Cindy stripped and began washing.

Laura wrapped herself in a towel, but otherwise didn't worry about drying off. The continuing rain made that pointless. Laura bent down and began washing each item of clothing in the tub as soon as Cindy finished bathing.

Cindy wrapped herself in a towel and helped.

Twenty minutes later, with all the clothes in a soapy pile on the concrete slab, Laura dumped the soapy-water filled tub, and repositioned it under the downspout to refill. It took only a few minutes. They then used the clean water to rinse their clothes. When done, they dumped the tub again and let it begin to refill while they wrung out as much water as possible from their clothes. They then picked up everything except the remaining soap, shampoo, and the bucket, and padded back down the hall. At the foot of the stairs Laura paused and leaned her head around the wall. Leroy, Damon, and Lincoln were still there, talking.

"I left the soap, shampoo, and the bucket at the back door," Laura said. "You boys definitely need a bath."

She saw Leroy look down at himself and nod.

Laura and Cindy continued up the stairs and into their room where they lit a candle, dried off with a fresh towel, and began hanging their clothes on a cord stretched between opposite wall lamps. With the clothes hung to dry, Laura turned her attention to her hair. A tangled mess stared back at her in the bathroom mirror.

Just as she had done all she could do with it, there was a light rap on the door.

Still wrapped in the towel, Laura opened the door to find Leroy standing in the dark hall, wearing only a white towel around his midsection. Light from the candle was enough to illuminate his physique. Laura could smell the soap he used to wash with, and for the first time she saw him clean shaven.

He extended a plastic jug full of water to Laura. "I filtered some water before I showered," he said. "Filled every container we have."

"Where're Lincoln and Damon?" Laura asked, as she took the jug from Leroy's hand.

"I went first. It was a bit of a struggle, but I finally got them to bathe as well. They're down there now."

"Thank you for the water," she said, as she let her eyes drop to Leroy's muscled arms and chest. "Will you be sleeping in the lobby?"

"I'll be in the room next door," Leroy said. "Damon and Lincoln will be downstairs."

Laura's expression turned more serious. "You think we can trust them?"

Leroy pursed his lips and exhaled. He glanced down the hall and then back to Laura. "To be honest, I don't know. Lincoln probably more so than Damon. But I'm a light sleeper."

"I'll block my door with a chair," Laura said, as she glanced back at Cindy lying on one of the beds.

"Probably a good idea," Leroy said, as he took a step back. "Doesn't hurt to be careful."

"What do we have planned for tomorrow?" Laura asked. She noted Leroy's millisecond eye drop to the edge of the towel, just above her covered breasts.

"Back to that house for the rest of what's there," Leroy said. "And at some point, I'd like to continue with the mini-storage units. You could still use some boots. And I was thinking that maybe we should hang here a few days more. If it's still raining in the morning, we could ferry water up to the rooms and use it to flush the toilet and take a splash bath inside an actual shower."

Laura nodded and smiled. "I'll see you in the morning then," she said, as she glanced at his arms and chest again.

"Looking forward to it," Leroy said with a smile, as he took another step back and turned toward his room.

Laura closed the door. She retrieved the arm chair in front of the desk and positioned the back under the doorknob. She then gazed at Cindy, still wrapped in the towel, sound asleep on top of the covers. Laura extinguished the candle and curled up in a ball on the adjacent bed. Her last thought was the white towel wrapped around Leroy's midsection.

◆◆◆

Laura opened her eyes to the dull light of an overcast morning and the sound of rain drops against the window. She looked at Cindy's still sleeping body, rolled up in her bed's comforter, and decided not to bother her. Laura rolled to a sitting position with her feet on the floor, glanced around the room, and at herself. She must have moved very little all night for her towel to be mostly still in place. She tightened the towel, stood up, and felt the clothes hanging on the cord, hoping they would be dry enough to wear. The clothes were still wet, almost as wet as the night before. They would take a lot longer to dry in the damp air. She looked around the room again and then padded over to her backpack. She pulled out a rolled up, thin pair of stretch yoga pants and a white t-shirt, the only dry clothes she had left. She slipped into the clothes, her boots, and removed the chair from the door. She went next door and knocked lightly. She waited several seconds and knocked again. Getting no response, she headed downstairs.

Finding no one in the lobby, she walked out the front doors and stood under the portico, wondering where Leroy, Lincoln, and Damon had gone. With no one in sight, she walked back through the lobby to the rear of the building and out the back door. In the distance, walking from the direction of the home improvement store, she saw the three of them headed toward the hotel carrying several large buckets and dragging two large, wheeled outdoor trash cans. They each wore their pistols on their hips. Laura waited in the doorway until they were within yelling distance.

"You should have woken me," Laura said. "I could have helped."

"It's okay," Leroy said. "We got what we needed. I want to collect as much water as possible."

Leroy stopped in front of Laura and let go of the wheeled trash can he had been pulling.

"What are you going to do with that?"

Leroy reached deep into the trash can and came up with a hacksaw. "I'm going to cut a couple of these water spouts so the trash cans will fit under," he said, as he stepped up to the downspout. He pulled the full water tub out of the way and began cutting.

After a couple of minutes of loud screeching from the thin metal, and water flying everywhere, the bottom three feet of the spout dropped to the ground. Leroy dragged the trash can over and positioned it under the spout. Water began filling the can.

Leroy grabbed one of the plastic buckets, dipped it in the water tub, and sat the full bucket on the concrete. He then filled a second bucket. "These need to go up to the rooms for the toilet."

Lincoln took a step forward and reached for the bucket, but Laura stepped in the way and picked both of them up. "Least I can do," she said, as she turned and shuffled inside.

"Keep both buckets in your room," Leroy said. "We have more buckets here for a couple of more rooms."

"Will do," Laura said, as she maneuvered the heavy load down the hall.

A moderate rain continued through the morning. After a few hours, water rushing from the roof and through the downspouts filled both trash cans, the tub, and all the buckets.

Laura positioned two buckets, ten gallons, in each of three rooms to flush the toilet and for showering. She also organized the food obtained from the day before and made sure it was equally divided between the five of them.

After Leroy, Lincoln, and Damon left to gather the remaining food from the red brick house, she and Cindy scavenged the hotel kitchen and the pantry. She found cans of beans, vegetables, and even two cases of spam. She couldn't imagine why a nice hotel would stock spam, but it was a welcome find. The food they found would last them several weeks, but they would have to stay at the hotel to eat it. The large commercial cans would be too heavy to carry in their packs.

By around noon, with the men still not back, Laura decided to take a whack at the storage units. She and Cindy slid into their empty backpacks, gathered the tools from Leroy's room, and walked the short distance to the storage facility. They went straight to where they left off.

Laura raised the hammer and smacked the padlock on the next unit. It took several swings, but finally the shackle separated from the body. She removed the lock, raised the door, and she and Cindy stared at various items of outdoor furniture along with a gas grill, including two white metal propane bottles.

Cindy dashed for the bottles and picked them up. "They're full," she said with a smile.

"We can definitely use the grill," Laura said. "Leave it for now; let's check the next unit."

Just as Laura slammed the hammer against the fifth lock of the day, and raised the hammer for the next whack, she heard scuffling and voices in the distance. She placed the hammer on the pavement and picked up the Glock from the pavement. The voices grew louder. She relaxed when she recognized Leroy and Damon's voices and then saw them round the corner at the end of the building. "You were gone a while."

"We checked several other houses," Leroy said. He slipped his pack off his back and unzipped the main compartment. "Nothing more of value, except what we went back for and these," he said, as he pulled a pair of leather hiking boots from the pack. "They're six and a half. Thought they might fit. They're good quality."

Laura approached, took the boots, and turned them in her hand. "I wear a seven, but these look like they might fit. I'll try them on at the hotel."

Leroy nodded and smiled.

"Did you see those men?" Cindy asked.

"No," Damon said, as he stepped closer to Cindy. "Did you guys find anything here?"

"We did," Laura said, as she stepped off and led everyone back to her first unit. She opened the door and pointed.

"We can use that," Leroy said, as he stepped in and opened the grill top. "The propane?" he asked as he bent down and took hold of one of the bottles.

"Full," Cindy said.

"We also found a bunch of industrial sized cans of food in the hotel kitchen," Laura said. "Spam, too."

Leroy raised his chin and smiled. "Our little community here is coming together."

"It is," Laura said. "Shall we get this stuff over to the hotel?"

Leroy put his pack on and lifted both the gas bottles. "Eat something and then we head back out. There's still plenty of daylight."

"Do you really need to go back out?" Cindy asked. "We have plenty, a lot more than we could carry."

Leroy looked around at everyone. His survey landed on Laura. "I suppose not."

"Have we given up on finding transportation?" Laura asked.

Leroy sat the gas bottles down. "I've been thinking about that. The chances of that diesel being any good are pretty slim. We were just plain lucky to find a pickup that still ran. I wouldn't count on that happening again."

Damon cleared his voice. "Even if you did find a vehicle that still ran, you'd probably have to fight someone for it."

"What about a boat?" Cindy asked. "Doesn't that river we crossed flow east?"

Damon laughed. "You'd still need fuel."

"Let it drift," Lincoln said.

Leroy stared at Lincoln while he rubbed his chin and jaw. "Something large enough to hold those of us moving on, but small enough to maneuver with paddles."

"Yeah," Lincoln said. "There are several marinas along the river. There should be something that would work. We could see what's available and take it from there."

"Sounds like a plan," Leroy said, as he hefted the two gas bottles and walked off.

CHAPTER 15

Everyone trailed behind Lincoln, through an open field, with the hotel still visible in the distance to their rear.

"Where is this place again?" Leroy asked.

Lincoln glanced back. "Only about a mile, where Broadway crosses the river. That's the closest marina to here."

"If we find a suitable boat, how far will it take us?" Laura asked Leroy.

Leroy looked at Laura. "If memory serves me right, the Arkansas turns south at Little Rock until it intersects the Mississippi. Little Rock is probably a hundred and fifty miles from here."

"Is this even worth the effort?" Laura asked.

Leroy twisted his lips as he stared ahead in the distance. "That's mileage we wouldn't have to walk. And the river would be faster, assuming we don't run into something at night and sink."

"That's a pleasant thought," Laura said.

"If we can find the right kind of boat, we should be okay," Leroy said.

Laura lowered her voice. "What about Lincoln and Damon?"

Leroy glanced at Laura to gauge her meaning. She wore a serious expression. "You mean should we make room for them to travel with us?" he asked, as he slowed his pace and let the gap extend between him and Laura, and Lincoln, Damon, and Cindy.

"Yeah."

Leroy rubbed his face with one hand while he thought. The extra manpower would be much appreciated if they ran into trouble, but Leroy had noticed the growing dynamic between Damon and Lincoln with regard to Cindy. Cindy had been paying more attention to Lincoln. Leroy wasn't sure how Damon would ultimately react. Without the extra drama, Damon was already a bit of a loose cannon. "How do you feel about it?"

"My only concern is for my daughter," Laura said. "I have to weigh every decision with her in mind."

"And?"

Laura took several long moments before answering. "I don't know."

Leroy nodded. "I don't know, either." He looked at Laura and locked onto her eyes. "I'm not even sure how you feel about me being around."

"Exactly," she said, with a slight smile, as she accelerated to catch up with Cindy.

Leroy shook his head as he picked up the pace.

They kept to the brush and trees as much as possible while they navigated their way south toward the river. They passed through overgrown communities of houses and apartments with a few people out and about, until the landscape finally transitioned to more industrial buildings. They crossed a set of railroad tracks, walked around a large warehouse, and faced the muddy water of the Arkansas River. A small marina, consisting of open and covered slips, was visible along the shore of an inlet.

"The place is wrecked," Leroy said, as he pulled up next to Lincoln, stopped on a rise above the marina. Leroy scanned the slips from one end to the other. There was nothing much bigger than a medium motor boat, and at least half of those were partially or completely sunk. The only boats still afloat were under the covered slips.

"Let's get a closer look," Lincoln said, as he started down the rise toward the covered slips.

Leroy and the rest followed close behind. Leroy brought up the rear and kept his head on a swivel for anyone around. So far he hadn't seen anyone in this part of town.

He wasn't sure what kind of boat he had in mind when he agreed that floating down the river might be a good idea. The boat would have to be large enough for five people for several days and nights. None of the engines would work on an inboard or outboard. The next best thing would be something with a flat deck, like a pontoon boat. There were two of those that he could see. Both were in serious need of repair. As everyone scattered to search the area, Leroy stood back and watched. He rubbed his face as he imagined himself on one of these boats drifting down the river. Going to the bathroom on the boat would be impossible. And if they had to beach every time someone wanted to go, it would take forever to cover the miles to Little Rock.

Leroy noticed Cindy standing in front of four covered slips, in a line a little farther down the inlet. Something had gotten her attention. Leroy watched as she ducked under one of the roofs. From his angle up on the rise, he could not see what she saw.

He skipped down the rise and began walking down the paved access road toward Cindy. He could see that she had boarded a pontoon boat and had taken a seat on one of the cushioned settees. When he stepped into the slip, he was able to take in the full view of the boat.

Everyone else suddenly appeared at Leroy's side and was also observing the boat and Cindy.

"What do you think?" Laura asked.

"It's in much better condition than any of the rest," Leroy said. "It's big enough, and it's close to the water.

Paddling and poling would be easier from a boat like that." Leroy stepped aboard and took a seat across from Cindy. He ran his hand over the vinyl coverings. They were dirty, but in good shape otherwise. "This could work."

Laura, Lincoln, and Damon took a seat on the boat.

Damon sat behind the wheel and smiled. He looked at Lincoln.

Lincoln cleared his voice. "Won't work."

"What do you mean?" Leroy asked.

"You won't be able to get this through the locks, there are several between here and anywhere east worth the effort," Damon said. "No power and no lock crew."

"When you said boat," Lincoln said, "we thought you meant something small, like an aluminum row boat. Something you can pick up out of the water."

"You'll need to carry the boat around the locks," Damon said. "The first one isn't very far down the river from here."

Leroy took in a deep breath and exhaled. He felt stupid. He didn't even think about the dam and locks along most rivers. "You're right, wasn't even thinking about that."

"Most people wouldn't think about it," Lincoln said.

"Can the locks be opened manually?" Cindy asked.

"On a small canal they can, but not the locks on a major river," Lincoln said. "The locks are closed at one end or the other, or both ends are closed. Can't open those by hand. Need hydraulics to open the paddles and gates."

"Luckily," Damon said, "water flows over or through the dams slow enough to keep the lakes upriver from flooding downriver. Everything is working normally, except for the locks."

"Do you guys plan to hang around here?" Leroy asked Damon.

Damon looked at Lincoln and then took a quick peek at Cindy. "I'd like to tag along," he said, "if none of you mind."

Leroy looked at Lincoln. "Linc?"

"There's nothing keeping us here," Lincoln said. "Eventually the food here will run out. At that point we'd be stuck."

"We have plenty at the moment," Damon said. "Do we need to be in a hurry to leave?"

"No hurry," Leroy said, "but we already have more than we can carry."

"We have a pretty good setup at the hotel," Damon said. "Showers and toilets."

Leroy saw Laura nod, apparently in agreement. "We can take advantage of that until the water runs out."

"Two days, tops, if it doesn't rain again," Lincoln said.

"I say two days whether it rains or not," Leroy said. He looked at Laura.

She smiled and nodded. "Two days."

"Okay," Leroy said, as he stood. "We need a different boat." He looked at Lincoln. "Something small enough to carry."

Everyone scattered to continue the search.

Leroy walked up and down the slips. There were several smaller fishing boats, bass boats and such, but they were all too heavy to pick up, even with five people. It became readily apparent that a suitable boat did not exist at this marina. He rubbed his face with one hand and stared up at the sky, thinking. Cindy's voice interrupted his thoughts.

"What about this?" Cindy yelled.

Leroy turned toward the voice and saw Cindy standing in front of a small metal building among those in the main part of the marina. Leroy started walking in that direction and converged with everyone else next to Cindy. They all stared into the small building.

"Canoes?" Laura asked, as she stepped inside the building and ran a hand along one of the fiberglass boats upside down on a rack.

Leroy stepped into the building and looked around at the six canoes, racked three against one wall and three against the opposite wall. The little boats looked almost brand-new. He glanced at a slew of paddles leaning against a far corner. "They're big enough," Leroy said. "We'd need three boats if we put a max of two people in each boat, plus our gear."

"If you want to travel down the river, this is probably the only way," Lincoln said.

"These things are easy to tip over," Damon said, as he ducked down and looked up, inside one of the boats.

"I've done that a time or two," Leroy said. "Usually when I was doing something stupid."

"I can't imagine you doing something stupid," Laura said with a smile.

Leroy thought of the pontoon boat and smiled back at Laura. He nodded as he turned in a circle and looked at the canoes. "Looks like we have transportation down the river."

Leroy knew there was something wrong as soon as he walked into the hotel lobby. The one gallon jug of water he left on the reception counter was gone. He shifted his rifle to the ready position and motioned for everyone behind him to remain quiet. He stepped farther into the lobby as he glanced in all directions. His eyes stopped on the windows looking out to the patio on the back side of the hotel. The gas grill and both gas bottles were gone.

He looked back at Laura and Cindy, standing several paces behind him. Both had their rifles up and ready. "We need to check our gear upstairs," he said, as he marched off toward the stairs. He looked over his shoulder at Lincoln and Damon still standing in the lobby doorway. "You guys keep an eye out down here. Maybe check the kitchen for anything missing."

Leroy bounded up the stairs, paused at the second floor landing, and then moved down the hall with his rifle shouldered, toward Laura and Cindy's room. He pushed the door open with the barrel of his rifle and stepped inside.

Laura pushed the door all the way open and stepped into the room, with Cindy close behind. She moved to the side of the bed, knelt, and peered under. She raised her torso, blinked one time slowly, and exhaled. "It's all gone."

"What all did you have under there?" Leroy asked, as he moved to the window and peered out.

"The tent, sleeping bags, and our portion of the food from that last house."

"We can probably replace the cans," Cindy said, as she knelt beside Laura and looked under the bed. When she raised up, her face had the same look of despair. "But we'll never be able to replace all those dry goods. They took that Winchester, too."

They both got to their feet.

"Art and Jason," she said.

"Probably," Leroy agreed.

"What now?" Cindy asked.

"We get our stuff back," Leroy said, as he marched out the door and down the hall.

Laura caught up. "What about your room?"

"I had the important stuff with me in my backpack," Leroy said. "The water filter is most important, we still have that. And the ammo and weapons. We still have those."

"Where do we look?" Cindy said, as she trotted behind.

"I'm hoping Linc and Damon can help with that," Leroy said, as he took the stairs two at a time.

Leroy, Laura, and Cindy met Lincoln and Damon at the foot of the stairs.

"The kitchen?" Leroy asked.

"A lot of it is gone, but not all," Damon said.

Leroy held his rifle in one hand while he rubbed his face with the other, thinking. "I would estimate it would take five or six guys to carry all this stuff off."

Damon and Lincoln nodded.

"Okay," Damon said. "What do we do about it?"

Leroy led everyone out the lobby doors and around to the patio. He stopped where the gas grill had been and then slowly walked over to where the concrete pad ended. He knelt down. "Wheel tracks from the gas grill," he said, as he pointed up close and then farther in the distance. "There's a clear path from the wheels."

Damon stepped closer and looked where Leroy was looking. "They dragged the grill."

"Yeah," Leroy said, as he stood up.

"Why would anyone leave such an obvious trail?" Laura asked.

"I can think of only one reason," Leroy said.

Laura raised her chin and squinted her eyes at Leroy.

Leroy returned her gaze. "Ambush. They want us to follow."

"So what do we do?" Cindy asked.

Leroy squeezed his lips together, dipped his chin in a slight nod, and looked at Cindy. "We follow."

"I'd prefer to not walk into an ambush," Laura said.

"I'll second that motion," Damon said.

Lincoln remained quiet.

"I'm guessing you have a plan," Cindy said, as she stared at Leroy.

"More of a tactic." Leroy turned to Damon and Lincoln. "Any idea where they would have gone and who was with them?"

"The same houses we've been targeting are in that direction, along with plenty of brush and trees. They could ambush us anywhere."

Leroy stared off in the direction of the wheel tracks.

"What are you thinking?" Laura asked.

He turned to Laura. "Me and Lincoln will follow the trail." He glanced at Lincoln. "The rest of you will travel parallel, about a hundred yards south of our path."

"You want us to flank them," Damon said.

"That's right," Leroy said. "Lincoln and I will depend on your ability to move quiet and low." Leroy looked at Laura and shook his head. "This is part of the risk of living in this new world."

"I get that," Laura said. "I'm just not sure I want to risk my daughter."

"She can stay back," Leroy said. "Actually, you both can stay back."

Laura looked at Cindy.

Cindy tightened her jaw and locked eyes with her mother.

Laura exhaled deeply. "We're going. The question is when."

"Just before dusk," Leroy said. He looked at the sun. "In about an hour.

Leroy motioned for everyone to follow him back inside the lobby, where he obtained a pencil and paper from behind the reception desk. He then took a seat at one of the lobby tables and began sketching.

Everyone else gathered around. He drew the hotel, the various features to the east, the edge of the housing area, and the north end of the forest they hid in before.

"Lincoln and I will form the tip of the spear. The rest of you will follow well back until you get to this church on the north end of the trees. Hold up there. Move into the trees when it gets completely dark. Be prepared to wait all night and into the morning. When you hear firing, circle around and come in from their flank, or rear. Start shooting as soon as you see a target. Stay well back. Don't do anything heroic. I mainly just want a diversion, something to take the fire off me and Linc."

"Are we sure we want to do this?" Damon asked. "Why not just replace what we've lost and head down the river?"

Leroy laid the pencil down and looked up. He scanned everyone's face. "You can all stay back if you want. I'm going to get our stuff back."

Laura blinked once, slowly, and then rested her face in both hands. She looked up. "How will you follow the wheel tracks when it gets dark?"

"I wouldn't be able to follow them in the daylight once they reach the streets of the housing area, assuming they went that far. I'll have enough light to get to that point."

"And from there?" Damon asked.

"I'll figure something out," Leroy said. He looked around at everyone. "Like I said, be prepared to wait as long as it takes. When you hear firing, move closer, but not too close." He looked out the window. "We have forty-five minutes. Let's make sure we're all locked and loaded."

CHAPTER 16

Fifteen minutes before sunset, Leroy set out with Lincoln at his side. They followed the wheel tracks across an open field to the mini-storage facility, and then into another open field. As the light grew dimmer, and the tracks became harder to follow, Leroy asked Lincoln to concentrate on the tracks while he focused on the surroundings.

The area consisted of wide swaths of open squatty brown grass alongside the interstate, that also covered the ground over a hundred yards south of the interstate. If the perpetrators had wanted to cover their tracks, they could easily have done so by walking along the highway. Leroy was even surer they intended to set up an ambush. The question was, where?

In the far distance to the south, Leroy saw movement, certainly that of Laura and the others as they planted themselves against the north wall of one of the mini-storage units. Leroy felt relieved that they were following directions, but still anxious about them moving into the trees. Unfortunately, he wouldn't be in a position to watch when they did. Leroy was taking a giant risk in that regard, but he was fairly confident that those waiting for whoever followed the wheel tracks would concentrate their force in one spot. He wasn't sure yet where that was, but he was fairly sure it wasn't the trees. Based on the wheel tracks so far, it had to be in the housing area. Even in the dim light, the paved road that ran along the north edge of the community was in sight. The first of the houses were just beyond.

Leroy pulled on Lincoln's shirt to get his attention. They both took a knee. "Let's give it a few minutes until the sun is completely down," Leroy said.

Lincoln focused on the houses in the distance. "The tracks are heading straight for those houses." He pointed. "If that's where they are, they've seen us."

"I know," Leroy said. He watched the very last rays of light as they sank beyond the horizon. "Okay, we're going to stay real low, move fast, and head straight out to the interstate."

"Why are we going away from the houses?"

"We're going to follow the gulley along the interstate east, past the houses, and come in from the east."

Lincoln nodded.

"Stay low," Leroy said, as he rose up and low trotted toward the highway. At the rise just before the gulley, Leroy suddenly stopped and went prone on the ground as he pulled Lincoln with him. "We crawl from here," he whispered.

Leroy crawled the remaining thirty feet. Once he was on the other side, well below the crest, he got to his feet hunched over, and ran flat-out. He didn't bother to look back at Lincoln. He was younger; he'd be able to keep up.

A thousand yards later, just as the interstate started a gradual curve to the south, he stopped. Breathing hard, he went to one knee while he caught his breath.

Lincoln pulled up beside him, breathing just as hard.

Leroy took several deep breaths, waited a few moments more, and then made his way up the rise. Just before the crest he went prone. Against the lighter sky he could make out the roofs of several houses, about a hundred yards off. He scanned left and right. "I think this is the northeast corner of the community. I want to move in among those houses, make our way west, and hole up until morning."

"Morning?" Lincoln whispered.

"We get into position, wait till morning, and watch for movement," Leroy said.

"If they saw us back in that field they'll be wondering where we went," Lincoln said.

"I know. They should be getting real anxious by morning. And someone will need to take a leak." Leroy glanced at Lincoln but couldn't see much in the dark. "Stay close," he said, as he ducked low, sprinted over the mound, and off toward the first house.

"This is crazy," Damon whispered, as he reclined with his back against a tree. "We're supposed to stay out here all night?"

Laura glanced in Damon's direction but said nothing. She kept her attention directed toward the houses just a few yards east of her position. Through the trees and light brush she could see the dark hulks of three houses from her little patch of paradise, the most northeastern corner of the forested area. Based on the direction of the wheel tracks and where they would likely intersect the community, she had to be within ten houses of where the perps would be waiting, if they were waiting at all. The possibility that this was all a ruse had crossed her mind. But more than likely, they were waiting for someone to show up, they did plan an ambush, and Leroy was headed straight into it. She only hoped his army training had prepared him to confront just such a situation. To say she was anxious about the whole thing would be an understatement. Her sense of anticipation was off the chart, made worse by not knowing when. When would Leroy do whatever he planned to do?

"Damon is kind of right," Cindy said, as she scrunched up next to Laura. "How long do we wait, and what do we do when the firing starts?"

"All we can do is wait," Laura whispered. "Like Leroy said, we're just a diversion. I'm thinking we throw a few rounds in the right direction and Leroy will take it from there."

"And what if Leroy goes down?" Damon asked, as he leaned closer to Laura and Cindy.

Laura tightened her lips and exhaled deeply, without looking at Damon. *Yeah, what then?*

Leroy nudged Lincoln in the shoulder as he reclined next to him against the red brick wall.

In the dim light of early morning, Lincoln's eyes opened. "Any movement?"

"Not so far," Leroy replied.

"Have you been awake all night?"

"Uh-huh," Leroy whispered, as he kept his gaze on the five houses in his view. He could see the front of each house; all five backed up to the open field over which the grill wheels had crossed. These particular houses were the most likely spots where whoever took the grill would be waiting. Leroy expected to see someone emerge soon, to urinate or to give up, thinking no one was coming.

Leroy played the previous evening's reconnoiter through his mind as he lay behind a clump of overgrown grass and bushes at the corner of the northeastern-most house of those that backed to the open field. He and Lincoln had spent hours working their way from house to house as they watched and listened for any signs. Leroy never did get any indication of where Art and Jason might be, but did settle on the five houses in his current view as the most likely candidates. Beyond waiting for someone to show themselves, Leroy didn't really have a plan. The chances that all of them would exit a house together was pretty slim. But even if they did, Leroy wasn't prepared to shoot them if they did not present an immediate threat. Even in this world, theft did not warrant the death penalty. Ideally, Leroy would like to get the drop on them. But without more intel, trying to form a plan was a useless endeavor. He would just have to wait.

"Damon and the others must be getting really anxious by now," Lincoln whispered.

Leroy nodded. Linc was right. They had been waiting in the forest all night, not sure when or if something would happen. They had to be tired, and likely over it. The only thing Leroy could do was hope they could hold on a bit longer.

Twenty minutes later, with heavy eyelids that insisted on drooping despite Leroy's intent to keep them open, Leroy heard it before he saw it. A door opening. He looked up and saw two men—middle aged, both wearing shorts, t-shirts, and sneakers—standing outside the front door of the fourth house down. Leroy came fully awake. "We have movement," he whispered.

Lincoln rolled to his side and crawled up beside Leroy. "Just two?"

"So far," Leroy said, as he watched both men walk a few yards away from the door, unzip their shorts, and urinate on what was probably once a nicely manicured yard.

The door opened again and two more men stepped out. Leroy recognized Art and Jason.

"That's Art and Jason," Lincoln said. "Assholes."

"Who are the other two?" Leroy asked.

"That's Jack and Jim Weatherman. Brothers."

"How dangerous are they?"

"Dangerous enough," Lincoln said. "If Jack and Jim are involved, you can bet Milo will be there, too."

"Who's Milo?"

"The biggest asshole, in size and temperament," Lincoln said. "That's probably it. Five guys."

Leroy studied the scene in front of him. Only one of them carried a rifle. Leroy focused and was fairly sure it was the Winchester from Laura's room. He could also see one holstered pistol, but didn't doubt there were others tucked here and there within easy reach. Jason and Art were unarmed before, but that could have changed.

"What now?" Lincoln asked.

"We wait until they go back inside," Leroy said. "Then we approach, enter, and whatever comes after that."

Lincoln bit at his lip for several moments. "What about Damon and the others?"

"I'm hoping we won't need them."

"I'm not waiting here another second," Damon said, as he got to his feet.

"My sentiments exactly," Laura said, as she got to her feet behind her tree.

"Now you're talking," Damon said.

Laura glanced back at the sound of Damon's voice as he began walking west, back toward the hotel. "I'm going this way," Laura said. She looked at Cindy, still sitting on the ground. Her head swiveled back and forth between her mother and Damon, each obviously intending to head off in opposite directions. "I want you to wait right here," Laura said to Cindy.

"For how long?" Cindy asked.

"Wait," Damon said, "you're heading into the houses?"

Laura looked up from Cindy. "Correct." She looked back at Cindy. "Right here," she said with a stern voice.

Cindy nodded.

"I'll wait here with Cindy," Damon said.

Laura nodded, took a final look at Cindy, and stepped forward, toward the houses. She exited the tree-line in a low trot and used any available brush to hide her advance around the back of three houses as she moved north. She paused in a clump of trees behind the third house. From that vantage point she could see a string of five houses arranged north and south, their rear yards faced west, toward Laura. The house farthest north formed the northwest corner of the community. Every house to the west of that point would back to the empty field that the grill wheels crossed. If the bad guys were lying in wait, they would be in one of those houses along the field. And since she had heard nothing from Leroy all night, she assumed he waited till morning for a reason. She had never served in the military, but she was smart enough to know that a direct approach from an open field would be stupid. Leroy didn't strike her as being stupid. Since her, Cindy, and Damon were holding down the western side of the community, that left only the east and south for Leroy and Lincoln. They would approach from one of those directions. But in the dark he had no way of knowing which house the bad guys were in, or if they were in any of them. He needed more info, which is why he waited until morning. So he could see. They would show themselves, eventually.

It had been only a few minutes since dawn; the light was still dim. Laura raced across an open patch of ground and slid to a stop behind a bush in the backyard of the next house, the first house in the north/south string. She felt fairly safe moving behind the first four houses. It would be that final line of homes where they would be.

Laura darted forward and didn't stop until she reached the fourth house. She flattened herself against the rear wall, next to a bedroom window. She eased an eyeball around the edge of the window. She didn't see or hear any activity inside, but just the same, she ducked under, and continued along the back wall. She eased past the back door, another bedroom window, and stopped at the corner. She dropped to the ground of mostly sand and scrub grass, inched herself forward and peered around the edge.

Six houses down. Four men stood in the front yard. Two were peeing in the front yard. She recognized the other two: Art and Jason. There was no sign of Leroy and Lincoln, but that was to be expected. They were hidden, probably watching the four men, just as she was. She was in a good spot. Far enough away from danger, but close enough to get there quickly if needed. She decided to wait and observe.

Leroy watched as Jack and Jim finished peeing. They zipped their pants and then moved back over to Jason and Art. Jack and Jim did most of the talking as they each pointed and motioned in various directions. This went on for several more minutes until, finally, the four of them sauntered back inside the front door. Leroy didn't hear the door close, which meant they might have left it open for ventilation. It was time to move.

CHAPTER 17

There were several ways Leroy could play this. He could wait until the four or five guys got tired of waiting in the house and then mount an assault when they left. He could move in on the house slow and easy, in stealth mode, while maintaining maximum cover. Or he could rush the house, bust through the door, and take them by surprise. The first option, which Leroy actually preferred, was out. He and Lincoln had already drunk all the water they had brought, and Leroy was dry as desert sand. There was no telling how long he would have to wait until the five of them decided to leave. Could be days. The second option still left the question of what to do when they reached the house. Plus, there was always the chance they would be seen on approach. And Laura would certainly be tired of waiting by now. That left the third option. *No guts, no glory.*

Leroy back-crawled until he was completely behind the corner and then got to his feet. He caught Lincoln's eyes. "I'm going in fast and direct. I want you to peel off and go for the back entrance. Door or window, doesn't matter. Be prepared to go in when you hear me hit the front door or when you hear a shot. And don't shoot me by accident."

Lincoln smiled, nodded nervously, and drew his pistol. He looked at the pistol in his hand like he had never seen one. His hand trembled.

Leroy took a final look at the target house. The only part of this plan he didn't like, actually he didn't like any of it, but the part he liked the least was having to depend on Lincoln, an unknown. He wasn't trained, and he had no experience. And yet, somehow, Leroy had confidence that Lincoln would do his part. That wasn't the case with Damon. Between the two, Leroy had made the right choice to bring Lincoln.

Leroy raced off at full bore with his rifle shouldered. He heard Lincoln behind him and saw him peel off when they reached the third house. Leroy accelerated straight for the front door of the fourth house.

Laura saw Leroy and Lincoln as soon as they emerged from around the corner of the fourth house west of the house where Art, Jason, and the other two walked back in the front door. Leroy was running for all he was worth, rifle shouldered. He obviously intended to go straight in the front door. She then watched as Lincoln turned off at the house just before, obviously going for the back. Two against at least four. And there were probably others in the house. The odds were not on Leroy's side. Laura knew she had to help, but how?

She knew how to use her rifle and she was a good shot. That wasn't the issue. The issue was the knots in her stomach. And the shaking. Especially her hands. The last thing she wanted was to get shot. Who would look after Cindy? She shook her head and tightened her lips. She knew traveling across the country with her daughter could get rough. Any number of things could have happened to them, and still could. But with all the possibilities, she did not envision having to rush four or more armed men. She had no doubt she would do it. It had nothing to do with the food and equipment the assholes had taken. It had to do with Leroy. It had to do with watching his back, because she knew he would do as much, or more, for her or Cindy.

When Leroy was within a few yards of the front entrance, Laura got to her feet and raced off toward the same house. The rifle she carried in both hands suddenly felt lighter and there was more spring in her legs.

With only a few feet to go, Leroy was at the point of no return. With the front door standing open, he was sure those inside could hear his footfalls against the concrete walk as he approached. He leapt over the threshold and slowed to a fast walk as he swung the barrel of his rifle side to side.

The foyer consisted of a short hall that led straight into a great room. The four men he had seen outside earlier immediately came into view. Three sat facing Leroy with stunned expressions on their face. The fourth sat with his back to the front door so he could watch out the rear glass sliding doors, through the screened enclosure, to the open field behind the house. Leroy did not see a fifth man, the Milo character Lincoln mentioned, among them or in the kitchen to the right of the great room.

Before any of the four men could react, Leroy fired off six rounds in rapid succession. All were aimed at the ceiling above the great room. He had no intention of killing anyone unless he had to. All four of the men rolled to the floor without hesitation and without going for a weapon.

Leroy brought the barrel down and swung it back and forth, generally aimed at the four men now lying on the floor. Even with Leroy's muffled hearing and the ringing in his ears, he heard the sound of glass breaking from a rear bedroom off to the right. He figured it was either Milo going out, or Lincoln coming in.

A few moments later, Lincoln appeared in the bedroom doorway, his pistol aimed at the four men on the floor.

Leroy saw the reaction on Lincoln's face before he heard the pistol being racked behind him. Given that it was only inches from his head, Leroy froze. Whoever held the pistol hadn't been in the kitchen when Leroy passed; he must have come from the garage, which opened into the kitchen.

"Drop the rifle," the deep voice said. "And Lincoln, you drop the pistol or your friend here is dead."

The four men on the floor hesitantly raised their heads in unison and looked toward the sound of the voice. With a look of relief, they all started getting to their feet.

That's when Leroy heard the faint *click*, the unmistakable sound of the safety lever on an AR type rifle. He heard rustling from behind, footsteps, and then Laura's voice.

"Should I shoot him?" Laura asked.

Leroy slowly turned his head until he saw the big man standing behind him, and Laura standing behind the big man. "Depends on whether he lowers his gun," Leroy said. He raised an eyebrow at the big man.

The big man slowly lowered the pistol a couple of inches.

When Leroy saw the confidence fade from the big man's face, he whipped around and snatched the pistol from his hand. He stuck the pistol in his waist band, raised the barrel of his rifle, and motioned for the man to join his four friends. "Art, are there any others in the house?"

Art hesitantly shook his chin side-to-side as he took a seat back where he had been sitting. "Lincoln and Laura, watch them while I check the rest of the house." When Lincoln and Laura stepped closer to the five men all sitting, Leroy quickly checked the two guest bedrooms on the left side of the great room, and the guest bath. He saw the gear and food taken from the hotel stacked in a corner of one of the bedrooms. He then returned to the center of the guest room and pointed his rifle at the big man. "Milo, I presume?"

Milo nodded. "Now what?"

"Theft in a time of martial law warrants the death penalty," Leroy said it with a straight face, in a deep voice. Everyone in the room instantly locked on Leroy's face, including Lincoln and Laura.

Art was the first to react. "Wait, we just needed the food."

"Uh-huh. What about the ambush you guys set up here, waiting for us to follow the grill tracks?"

"We were just going to scare you off if you came for it," Jason said.

Leroy motioned at Lincoln. "Linc, can you get their weapons?"

Lincoln proceeded to gather the three pistols and one rifle, the Winchester. He placed the guns on the counter in the kitchen.

Leroy walked through the great room to the glass sliding doors at the rear and peered into the screened porch. The gas grill and the two propane bottles were against a wall. He then turned back to the five men. "I want you five to gather everything you took from the hotel and put it all back where you found it. Plus all the extra ammo you have here."

"And then you'll let us go?" Milo asked.

"Depends on how long it takes you to return everything, the sooner the better."

Milo glanced at the other four men and then got to his feet. "Let's do what the man says."

With everything back in place at the hotel, Leroy turned to the five men standing in the center of the lobby. "You can go."

Everyone except Milo took a step toward the front entrance.

"Our weapons?" Milo asked.

"We'll keep those," Leroy said, as he motioned with his chin toward the door.

Milo nodded but didn't look happy as he turned and followed the others out the door.

"Think that's the last we'll see of them?" Cindy asked.

"Hopefully we'll be out of here before they regroup," Leroy said.

"You know, we could have had them carry all this stuff straight to the boats," Damon said. "It would have saved us a lot of trouble."

"Yeah, but then they would have known about the boats," Leroy said. "They could have moved them or set up some kind of ambush. Better they don't know."

"So why are we waiting around?" Cindy asked. "We could leave now."

Laura took a step toward the pile of gear and food. "Let's take a day to get this stuff organized."

"She's right," Leroy said. "Set up your packs as though you had to run in the middle of the night and the pack was the only thing you had time to grab. You'll need some food in each pack, water, clothes, and any other gear you have."

"And the rest of the food?" Lincoln asked.

"We take it of course, eat from the bulk stock," Leroy said. "When the boats play out, we'll have to walk. We won't be able to carry everything. So like I said, put the most important stuff in your pack, but keep it light enough to carry."

"Getting organized won't take all day and night," Damon said.

"True," Leroy said. "But I could use some sleep before we depart, preferably in the bed upstairs."

Damon nodded. "Lincoln and I can grab our gear when we head out, it's on the way."

Leroy nodded. "Right now, I need to eat something and maybe take a nap."

"I'll second that," Lincoln said.

"I don't think any of us got any sleep last night, food and nap sounds like a plan," Laura said.

Just after dawn the next morning, Leroy opened the small metal building containing the canoes. They were still there, just as before. He leaned his rifle and gear against the building, stepped inside, and went to the far end of the closest canoe. He motioned for Lincoln to help with the other end.

Lincoln dropped his gear and helped Leroy lift the canoe, carry it out, and flip it right side up on the ground.

"Laura and I can get the canoes down to the ramp and get the gear we have here stowed. The rest of you should be able to get the remaining food and gear in one trip."

"And bring that plastic storage tub," Laura said. "We may need to collect some water." She looked at Leroy. "It should fit okay in the bottom of a canoe. We can put other gear inside the tub."

Leroy nodded.

Damon and Cindy dropped their packs. The two of them, along with Lincoln, walked off carrying just their weapons.

"I'm starting to wonder if this is really a good idea," Laura said.

"You mean letting her go with those two, or leaving?" Leroy asked, as he stood up straight and faced Laura.

"Leaving. The threat here doesn't seem all that great. There are resources still here, with very little competition. And frankly, the set up at the hotel is pretty good."

"I agree with everything you just said," Leroy said.

"Then why are we leaving?"

"It won't last," Leroy said. "The food will run out, eventually. We have the resources to travel now, that might not be true in the future. Plus, I think there's a good chance civilization is forming back east."

Laura rubbed her face, took a deep breath, and exhaled.

"If you don't think the time is right, I would understand," Leroy said.

"If Cindy and I decided to stay here, at least for now, what would you do?"

"Damon and Lincoln would stay behind as well," Leroy said. "The only reason they're going at all is because of Cindy."

"I know," Laura said. "And that worries me a bit, but you didn't answer my question."

Leroy raised his chin and stared off into the distance for several moments. He then looked back at Laura. "I guess I'd wait."

Laura pursed her lips, took another deep breath and exhaled. She rubbed her face again and looked off in the distance for several moments.

"Your original intent was to head east," Leroy said. "If you wanted to stop at any point, there are probably better places than here."

Laura nodded. "Let's get the next canoe."

As he lifted his end, and they walked the canoe out of the building, he contemplated what he had said about waiting to leave. Would he really wait very long? How important had Laura and Cindy become to him? Was being with Laura more important than getting to Virginia? The answers were too complicated to figure out at that moment. But it was definitely something he would think about.

By the time Cindy, Damon, and Lincoln returned with the rest of the food and gear, Laura and Leroy had three canoes side-by-side next to the water. Each was loaded, with gear secured with cord.

After everyone helped stow the rest of the gear and food, Leroy stood up and did a three-sixty around the area. His focus turned back to Laura. "I guess we're ready."

Laura nodded.

"Who goes where?" Cindy asked.

"That's an excellent question," Leroy said.

Damon stepped closer to the boat next to Cindy. "Cindy and I can take this one."

Leroy looked at Laura. "You and Cindy know how to paddle?"

"Pretty much every summer since she was born," Laura said. "We'll be fine."

Leroy looked at Lincoln and Damon. "How about you two in the canoe with your packs? Laura and Cindy in the boat with their packs. That leaves me and the rest of the gear in this boat," he said, as he kicked the boat with his boot.

"I like it," Laura said. Without hesitating she motioned to Cindy, and the two of them pushed their canoe into the water.

Cindy stepped into the boat first, without getting her boots wet, and took a seat up front.

Laura finished pushing the boat into the water, stepped in the rear, and took a seat. Her movements and execution showed she did, in fact, know her way around a canoe.

After watching Laura and Cindy, Damon shrugged, and then helped Lincoln get their boat into the water and the two of them boarded.

Leroy brought up the rear. "Nice and easy," he said, "we're not in a race."

Everyone quickly fell into a routine that moved the boats along as fast as could be expected, given the situation. After a few minutes of paddling the relatively calm water of the inlet, they reached the much faster-flowing convergence with the main part of the river.

"A few yards offshore should keep us out of trouble," Leroy said, as he dug in with stronger strokes to get through the turbulence. He wanted to make sure the three boats stayed together.

"How fast are we going?" Damon asked, as he watched buildings on shore pass by.

"Two or three knots," Leroy said. "Maybe four, at times, when the river narrows."

Each person fell into their own thoughts as they quietly paddled along. Soon they reached the first dam and lock system that Damon mentioned. In the front canoe, he motioned that everyone should head for the shore. He paddled for a patch of white sand in front of the tree-line along the north bank, well before the dam.

Without being told, everyone pitched in to beach the canoes, remove all the gear, and carry everything separately around the dam to the riverbank on the other side.

Start to finish took an hour, and then they were back on the water.

CHAPTER 18

The flotilla floated silently past abandoned buildings, empty roads, and all manner of dilapidated boats. For some, only a small part of the boat was visible above the surface. The unseen portions rested below the surface of the heavily silted water, likely stuck in the thick mud along the shore.

On rare occasions, a person or two would stop whatever they were doing and wave from the bank. Leroy made a point to wave back. He felt a deep sense of despair over what the country, probably the world, had become. A small population, scattered over a large world, with nothing to do each day except scavenge for their next meal. What struck Leroy the most was how quiet it had become. The hustle and bustle of the past was no more.

Leroy used to read novels about life after an apocalypse. Nearly every story depicted hordes fighting over scarce and dwindling resources. That wasn't what Leroy witnessed before his eyes. To a large degree, the resources remained. It was the people who were gone. There wasn't a lot of fighting and killing. There were exceptions, of course, like the family slain in the desert, and Milo's attempt at thievery. He wondered if Milo would have actually gone through with the ambush. Probably. He seemed the type. The dark side of humanity would exist as long as a single person walked the earth. It dwelt in everyone. The difference was whether a person walked in the dark, or in the light.

Which a person chose probably had a lot to do with his or her belief system and their faith. But Leroy had seen, during his lifetime, people of the dark who professed a strong belief in a higher power, and people with little or no belief who spent their life putting others first. He wasn't sure a higher power had a lot to do with which a person chose. It was largely, in Leroy's estimation, a matter of intellect, education, and upbringing. Something Leroy often repeated during his times in battle came to mind. *This planet would be a great place to live, if it wasn't for the people*. He realized it was pessimistic, but true.

Leroy had read once that overpopulation was behind every problem faced by man. The world population had more than doubled in his lifetime: three billion to seven billion. In his mind he ticked off the results. There was the rise of growth-modified organisms, herbicides, insecticides, antibiotics, and the loss of animal habitats in an attempt to feed an exponentially growing population. The lands and waters, including the oceans, had become polluted to satisfy man's hunger for technology, the next new gadget, and convenience. Cancer, heart disease, and once dormant illnesses were up because of overcrowding and diets with little nourishment. The list went on. Leroy stared at the empty landscape. *This was the result.*

Maybe it would be different this time around. He doubted it, human nature being what it was. All he could do was his part, do what was right as best he could at each intersection.

Leroy accelerated his strokes until he was alongside Laura and Cindy. "I didn't get a chance to thank you for backing me up yesterday," he said to Laura. "Thank you."

"You would have done the same for me," Laura said, as she paused her strokes and looked at Leroy.

"I would," Leroy said. "You handled that rifle pretty good. You learned that from your dad?"

She resumed her paddling. "I got comfortable with firearms with my dad," she said. She wiped sweat from her chin with her sleeve. "My husband was into tactical shooting. He did it as a hobby. He got me involved some, but I was never as good as he was."

"Was he military?"

"No, heavens no, Dave went to college straight from high school. Accounting. He worked his way up to CFO of a medium sized company. He was the office type. But he kept himself in shape. Working out was something we did together. He started shooting at the tactical range for something to do on the weekends with his friends. A co-worker got him started. Dave hated golf." She smiled, but the smile quickly dissipated as she stared off into the distance.

"You and Cindy must miss him."

Laura nodded. "Yeah, but life goes on. At least it has for a few of us."

Leroy stared at a group of buildings passing slowly in the distance.

"I'll always love him, but he died two years ago," Laura said.

Leroy looked at Laura. "I know exactly how you feel."

By late afternoon Leroy estimated they had covered about fourteen miles. It was time to look for a place to stop. "We'll need to pull up and tie off at night," Leroy yelled loud enough for everyone to hear, as he scanned the river ahead.

"What about one of those little islands up ahead," Cindy said, as she pointed.

"If I were a snake, that's where I'd hang out for the night," Leroy said. "I'd like to find some place a little more substantial." He surveyed both shores and saw mostly mud. The last thing he wanted was to get bogged down in waist-deep mud.

Just after they floated past three tiny islands in the middle of the river, Laura pointed off to the right. "What about that?"

Leroy looked where she pointed and saw a single boat ramp. Behind it, he saw what appeared to be a small RV park with room for about twelve units. Only one RV occupied a space in the park. "Looks good," he said.

Everyone paddled in that direction until all three boats bumped up against the sand bottom boat ramp.

Laura, holding her rifle, jumped out with a shallow splash and walked up to the mostly empty parking lot. "This is good," she said, as she turned in a slow arc to scan the entire area. She then bent at the waist, almost to the ground, to stretch her back. "Seems deserted," she said, as she stood up.

"We should check that RV," Leroy said, as he jumped to the ramp and joined Laura. He shifted his rifle to one hand.

They both stepped off in the direction of the lonely vehicle, a class A motor home, fifty yards down in the middle of the park.

Leroy swiveled his head, looking for any signs of human occupation. He saw a trash pile, composed of cartons, cans, and bottles, to one side of the vehicle, and the remains of a campfire a few feet in front of the vehicle's side entrance. There was a single fold-up chair next to the fire pit. The door to the RV stood open. He then saw a shadow pass behind a curtained window just to the left of the door.

Laura stopped and raised her rifle, obviously having seen the shadow as well.

Leroy stepped a few feet beyond Laura, stopped, and yelled. "Ahoy, inside the motor home."

"I've got a bead on you," came an elderly man's voice from inside the vehicle. "Don't come no closer."

"We mean you no harm," Leroy said, without raising his rifle. "We're just stopping for the night. We'll be continuing down the river in the morning."

An old man, late sixties or early seventies, wearing a blue plaid shirt, work pants and boots, and a bright orange cap, stepped into the doorway. He held a bolt action hunting rifle in both hands. "I have nothing you would want here," the man said in a gruff voice. "Might as well move on now."

"We can't do that," Leroy said, as he took a few steps closer. "My name is Leroy, this is Laura. We're with three others still down at the river by our canoes."

The man looked into the distance and raised his rifle in the direction of the boat ramp.

Leroy looked around and saw Cindy, Damon, and Lincoln, all armed, meandering toward the RV. He looked back at the old man. "Like I said, we mean you no harm."

The man studied Leroy for several moments. "You army or something?"

"I am," Leroy said, "army. We're just traveling east. Stopped here for the night."

"What'd you say your names are?" the old man asked, as he lowered his rifle.

"I'm Leroy, this is Laura. That's Cindy, Damon, and Lincoln bringing up the rear." He glanced back at the three and saw they were still headed toward the RV, stepping a little quicker now. "You have nothing to worry about from us. Maybe we could share your campfire; we have our own food."

The old man stepped from the RV and stuck out his hand as he approached Leroy. "Rufus Sims," the old man said. "Memphis, Tennessee. Former eighty-second airborne."

"Glad to meet you, Rufus," Leroy said, as he shook the man's hand with an equally extra firm grip.

Laura came forward and shook Rufus' hand. "You're here alone?" she asked, as she looked past the man and into the RV.

"Lost my wife years ago," Rufus said. "Kids are scattered. Don't really know if they're alive or dead."

"How'd you end up here?" Damon asked, as he, Cindy, and Lincoln joined the group. Damon stuck out his hand. "Damon." They shook.

Cindy and Lincoln stepped forward and shook.

"Left Memphis before the plague got really bad. Crossed the river at Ozark and found this place about the time I ran out of gas. Been living here ever since. Hunted to stay alive after my food ran out."

"And there's been no one around in all that time," Leroy said.

"A few, but no one lately," Rufus said. "This is pretty far from everything."

"Where were you headed?" Laura asked.

"I have, or had, a son in Denver. We lost contact when the power went out. This is as far as I got."

Leroy looked around. "Well—"

"I have some extra chairs if you folks would like to join me for a spell," Rufus said. "I'd love to hear about what's going on out there."

Leroy glanced at Laura and saw her nod. He turned back to the old man. "Sure," Leroy said. "Can I give you a hand?"

"Nope," Rufus said, as he turned, stepped back, and disappeared inside the RV. He returned with three more fold-up chairs. He opened them and positioned them around the fire.

While everyone stood there and watched, Rufus disappeared around the corner of the RV. He returned a few moments later rolling a short tree trunk, pushing it with his foot. He bent down and flipped the log on end to form another seat. Rufus then looked at Damon. "Young man, there's another one of these around there," he said, as he pointed.

Damon looked at Lincoln.

Lincoln went after the extra log.

"Please," Rufus said, as he motioned to the chairs, "have a seat." He sat in the original folding chair.

Lincoln returned, rolling the log with his foot just as the old man had done.

Everyone sat.

Leroy filled the old man in on what had transpired over the previous few days and covered a little of everyone's background. He talked about the rumor of a government trying to form back east and that they were headed that way in hopes of finding civilized society taking shape. It seemed the best option, he explained, given that food was starting to run low, even with the much-reduced population.

The others piped in with comments or clarifications.

Rufus listened intently, nodded occasionally, and rubbed his stubbled jawline when he heard something of particular interest. When Leroy finished talking, and the others had no more comments, the old man turned his gaze to the river. "That river won't take you to Virginia."

"Little Rock," Leroy said. "When the river turns more south, we'll have to start walking."

"You say you started at Fort Smith?" Rufus asked.

"That's right," Leroy said.

Rufus nodded and raised both eyebrows. "How'd you get through the lock, there at the dam?"

"Canoes," Leroy said. "We walked them and our gear around the dam."

"There's three more, Ozark, Russellville, and Conway, four if you count this side of Little Rock," Rufus said.

Leroy nodded.

"Have you run into any desperados?" Damon asked.

"No," Rufus said. "This place is out of the way. I've seen some people on the river, weeks ago was the last one. He was in a canoe, too. Had a dog with him."

"Didn't stop?" Laura asked.

"Nope, went right on by. Course it was midday; he still had plenty of light left."

"You plan to just wait it out here?" Cindy asked.

"Unless I hear of something better," Rufus said. "The hunting is still okay."

Everyone talked on until the light dimmed as the sun went behind the trees.

Leroy looked at Laura. "We better get our tents set up before it gets dark."

Laura stood up, followed by Leroy and Cindy.

Leroy looked at Lincoln and Damon. "Tents?"

Lincoln shook his head.

"We have a tarp and some blankets," Lincoln said. "We'll be fine."

"You're welcome to set up in the camper," Rufus said. "There's room on the floor. It'll keep you out of the mosquitoes."

Damon glanced at Lincoln. "Thank you. We'll take you up on that."

"After we get the tents up," Leroy said, looking at Rufus, "you're welcome to join us for dinner."

"That's mighty nice of you," Rufus said. "Something besides rabbit and squirrel would be most appreciated."

Laura, Cindy, and Leroy cooked rice, beans, and spam over the open fire, with the aid of a lidded pot and frying pan from Rufus. Everyone sat around the fire, ate, chatted, and exchanged stories. Rufus talked about the condition Memphis was in when he left, basically a few people with guns taking what they wanted from the few other people without guns. But that was months earlier. A lot could have changed since then, Rufus pointed out.

"Any interest in going back?" Leroy asked.

Rufus took several seconds to think about the question while he stared at Leroy. "I haven't thought about it. Without gas, it wasn't possible."

Leroy looked at Laura.

Obviously catching on to where Leroy was headed with his question, she raised her chin slightly.

Leroy looked back at Rufus. "I have room in my canoe, if you'd like to join us. We'll be going through there from Little Rock."

"That's a hundred miles from Little Rock," Rufus said.

"Uh-huh," Leroy said. "Figure ten or fifteen miles a day; shouldn't take that long if you can walk it."

"I can do the walk," Rufus said. He looked around at the motor home. "Let me sleep on it."

"Fair enough," Leroy said. He turned toward the two tents, both pitched a few yards to the right of the motor home, and then to Laura. "I'm going to wash out these pots down at the river, make sure the canoes are secure."

"I'll give you a hand," Laura said.

Cindy shrugged and stepped off toward the tent she would be sharing with her mother.

Damon used a long stick to move the ashes around in the fire. "Cindy, care to chat some more? Lincoln and I aren't tired yet." He glanced at Lincoln.

Lincoln yawned.

Cindy stopped and looked back. "Thanks, but I'm really tired. I'll see you guys in the morning." She continued on to her tent.

Leroy and Laura gathered the pots, plates, and utensils, and walked off toward the river.

"You didn't mind inviting Rufus along?" Leroy asked. "He seems to know the area between here and Memphis."

"Didn't mind at all," Laura said. "I like the old man. And I like his stories."

Together, squatting in the dark at the edge of the water, they washed each plate, pot, and utensil as they continued to chat. Stacking the clean dishes in the front seat of the nearest canoe, they mostly talked about what could be expected along the river, the long walk that would come after that, and whether they should try to go through or walk around the larger cities. Leroy didn't have a lot of answers. They also talked about Lincoln and Damon. Lincoln was fine, they agreed. He would be a definite asset. But Damon was beginning to show his true colors. He was lazy, and his main interest, perhaps his only interest, seemed to be Cindy. Leroy and Laura both agreed to keep a close eye on Cindy and Damon.

They continued to chat long after the dishes were done, until finally Laura stood up. "We better get these back to the camp."

Leroy stood up next to her.

With Laura's first step, in the nearly pitch dark, her leg hit the rope stretched from one end of the canoe to a nearby tree. She lost her balance, stumbled, and started to fall.

Leroy stuck out an arm and caught her.

She rolled into his arm and up against his chest. She held that position for several moments before she recovered her balance. She backed away a step. "Sorry."

"Not a problem," Leroy said.

"Well, we better get this stuff back to camp," Laura said again, as she stepped over the rope, and gathered half the dishes in her arms.

Leroy nodded, picked up the remaining dishes, and waited for Laura to go first. He fell in behind with just one thought. *She felt good.*

CHAPTER 19

Leroy dropped an armload of sticks and twigs into the fire pit just as Rufus opened the door and stepped from the motor home.

"I thought I was an early riser," Rufus said, as he joined Leroy.

Leroy bent down and used a lighter to get the fire started. He glanced at Rufus. He stood mesmerized, watching Leroy light the fire. He was obviously deep in thought, probably still thinking about whether to stay or go.

"How does a bowl of oatmeal sound?" Leroy asked, as he stood up.

Rufus jerked from his reverie and looked at Leroy. "Fine. Sounds good. Haven't had any oatmeal in forever."

"Any decision on whether you'll be leaving with us?"

"Been thinking on it all night, practically," Rufus said. "There're pros and cons both ways. As for the walking, I'm not as young as I used to be. I can do it, but it won't be as easy as it once was."

"I understand," Leroy said. "It's up to you."

Rufus nodded. "Let me think on it some more."

"No hurry," Leroy said.

The door to the motor home opened again and Damon stepped out. He yawned, stretched, and looked at Leroy. "What's for breakfast?"

Leroy cocked his head at Damon.

"Like I said, I'll think on it some more."

Leroy nodded.

After breakfast Rufus disappeared into his motor home while Cindy and Lincoln took care of washing the dishes.

Leroy and Laura took down the tents, rolled up the sleeping bags, and secured everything to their packs.

Damon spent the whole time fiddling with his backpack.

Leroy looked around the campsite for anything they might have not packed. He picked up his, Laura's, and Cindy's packs. "I'll get these down to the boats," he said, as he turned to leave. He stopped, put the packs on the ground, and turned back to the motor home when he heard the door open. He saw Rufus standing there, a full backpack in one hand and his rifle in the other.

"I guess you decided," Leroy said.

"Guess I did," Rufus said, as he stepped down from the coach. "You sure you got room?"

"We've got room," Leroy said, as he picked the packs up and started off toward the boats.

With everything packed, including a nylon bag full of the pots, plates, and utensils from Rufus' motor home, they were ready to depart.

Cindy and Damon got in their respective canoes first.

Lincoln and Laura pushed off and then stepped inside.

Leroy stood waiting for Rufus.

Rufus stared at the motor home in the distance.

"Not too late to stay behind," Leroy said.

"Naw, I'm going," Rufus said, as he turned to the canoe and stepped in. He made his way over the equipment to the front seat. Grabbed a paddle and sat. He looked back at Leroy. "You coming?" He then faced front.

Leroy nodded, smiled, and stepped in with one foot, pushed off with the other, and got situated in his seat. He picked up the paddle and began stroking. "You paddle a canoe before?"

"Of course I've paddled a canoe before," Rufus said, as he stuck his paddle in the water and pulled.

There wasn't much to see as they glided along, hugging the south bank. Just trees mostly. The sun was bright.

"Ozark is another ten miles or so up," Rufus said. "We can make it, easy, before dark."

"That's the next dam, you said?"

"Right," Rufus said. "I recommend we get this stuff past the dam before we break for the night."

"My thoughts exactly," Leroy said, as he paddled.

When they entered the outskirts of Ozark, they once again hugged the south bank to keep some distance between them and the main part of town.

Leroy glanced often at the town's buildings and structures along the north bank. He saw some people moving around, more than he would have thought. He didn't see any signs of violence; there was no shooting or screaming. A few people waved, but most ignored the three canoes moving in single file with the flow of the river.

With Lincoln and Damon still in the lead, and Leroy and Rufus bringing up the rear, the group of boats rounded the bend in the river, passed under a causeway, and approached the dam.

Just prior to the dam, they passed another RV park on the right. Unlike Rufus' park, this one was full. Every parking space was occupied with some sort of large motor home.

Everyone in the three canoes watched the park, and the few people that milled around, as they slowly paddled past.

Lincoln looked back at Leroy and silently, with a questioning expression, asked where they should pull over.

At the very end of the park, five hundred feet or so short of the dam, Leroy spotted a stand of trees and an open area. He waited for Lincoln to look back again. When he did, Leroy pointed to the spot.

Lincoln nodded and said something to Damon. They began turning the canoe toward the spot.

Without questioning the change in direction, Laura and Cindy followed close behind.

There was no white sandy beach, but there was a dock. It looked a bit dilapidated, but Leroy thought it would stand the weight of six people. Besides, the rest of the shore in that area was covered with muck, accumulated detritus from the river, and rocks. Getting the canoes out of the water anywhere other than the dock would be a chore.

Damon grabbed one of the vertical supports and pulled. "Seems sturdy enough," he said, as he looked back at Leroy.

"Well, get on up there then," Rufus said.

Even from several yards away he could see the muscles in Damon's jaw tighten as he turned back to the dock, took hold, and carefully stepped from the boat, making sure he kept the canoe balanced as he stepped out. He then reached down and steadied the canoe while Lincoln got out.

The dock was short, only enough room for two of the canoes parked broadside, end-to-end.

Leroy and Rufus, a couple of yards behind Laura's canoe, stuck their paddles in the mud to hold their position against the current.

Lincoln and Damon removed their gear from the boat and then lifted the boat out of the water. They flipped it above their heads and walked it across several yards of rocks to an unkempt patch of greenish-brown grass. They then retrieved their gear from the dock and helped Laura and Cindy through the same procedure.

It took several trips to walk the canoes and gear the hundred yards past the dam, around a power relay station, to a small patch of sand at the water's edge, relatively clear of the junk that had accumulated along most of that part of the river.

"Camp here or move on?" Laura asked.

Everyone did a slow three-sixty. There were no people in sight; even the opposite bank was devoid of people and structures. Just trees and scrub were visible.

Leroy thought about the people back at the camp only a few hundred yards back. He only saw three or four, but there could easily have been many more. "I hate stopping this close to a major town."

Damon looked around again. "We're a good ways down. No people in sight."

Leroy looked at Rufus and Laura.

They both shrugged.

"We have maybe two hours of light left," Damon said. "Loading again and unloading an hour later, doesn't seem worth it."

Leroy scanned the area again. There were trees and brush to block the campfire they would light. He didn't like the area, but Damon was right. Loading and unloading again for an hour of paddling probably wasn't worth it. Plus, Leroy did not know what awaited them an hour down the river. There may not be a place to stop. He took in a deep breath and exhaled. "Okay, but I think we should keep watch during the night. We'll take turns."

Rufus nodded as he looked around the area. "How about we set up over there in those trees?" Without waiting for an answer, he picked up his pack, rifle, and two jugs of water, and began walking in that direction.

Leroy cocked his head, lifted his chin, and grabbed two handfuls of gear. "I guess we're this way," he said to Laura, as he started walking.

Later, with only the campfire for light, everyone sat on a log or a rock in a circle chatting. The fire crackled. Sparks jumped out just short of Leroy's boot. The two smaller tents and a larger tent of light fabric stood a few yards back.

Rufus massaged his left shoulder, stretched it in the air above his head, and then noticed Leroy looking at him. "I'd like to say it was a war wound, but I'm just getting old."

"Were you in the war?" Cindy asked.

"Vietnam. Came through without a scratch. Only one tour."

"After that?" Leroy asked.

"I owned a tree cutting and landscape business. I had over forty people working for me at one point. It was a big operation. Made good money." He looked at Damon. "It was hard work though. Not sure kids these days would be up to it."

"Uh-huh," Damon said. He smirked.

"We should get some sleep," Leroy said. "It's about seven-thirty. Two-hour shifts. Who wants to go first?"

Laura raised her hand.

Leroy nodded. "Laura, then Cindy. Wake me up next. Then Damon, Lincoln." He looked at Rufus. "You up early okay?"

"Sounds fine," Rufus said. He looked at Damon and Lincoln. "You boys are welcome to the tent. Plenty of room."

"Thank you," Lincoln said. "We'll take you up on that."

"Yeah, thanks," Damon said.

Everyone except Leroy and Laura moved off toward their respective tents.

Leroy got up and stepped closer to Laura. He bent down. "Wake me if you hear anything strange, or if something doesn't feel right."

Laura looked up and smiled. "I will."

"Let Cindy know," Leroy said, as he went to touch Laura on the shoulder. He pulled his hand back before making contact.

"We'll be fine," Laura said. "You get some rest." She smiled again.

Leroy paused a moment, stared at her with a smile, and then moved off toward his tent.

"Leroy."

The sound of his name brought him halfway to consciousness. He wasn't sure if the sound was real or in a dream. As he struggled in his mind to determine which it was, he heard it again.

"Leroy."

Leroy opened his eyes to the sound of Cindy's whisper. At the sound of his tent's zipper being opened, he raised up. "I'm here. What's up?"

"I heard something," Cindy said.

Leroy finished unzipping the tent and stuck his head out. Only the stars provided light, just enough to make out the outline of Cindy's form as she knelt next to the tent. "What did you hear?" he whispered.

"Voices. They were low, but I'm sure I heard them."

Leroy pulled himself out of the tent, still fully dressed, and knelt next to Cindy. He peered into the darkness as he listened. He heard nothing except a distant owl. "Which direction?"

"Toward the RV park, but much closer. Probably around the power relay station."

Leroy reached back into the tent, pulled his Glock out, and slid it quietly into his holster, still slipped inside his belt. He then reached back into the tent and pulled his rifle out. "I'll take a look. You stay here." He saw Cindy's chin move up and down in the dim light. "If I'm not back in a few minutes or if you hear the sound again, wake your mom, and the others, but keep it quiet." He saw her nod again.

Leroy stepped off quietly to the east, perpendicular to the north/south flow of the water at their current position on the river. When he reached the tree-line only a few yards away, he paid particular attention to his foot placement. With the toe of his boot he felt the ground before placing his weight on that foot to make sure he wasn't stepping on twigs or sticks that would give away his position. Every few steps he stopped and listened. The fourth time he paused, probably thirty yards from the camp, he heard it. A whisper on the wind. Barely audible, but it was there. And Cindy was right, it came from somewhere around the power station. He turned north and continued his careful trek with the intent of flanking whoever was in the area.

At the next pause, he heard the whispers again, except a little louder, closer to the camp. There were obviously more than one and they were moving toward the camp. Leroy began making his way back to the west, through the trees. Slow and methodical. He judged that he would be on their flank about the time they reached the camp. Their intent was clear. There was only one reason why a group of men, it sounded like men's whispers, would be skulking toward the camp in the middle of the night. They either wanted the food and weapons, or they wanted Laura and Cindy, presumably having seen them in the canoe earlier. Probably both.

A few minutes later, Leroy reached a point where he could see silhouettes a few yards in the distance just as they were about to reach the tree-line on the edge of the camp. He counted five. Based on their size and shape, they were all men, and they carried weapons. Leroy counted three rifles. He couldn't tell if the others had pistols, but he had no doubt they did.

The dam, where anyone traveling the river would have to get out of the water, was the perfect spot for bandits. A group could make a pretty good living off travelers. There probably weren't that many traveling these days, but any would be worth the effort. Leroy thought of the canoe Rufus had mentioned seeing and wondered if that guy had made it past this spot.

Through the trees, Leroy could see the outline of the tents in the clearing. He didn't see any movement and no sign of Cindy. Either she was concealed and everyone was still sleeping, or she woke everyone and they were all hidden. Waiting. Leroy hoped it was the latter.

With only thirty yards or so between Leroy and the five men stopped at the edge of the trees, despite the darkness, he had a shot. In fact, if Cindy and the others in the camp were awake and waiting, the five men would be caught in a crossfire. But there were two reasons Leroy didn't start shooting. No matter how much of an advantage he had tactically, there were no guarantees when bullets started flying. Leroy didn't want to see any of his people hurt. The other reason had to do with the five men. Leroy didn't know their ages or what they actually had in mind. They could be children. Leroy didn't think so, given their size, but they could certainly be young adults. And even if they were adults, intent on evil deeds, they had not done anything yet. Which meant Leroy would not be firing in self defense. However, given his feelings toward Laura and Cindy, self defense was the more minor of the two points. He deemed any risk to their health as justification for pretty much any action.

With that in mind, Leroy shouldered his rifle and took aim at the dark silhouette in front of the group, most likely the leader. With his thumb, Leroy flipped the safety, riding the lever so it didn't click.

CHAPTER 20

The five men were obviously contemplating the best way to approach a dark camp with no one in sight. They had to be wondering whether everyone was asleep, or whether they had heard the men's approach and were waiting, ready to spring into action.

Leroy wondered the same thing for several long moments, but then he saw the outline of the rifle held by the man in front coming up to the man's shoulder. Leroy cocked his right cheek down to the rifle's stock and easily lined up the tritium glow-in-the-dark dots on the iron sights with the man's torso. Leroy then moved his index finger to the trigger and lightly massaged the smooth arc of what felt like an upgraded system. *Fred, back in Sayre, apparently believed in good equipment*. When Leroy saw the man's head duck to take aim, he squeezed the trigger.

The resulting *boom* disintegrated the nighttime silence and muffled Leroy's hearing. The muzzle flash would have given away his position behind the trunk of the large pine tree, so he had only milliseconds to acquire a new target.

Before the front man even dropped, Leroy swung the barrel to the left and stopped on the next dark silhouette. He squeezed the trigger again and saw the second man drop. At that point gunfire from the remaining three opened up as Leroy ducked behind the tree trunk. He heard rounds *thump* into the tree's flesh. He also heard gunfire from the area of the camp. *Cindy had gotten everyone up and they were returning fire.*

Leroy dropped to the ground at the base of the tree and did a rapid crawl to the left, away from the camp and more toward the rear of the five men. At the next large tree, he got to his feet and peeked around the trunk. He saw gunfire from the three men aimed at the tree where Leroy previously stood, and at the camp. He only hoped Laura, Cindy, Rufus, Lincoln, and Damon knew how to duck and keep low.

Leroy shouldered his rifle and raised the barrel as he brought it around the tree trunk. He took half a second to plan his shots on the third man. He aimed, fired, and saw his target drop. His next planned target was no longer in the picture, apparently having dropped to the ground. In fact, Leroy wasn't able to get eyes on either of the last two men.

He dashed to the next large tree, shouldered, aimed, and waited for something to appear. A few seconds later, gunfire from the camp died off, and the night went quiet, doubly so since Leroy's hearing was still muffled. All he heard was ringing in both ears. In a wide arc he scanned the area previously occupied by the five men, but saw nothing. He also saw no movement from the camp. They were waiting. He turned his attention back to the area of the five men and waited. Either they were down, hiding, or they had crawled away.

He couldn't hold this position all night; he needed to get back to the camp and make sure everyone was okay. Leroy turned and low trotted in a zigzag directly away from the target area. He ran forty yards and turned toward the camp. At the camp's southeast edge of the tree line, slightly to the rear of the clearing, he stopped at the largest tree trunk. He peered around the tree at the dark camp and still saw no movement. "Coming in," he said, in a slightly raised voice. When he got no response, he repeated the warning again in a slightly more raised voice.

"Well, come on then," he heard Rufus say from the dark in the distance.

Leroy ducked low and hauled ass until he ran up on Rufus, prone behind a log in front of the tents. Leroy plopped down beside him. "Everyone okay?"

"Not sure," Rufus said. "I'm okay."

"Where're the others?" Leroy asked.

"Scattered behind cover to my right," Rufus said.

Leroy turned his attention back to the tree-line at the northwest edge of the clearing. "Out of the five I saw, any idea how many are left?"

"I think they're all down," Rufus said. "You got three, no doubt about it. I definitely got one, and I think one of the others got the fifth man."

Leroy looked to the right of Rufus. "Laura, you okay?"

"Okay," Laura said from the dark. "And Cindy's okay."

"Lincoln's hit," Damon yelled in a frazzled voice.

Leroy glanced at the woods, immediately jumped to his feet, and dashed toward Damon's voice. Leroy found him huddled behind a rock, kneeling next to Lincoln's prostrate body. Leroy plopped to the ground next to Damon. "How bad."

"A lot of blood, but I can't see how bad," Damon said.

"It hurts like hell," Lincoln said.

Leroy felt the dark spot on Lincoln's left shoulder. He placed Damon's hand on the spot. "Lots of pressure. I have a trauma kit in my pack."

"How bad?" Damon asked.

"If it had hit an artery, he'd already be dead," Leroy said. He then jumped to his feet and ran toward his tent. "Everyone stay down," he whispered, as he passed Laura and Cindy, prone on the ground behind a different rock. "Keep an eye on that tree-line." He slid to a stop at his tent, reached inside, and pulled his pack outside. He rummaged a few seconds, found what he wanted, and then raced back to Lincoln.

"Help me roll him to his side," Leroy said, as he opened his med kit and extracted rubber gloves, a bulky dressing, and some tape. Next he pulled a pocket knife and a lighter from his pocket and cut the sleeve of Lincoln's t-shirt to expose the shoulder. He slipped on the rubber gloves, moved Damon's hand from the wound, and handed him the lighter. "Light it with your hand cupped around the flame so I can see. Make sure you stay behind the rock."

Damon flicked the Bic and held the light close to Lincoln's shoulder.

Leroy could see the entry wound. He lifted the shoulder and looked to the back. He applied the bulky dressing to the front, another from his kit to the rear, and wrapped both tight with gauze. "I think the bullet went through," he said, as he taped the gauze. He then helped Damon roll Lincoln to his back. "How do you feel?"

"Like shit," Lincoln said. "Is it bleeding a lot?"

"From what I can tell, not that much, really. I don't think it hit anything vital."

"What do we do with him?" Damon asked.

"We need to find him a doctor or EMT, even a nurse, who can do a proper job of fixing him up."

"Where are we going to find a doctor in the middle of the night?" Damon asked.

"You and I are going to take him into town at first light," Leroy said.

"What about those guys in the woods?"

"Pretty sure they're either down or gone," Leroy said. "Otherwise they'd be shooting."

For the few hours until dawn, Leroy kept one eye on Lincoln and one on the tree-line, just in case. At the first sign of light in the sky, Leroy motioned for Rufus to follow him as he got to his feet. He low trotted at an angle into the brush, followed by Rufus. They took cover behind the first sizable tree.

Leroy immediately saw three men a few yards farther into the brush. He left his cover, stayed low, and checked each of the men. All dead. He then caught sight of two more a few yards farther back. They, too, were dead.

Rufus walked up as Leroy stood up straight. "Likely somebody will come looking first thing."

"Especially with all the gunfire last night," Leroy said.

"Don't think we can stay here," Rufus said, as he scanned the area in a wide arc.

"Damon and I need to take Linc into town," Leroy said, "try to find him some decent help."

"And the rest of us?"

"Think you can get everything packed up and moved downriver?"

"You think I'm an old man or something, can't find my way down the river?"

"No, I—"

Rufus put a hand on Leroy's shoulder. "I'll take care of getting out of here first thing. How far down the river?"

"At least two miles," Leroy said. "No more than five. I'll look for you along there."

Rufus nodded, turned to start off, and stopped. He looked back at Leroy. "What if you don't show up in a reasonable amount of time?"

"If I'm not there by dark, make camp. Give me another day, but it shouldn't take that long."

"And if you don't show up after another day?"

"I guess I pulled you away from your RV for nothing."

"Not nothing," Rufus said. "It was my decision to trail along with you back to Memphis." He looked at the camp. "I won't leave the ladies stranded, that I can promise you."

"Thanks, Rufus. I'm glad you decided to come along."

Leroy and Rufus returned to camp. Leroy filled everyone in on the five men in the woods and that it wouldn't be safe to remain at the current location. He explained about him and Damon taking Lincoln into town to find help, and that he would catch up by that night, maybe the following night.

Leroy turned to Damon. "We need to get Lincoln in my canoe. Bring your shotgun and your pack."

Damon nodded and bent down next to Lincoln.

Leroy then turned to Laura. "I'll catch up as fast as possible."

Laura took hold of Leroy's hand. "I know you will. Just be careful."

Leroy gave her hand a slight squeeze, smiled, and winked. "See you soon," he said, as he dropped Laura's hand, retrieved his pack, and helped Damon get Lincoln to his feet. "You'll take care of the tent?" Leroy said, looking back at Laura.

"Don't worry about anything except being careful," she said.

Lincoln was able to walk, although with a grimace, as Damon and Leroy carried the canoe back past the dam. They dropped it in the water, loaded Lincoln, and started paddling against the current. When they reached the bridge, they began paddling at an angle toward what appeared to be the main part of town. Twenty minutes of hard pulling got them to a grass-covered bank next to double railroad tracks. They unloaded Lincoln and carried the canoe to a thick stand of trees and brush next to the highway at the north end of the bridge. Wearing their packs on their back and carrying their rifles in one hand, they helped Lincoln down the road until they reached the first intersection. Right there, on the northwest corner, stood an urgent care clinic.

Damon looked at Leroy. "What are the chances?"

"Let's find out," Leroy said, as he started walking toward the clinic with his right arm around Lincoln's waist.

Before they even got to the front doors, it was obvious the place was deserted. A large plate-glass window at the front was shattered, and the inside was dark, dusty, and littered with trash and broken pieces of reception area furniture.

Leroy walked Lincoln back out to the street and looked both ways. "That looks like a hospital down the block," he said, as he motioned with his gun hand.

Damon caught up and all three began walking.

The hospital entrance gave some cause for hope. The windows weren't broken, and there was an older man standing outside.

"Is the hospital still operational?" Leroy asked the man.

"Some," the man said, as he looked at Lincoln. "There's a nurse and an orderly that might be able to help, if it's not too serious."

Leroy opened the door and maneuvered Lincoln through the opening.

A man wearing green scrubs approached, presumably either the orderly or the nurse. "Bring him over here," the man said. He pointed to a small exam room off to the side. "Put him in that chair."

"Are you the nurse or the orderly?" Leroy asked, as he helped Lincoln into the chair.

"Mack Daniels," the man said. "Nurse. They all call me that, but actually I was an EMT. The only one left around here that I know of." He examined the front and back bandages. "Gunshot?"

Lincoln nodded. "And it hurts like hell."

"Marauders during the night," Leroy said.

"You don't look familiar," Daniels said, as he lifted the bandage and peeked underneath.

"Just passing through," Leroy said.

"I've heard of bandits down by the dam," Daniels said, as he cut the gauze with scissors.

"May not be much of a problem anymore," Leroy said.

Daniels paused and looked up. He nodded and then went back to work on Lincoln. "How you feeling, other than the pain?" he asked Lincoln. "Your color doesn't look so good."

"I'm feeling a little weak and nauseous," Lincoln said.

Daniels removed the bandage, front and rear, and examined both wounds. "I can clean the wounds, sew him up, and give him some antibiotics. Not sure they will work."

"And something for the pain," Lincoln said.

"And something for the pain," Daniels repeated. He looked up at Leroy. "You can wait in the reception area. Shouldn't take too long."

"You said they all call you Nurse, how many people are left around here?" Damon asked.

"About twenty percent of the original population, a little better than average, I think. We even still have an active police department."

"Really?" Leroy asked.

"Well, just two officers, but they do a good job with what's left of the people around here."

"We'll be back in a few," Leroy said, as he looked at Damon.

"Give me thirty minutes or so," Daniels said.

"Will do," Leroy said.

He and Damon then walked back through the reception area and out the front doors. The man that had been there previously was gone. "I think we got lucky."

"Looks like it," Damon said, as he looked up and down the street in front of the hospital. "Here come those two officers the nurse mentioned." He motioned with his chin up the street to the west.

Leroy saw two men in uniform, both young, and the man he talked to in front of the hospital. All three were walking toward the entrance.

Leroy shifted his rifle to his left hand and stepped a few feet forward.

When the first officer arrived ahead of the others, he extended his hand. "Officer McFarland. Heard you had some trouble."

Leroy shook hands. "One of our party was wounded last night during an attack by bandits. We were camped the other side of the dam on the opposite side."

"Sorry to hear that," Officer McFarland said. "This is officer Stevens, and you already met Bob."

"This is the only town I've come through with an active police force," Leroy said.

"What's left of us. No vehicles, just foot patrols."

"So what happened during the attack last night?" Officer Stevens asked.

Leroy cocked his head, glanced at Damon, and then back to Stevens. "Middle of the night, we defended our camp."

Stevens nodded. "Who fired first?"

"Does it matter?" Leroy asked. "We didn't attack them, they attacked us. I don't see where who fired the first shot is important."

"It's not," McFarland interrupted. He rubbed his chin. "How many of the bandits went down?"

"All of them," Leroy said. "Five."

McFarland looked Leroy up and down. "You army?"

"Regular army," Leroy said.

McFarland nodded. He looked through the glass entrance doors. "Your man going to be okay?"

"Daniels is fixing him up," Leroy said. "I think so."

"So you'll be moving on?" Stevens asked.

McFarland glanced at Stevens.

"As soon as he's ready to move," Leroy said.

McFarland looked up and down the street. He tapped Stevens on his arm. "We have more streets to patrol," he said, as he turned back to Leroy. McFarland stuck out his hand. "Safe travels."

Leroy shook. "Thank you," Leroy said.

The two officers and the other man turned and walked off.

"Depending on the town, that could have gone a lot different," Leroy said when the three men were out of earshot.

"We're not out of town, yet," Damon said, as he watched the three men walk away.

"That's true," Leroy agreed.

CHAPTER 21

After breaking down the camp and loading the two remaining canoes, Laura, Cindy, and Rufus set out down the river. The river quickly turned south and narrowed, which increased the current. With Laura and Cindy in one canoe, and Rufus in the other, they soon passed a series of ten breakwaters and white sandy beaches on the right, along the west bank, that covered a stretch of nearly two miles. Past the breakwaters, the banks turned mostly to rock and mud as far as Rufus could see. He was about to turn around and go back to the last beach when he spotted a small stream, a ditch really, leading into a stand of trees on the west bank just ahead. Rufus pointed at the stream, paddled in that direction, and then turned into the murky outflow. Within two-hundred feet the stream turned into a shallow mud flat.

"Let's back up closer to the river, it's too muddy down here," Rufus said, as he pointed behind him.

Laura and Cindy back-paddled, followed by Rufus, and then they turned the canoes into the bank. It wasn't white sand, but it wasn't mud, either.

Rufus pulled both canoes up on the ground and then scanned the area in a three-hundred-sixty degree sweep. "This will work." He pointed. "There's a clearing if we need to make camp."

Cindy walked off to explore the clearing.

"Will Leroy be able to find us here?" Laura asked, as she scanned the area.

"Shouldn't be a problem for an Army Ranger," Rufus said with a slight smirk. "According to the patch on his shoulder, he's a Ranger."

Laura tightened her lips and stared at Rufus.

"He'll find it," he said.

"How long do we wait?" Cindy asked, returning to the boats.

"As long as it takes," Laura said without hesitation. "Do we unload?"

"Naw," Rufus said, "we have most of the day ahead. If he's not here by mid-afternoon, we'll set up."

Laura nodded and looked around. She pulled her rifle from the canoe. "I think we should keep watch closer to the river."

"In fact, I'd like to set up a perimeter, someone at the river and someone in the trees to the west," Rufus said. "We're only two-and-a-half miles from last night's camp." He stepped to his canoe and retrieved his rifle. With the rifle in hand, he turned back to Laura. "We should probably eat something first."

"Something easy," Laura said.

"While you do that, I'm going to check the area," Rufus said. Looking at Laura, he raised an eyebrow.

Laura nodded.

"Won't be long," Rufus said. He then walked off into the scrub.

"Ten minutes," Laura said.

"Gotcha," Rufus said. He walked east through the trees, which turned out to be a narrow band no more than fifty feet wide, alongside a large field of scrub grass. In the distance he could see a wide area of white sand, including flats and hills. There were tracks indicating the field had been used by dirt bikers and such. He walked along the tree-line away from the river, entered another band of trees, and then a hundred feet later into another wide open field. In the field right at the edge of the trees stood the back of a long, wood, single-story structure. A barn of sorts, Rufus figured. Rufus walked the circumference and peered in the windows on three sides, at the interior, mostly wide open and empty except for some work benches along the walls. From what Rufus could see, the inside looked relatively clean. Rufus returned to the camp to find Laura and Cindy tending to a campfire.

"Decided we had time, so I thought I'd fry some Spam. You want canned vegetables or oatmeal on the side?"

"Let's use the cans, it'll leave us less weight to carry."

Laura nodded and set to work preparing the food. "See anything?"

"A barn," Rufus said. "Empty. Didn't see anyone around. Just trees, fields, and that's about it."

"I was thinking," Laura said. "If Leroy, Damon, and Lincoln are not back by dark, I think we should go looking for them."

Rufus licked his lips and then rubbed his jaw. That's not what Leroy wanted but, in fact, Rufus agreed.

"I cleaned both wounds, closed, and bandaged them," Daniels said, standing over Lincoln sitting in a chair. "His arm should stay in the sling for a couple of days, no longer. He doesn't want a frozen shoulder." Daniels handed Lincoln a small bottle of tablets. "Antibiotics. Don't use them unless you come down with a fever."

"Shouldn't he start taking them now?" Damon asked.

"He doesn't have an infection now," Daniels said. "He should take them when he gets an infection.

Antibiotics used as a prophylactic is part of the reason we're in this fix."

Leroy looked at Lincoln, whose face was still a little pale. "How you feeling?"

"Arm feels better," Lincoln said.

"I gave him a local anesthetic," Daniels said. "It will wear off quickly. You might feel some discomfort for a few days. Try not to move your arm too much for at least a couple of days. Don't want it to start bleeding."

Lincoln nodded. "Thanks, Doc."

Daniels patted Lincoln on his good shoulder. "You should be okay in a few days. In two or three weeks, you'll be back to normal." Daniels looked at Damon and then Leroy. "Anything else?"

"No," Leroy said. "How much do we owe you?"

"The medical goods here aren't mine to sell," Daniels said. "I'll do the best I can until supplies run out."

"Thank you," Leroy said, as he shook Daniels' hand. Leroy helped Lincoln to his feet and then helped him walk from the room.

"I'm okay," Lincoln said. "I can walk. Just point me in the right direction."

Leroy led Lincoln through the reception area, out the front doors, and into overcast light. Leroy looked up at the clouds. "Looks like rain."

The three of them walked back to where the canoe was hidden. They paddled back to the dam, pulled the canoe out and then back in on the other side, and resumed paddling.

"How far down you think they are?" Damon asked.

"I told Rufus two miles, so at least that far," Leroy said. "Look for some sign, might be either side of the river."

They paddled past their former campsite and past the first two white sand beaches and breakwaters.

"That beach would have been a good place to stop," Lincoln said.

"Too open," Leroy said. "Rufus would have passed these."

At the tenth breakwater Leroy began searching both shores in earnest. He had no idea what kind of sign Rufus would have left, but he was sure it would be something. Another half mile down, the sign turned out to be Laura jumping up and down, waving her arms. She stood at the point made by a small stream, lined both sides by trees and brush.

Leroy and Damon paddled for the point, then up the stream a bit, and beached next to the other canoes. Laura, Cindy, and Rufus stood there ready to greet them like they had been gone for a month.

Leroy stepped out, pulled the canoe farther up on the sand, and then turned around. He found himself face-to-face with Laura.

She gave him a quick hug and then stepped back. "I'm glad you're back." She looked around at everyone staring at her. "We're glad you're back."

"Looks like rain," Rufus said.

"I guess we should pull out the tents," Damon said.

Rufus took hold of one of the canoes and pulled it completely out of the water and onto the sand. "I have a better idea," he said, as he stood up. He pointed through the trees to the west. "Found a large barn about a hundred yards through the trees. Wood floor. Clean. Let's take cover there."

Leroy looked at the sky and then began untying the gear in the two canoes. "Everybody grab something."

"Canoes, too, right?" Rufus asked.

"Yep."

It took three trips for everyone to get everything into the barn which, just as Rufus described, turned out to be a long, wide structure with a completely open floor space. Leroy figured it had been used for storage years earlier. Storage of what he didn't know, since the wood plank floor was completely clear of any debris. Just some dust was present.

And just as they stepped in with the last of their gear and the canoes, the sky opened up.

Laura immediately gathered every pot and the plastic tub and set them out to collect as much water as possible. And everyone except Lincoln took the opportunity to shower, taking turns under the water rushing off the roof onto a concrete slab on the one side of the barn without a window, just a door. Leroy recommended Lincoln not get his bandages wet. Instead, he took what amounted to a sponge bath with some soap and a hand towel.

Leroy, the last to shower, stepped back into the barn wearing just a towel around his midsection. His hair dripped water.

"You could use a good snipping," Laura said, as she stared at Leroy. "Take a seat."

As ordered, he sat on the only seat in the barn, a short three-legged stool that had seen better days.

Laura retrieved some scissors from her pack and began snipping away.

"Cut it as short as you can," Leroy said. "And thanks."

"No problem," Laura said. "Cindy and I cut each other's hair all the time." Ten minutes later Laura stood back and admired her work. She left a little hair on top, but cut the sides and back as close as possible. "You look like you belong in the army again."

Leroy felt the sides, back, and top. "Feels good."

"Hold on," Cindy said, "we have a mirror." She rummaged through her pack and then stepped up with a small mirror in a fold-up case. She handed it to Leroy.

He checked all angles and then nodded. "Perfect," he said with a smile. He looked at Laura. "Thank you."

"Like I said, no prob." She looked around the room. "Who's next, you could all use a serious trim. There may not be another opportunity."

Leroy went back to the roof shower to wash off the excess hair.

Laura ended up cutting all the men's hair, and even gave Cindy a trim while she was at it.

The rain continued the rest of the day and into the early evening. Dinner was cold, since there was no place to light a fire and Leroy wanted to preserve his stove gas as long as possible. Laura was able to filter and top off every jug and water container they had, which amounted to about eight gallons total.

When darkness arrived, Laura lit one of the candles and placed it on the three-legged stool in one of the corners. Everyone sat on the floor in that corner and leaned back against one of the two walls.

"Are we moving out tomorrow?" Damon asked. "I'm not sure this rain is going to let up."

"I'd like to give Lincoln at least a couple of days' rest, with that shoulder," Leroy said. "If he ends up with an infection, he'd be better off here than out on the river in a canoe."

"How are you feeling?" Cindy asked, looking at Lincoln.

"A little tired," Lincoln said. "The shoulder is achy, but not too bad."

"Does it hurt if you try to move it?" Rufus asked.

Lincoln moved his arm slightly with a wince. "Yeah."

"We'll see how you're doing in a couple of days," Leroy said. "In the meantime, at least we have this barn."

"A couple of us could go back to town," Damon said.

"What for?" Rufus asked. "You meet a girl while you were there?"

Damon glanced at Cindy. "No. I just thought maybe we could trade or something. The town seems pretty civilized. Police force and a doctor."

"We don't really have anything to trade," Laura said. "We need all our food. We have no equipment to spare."

"Same with guns and ammo," Leroy said. "None to spare, really. We should hang close to here until we're ready to move."

"We could do a little hunting," Rufus said. "Maybe scare up a rabbit."

"Good idea," Leroy said. "Maybe you can take Damon out tomorrow, if this rain stops."

"I could do that," Rufus said, as he glanced at Damon.

Damon cocked his head. After several seconds he nodded. "Whatever."

"I think we should all get some rest," Laura said. "Especially Lincoln. You heal most while you're sleeping."

Everyone nodded, or grunted in Rufus' case, and began unrolling sleeping bags at various spots around the barn floor.

Cindy unrolled her bag fairly close to Lincoln. "I'll keep an eye on Linc," she said.

Damon took a spot nearby, likely to keep an eye on both of them.

Rufus staked a spot in the far corner, the farthest possible from everyone else. He mumbled something about his snoring as he walked in that direction.

Laura took a corner in the front of the building.

Leroy set up a few feet away. He removed his boots and then scrunched into the sack. He lay flat on his back, with his fingers intertwined behind his head. He stared into the darkness, thinking. His thoughts pinged from one thing to the other. Would Lincoln's shoulder get infected? Should they consider remaining here, close to Ozark, longer? Damon was right. With the marauders gone, the town was much more civilized than most he had come across. How would his motley crew fare when the river played out, and they had to start walking? And he thought about Laura, lying only a few feet away.

CHAPTER 22

Damon woke to something pushing on his shoulder. Not wanting to be roused, he kept his eyes closed and pretended to be asleep. The interloper persisted with more nudges.

"I know you're awake," Rufus said in a gruff whisper. "You sleeping this morning, or hunting?"

Damon opened his eyes a slit, enough to see that it was still dark, and immediately closed them. "It's still dark," he said, as he pulled his knees up closer to his chest. "We can hunt later."

"It's now or never, sweet pea," Rufus said. "Coming or not?"

Damon opened his eyes fully. "Seriously, bro, it's pitch dark." He paused for a moment. "And it's still raining."

"A mere drizzle, it'll let up soon enough. Let's go."

Damon rolled to his back and stared up at the dark hulk standing above him.

"Early bird, and all that," Rufus said.

Damon snorted as he crawled out of his sleeping bag. He looked around at everyone else still sleeping. "Dude—"

Rufus held up his hand to stop Damon mid-sentence. He motioned with his head to follow.

Damon put on his sneakers, got to his feet, and followed Rufus out of the barn's front door. He noticed Rufus was not carrying a rifle, not even a pistol. "You plan to attack something with your bare hands?"

"I'm going to show you how to set some small game snares," Rufus said, as he continued walking. "Everything I need is in my pocket."

"Let me arm up, just in case," Damon said, as he stopped walking.

"Don't need it," Rufus said. "You and I are the only ones up at this hour."

Damon continued walking and caught up to Rufus. "What hour is it?"

"Four or five. Sun will be up soon." Rufus pointed to the horizon in the east. "Already getting light over the trees."

"What kind of snare?" Damon asked.

"The kind that will catch small game," Rufus said. "Just watch and listen."

Rufus led Damon due west, away from the river, a hundred yards across the open, short-grassed field to a line of trees. They entered the trees and kept walking another two hundred feet to the other side of the narrow strip. An even larger, wide open field occupied the vast empty space to the west.

Damon immediately set his eyes on a small pond, almost perfectly round, about two-hundred feet out. "Let's check out the pond."

Rufus nodded and set off across the open field toward the water.

Damon scanned the area as they walked. He saw no people and no structures, except a barbed wire fence alongside a north/south running two-lane paved road. "Meant for livestock you think?"

"Yep, probably cattle," Rufus said, as they reached the edge of the pond. "This is manmade, watering hole for the cattle."

"Looks pretty clean, sand bottom," Damon said, as he squatted and swirled his hand in the water. He stood up, looked toward the fence, and pointed. "What's that over there?"

Rufus looked where Damon pointed. "What?"

"That field," Damon said. "Looks like some kind of garden. Might be something we can eat." He started walking. "Let's check it out."

The two of them stepped through the barbed wire fence, walked a few hundred feet into the field on the other side of the road, and stopped at the edge of a large area, the remains of what was once a garden. The rows were still visible, despite the weeds.

"Personal garden for whoever owns or owned this property," Rufus said. "It hasn't been planted since the plague, mostly weeds."

Damon pointed to the far end. "What about that?" He pointed.

They both walked to the far end, where they found several rows of intermittent short plants with yellowing leaves.

"Potatoes," Rufus said. "Must have sprouted from what was left in the ground."

"Think there's any we can eat?" Damon asked, as he stooped toward one of the plants.

"We're at least a month past harvest time," Rufus said, "but yeah, there might be a few."

Damon pulled gently on the stalks, wiggled them back and forth to help free them from the loose soil, until finally the ground let go and potatoes emerged. He fingered the potatoes. "I think some are good."

"Let's go back to the trees to set the snares," Rufus said, as he looked around the area. "We can come back here after and see if we can collect enough for everyone." He turned and marched off.

Damon rose and followed.

Back through the fence, Rufus stopped just inside the trees and looked around at the brush. He must have spotted what he was looking for because he suddenly marched off a few yards and stopped next to a small path mashed into the ground cover. "Game trail," he said. He reached into his pocket and pulled out a pocket knife. He flipped it open with one finger and looked around.

"Looks like a nice one," Damon said, staring at the knife.

"ZT titanium," Rufus said, as he grabbed hold of a very young sapling, about one inch in diameter. He looked at the knife. "S35VN steel. Titanium handles. Yeah, it's a pretty good knife."

"You mean scales," Damon said.

"No, I mean handles," Rufus countered. "On a pocket knife scales are the metal linings of the slot where the blade folds into. Handles cover the scales. Sometimes there are no scales, just handles. Like with this knife."

"Small point," Damon said.

"You're right," Rufus said, as he started cutting at the sapling. "You can call them scales if you want. You can call them lickity dickities if you want. But I'll call them by their proper name. Handles."

"Fine," Damon said. "Are you always this ornery?"

"If by ornery you mean accurate, then yeah, I try to be," Rufus said.

Damon shook his head.

Rufus cut the sapling, trimmed the end, and cut off a section about four inches long. He cut off another fourteen inch section and let the remainder drop to the ground. "Now watch how I do this, you might learn something."

Damon stretched and rubbed the back of his neck, exhaled, and tightened his lips. But he watched.

Rufus cut a square notch in one end of both sticks, so that when the ends were brought together at both notches, the sticks would more or less lock together lengthwise. He then sharpened the other end of the long stick and whittled a shallow notch around the other end of the short stick and a second shallow notch around the middle. He then pulled some twine from his pocket. "Thin wire would work better, but I don't have any thin wire. This string will work." He unrolled enough string to form a ten-inch-diameter circle, cut it, and tied a slip knot in one end. He ran the other end through the slip knot and tied the loose end to the middle of the short stick. He then found another sapling next to the game trail and stripped it of its limbs and leaves. He cut the top off of the sapling, bent it toward the ground, and let it whip back. "That'll work." He took a longer length of string and tied one end to the sapling and the other end to the short stick, opposite the notch.

"I see," Damon said. "Long stick goes in the ground and hooks to the short stick by the two notches. You drape the loop on the trail. Animal comes through, trips the two sticks, and he flies up in the air."

"Correct, young lad," Rufus said. He pushed the long stick in the ground, pulled the sapling down, and hooked the short stick to the long stick. He then spread the looped string over the game trail, and camouflaged the string with a little grass and tiny twigs. "That's it," he said, as he stood up. He handed the knife to Damon.

"We need four of these around the area, either farther down this trail, or other trails would be better."

Damon took the knife, looked around, and set off, followed by Rufus.

"Rufus and Damon are coming back," Laura said, as she stared out the front window of the barn. "Looks like they're carrying something in their arms."

Leroy, Cindy, and Lincoln joined Laura at the window, peered out, and then everyone stepped out the door.

When Rufus and Damon got close enough for Leroy to tell what they were carrying he smiled as he glanced at Laura. "You were able to snare some potatoes."

"And some rabbit, if we get lucky," Rufus said, as he stopped in front of Leroy. He opened his arms and let a bunch of potatoes drop to the ground.

Damon walked up and did the same thing.

"Where'd you find those?" Cindy asked, obviously delighted at the find.

"An old garden across the way," Rufus said. "Found a pond of fresh water over there, too."

"We set some small game snares," Damon said. "We'll go back to check later."

"Is there anything else in the garden?" Leroy asked.

"Don't think so," Rufus said. "These probably sprouted from old plants or something."

"You said there's a pond," Laura said.

"Yep," Rufus said, "manmade for when there was livestock. The water's clear. Sand bottom."

"We can filter more water when we need it," Leroy said.

Lincoln bent down and picked up a potato with his good hand. He examined it closely. "If you do get a couple of rabbits, we could make some stew."

"We have a can of carrots," Laura said, as she bent down and started gathering the potatoes.

Cindy and Leroy helped.

"Let's hope we get lucky with the snares," Rufus said. "We'll check them later in the day."

Rufus looked at Lincoln. "You're looking a little peaked. How are you feeling this morning?"

"Didn't get much sleep," Lincoln said. "Shoulder is stiff, hurts when I move it."

Leroy placed the back of his hand against Lincoln's forehead. "Hard to say, you might be a little warm."

"Should we give him the antibiotics?" Damon asked.

Leroy paused, took in a deep breath, and let it out slowly. "Let's see how he's feeling later in the day." He locked eyes with Lincoln. "In the meantime, you need to rest. Stay in the shade." He looked at the sky. "If the sun comes out, that is. And drink plenty of water."

Lincoln raised his chin, gave a weak smile, and returned to the barn.

"What's for breakfast?" Damon asked.

"What do you think?" Leroy said.

"Oatmeal."

"That's right," Leroy said. "We were just about to make some, if we can find some dry wood."

Rufus tapped Damon on the back of the head. "It's been long enough, we better check those snares. Otherwise some varmint will take what's ours."

Damon got up from the floor and stepped out the door, holding the door open. "You coming?"

Rufus chuckled with a smile, then got up and followed Damon.

"Hold up," Leroy said, as he looked at Laura. "We're coming, too."

Laura cocked her head and fell in behind Leroy. At the door with Leroy she glanced back at Cindy and Lincoln sitting in a corner. "Can you keep an eye on Lincoln?"

With no break in her conversation with Lincoln, she looked up at her mother and nodded. She and Lincoln then resumed talking.

Leroy and Laura followed Rufus and Damon into the woods and to each of the snares. All four snares had been set off; the first two held a rabbit each, strangled by the neck.

At the fourth snare, Rufus held up a rabbit in each hand. "This is enough for today. We can reset the snares this evening, maybe get something for tomorrow." With the two rabbits in one hand and his rifle in the other, he turned to head back to the barn.

Damon fell in close behind.

Leroy stopped Laura as she took a step. "Let's check out that pond and the garden, there might be something left."

Laura nodded, shifted her chin to one side as she pursed her lips, and smiled. "Okay."

"We'll meet you guys at the barn," Leroy said in a raised voice to Rufus.

Rufus stopped, glanced back, smiled, and kept walking.

Leroy and Laura exited the trees and started out across the field.

"Let's check out the garden first," Laura said, as they walked. "We don't seem to be making very good progress toward Virginia."

Leroy ground his teeth trying to think of something to say, but for the life of him, words didn't come to mind. "Uh-huh."

Laura continued to talk as they walked. She talked about how adding Rufus to the group turned out to be a good idea, and how he had kind of taken Damon under his wing. Every young man needs a mentor, she pointed out. She looked at Leroy. "Not that you wouldn't make a good mentor."

Leroy returned her gaze and nodded.

At the fence, Leroy used a boot and a hand to part the fence strands while Laura stepped through.

Then she did the same for Leroy.

The garden was pretty much as Rufus described. There were remnants of a variety of vegetables, but nothing salvageable except the potatoes that Rufus and Damon dug up.

Laura did a slow three-sixty of the area. "Shall we check out that pond?" she asked, as she started walking toward the water hole.

Leroy followed.

At the pond, Laura bent down and fingered the water. "Feels nice." She looked up at Leroy.

"Full from the rain," Leroy said, as he felt the water. "It does feel nice."

Laura walked to a stump sawed clean and the former adjoining tree trunk, lying flat, a few yards from the edge of the water.

Both the stump and the trunk were completely stripped of bark, leaves, and most limbs, but were otherwise intact.

Laura took a seat on the trunk and started removing her boots.

"What are you doing?" Leroy asked.

"I'm going for a swim," she said. She stopped what she was doing and looked up at Leroy. "You're welcome to join me." She smiled and resumed untying the laces and slipping off her boots.

"Not wearing trunks," Leroy said.

"Neither am I," Laura replied.

"What about the others?" Leroy asked. "What if Damon or Rufus shows up, or, heaven forbid, Cindy?"

"They're welcome to join us, too," Laura said, as she slipped her t-shirt off, undid her waist snap, and let her khaki shorts drop, leaving her in black panties and a sports top. She paused for a moment and looked at Leroy.

Leroy stood with eyes wide.

Laura then slipped her sports top off, pulled her panties down her legs and off, and nonchalantly walked nude into the water.

Leroy watched until Laura was thigh deep. He then slowly scanned the area. Except for a tree here and there, the area was completely open and visible from the trees and brush back toward the barn, the fence and paved road, and much of the land beyond. With no one in sight, Leroy turned his gaze back to Laura who was wading deeper into the water. He hoped Rufus would not return to the forest to reset the snares. If he did, Leroy and Laura would be in plain view.

Leroy walked over to the tree trunk, leaned his rifle against the stump, and stripped off everything quickly. He then waded into the water until he stood in breast deep water next to Laura.

"Perfect depth," she said, as she stared off in the distance. She looked down. "Clear water and a sand bottom."

Leroy smiled as he subtly shook his head back and forth. "Trust me; I am well aware of how clear the water is."

Laura smiled, laughed, and looked down toward Leroy's waist. A bit lower. She tightened her lips as she raised her head and looked off in the distance. A slight smile reappeared.

Leroy caught her expression, looked down into the water, and watched himself growing by the second.

Laura suddenly dropped below the surface until totally submerged. After a few moments she sprang up in a cascade of water, faced Leroy, and wrapped her arms around his neck.

They kissed, long and hard.

On the way back to the barn Leroy and Laura ran into Rufus and Damon in the forest, resetting the snares.

"How's everything at the barn?" Leroy asked, as he approached Rufus.

"Fine," Rufus replied, as he stopped what he was doing and looked up at Leroy. "How are you two doing?"

"Fine," Leroy said. He looked at Laura.

"Fine," Laura said, with a smile.

Rufus returned his attention to his snares. "Uh-huh."

Leroy looked at Laura and raised an eyebrow.

Laura shrugged. "We'll see you two back at the barn," she said, as she stepped off.

Leroy nodded at Damon and fell in behind Laura.

As they exited the trees and the barn came into view, Leroy saw Cindy and Lincoln headed their way across the open field. Cindy carried one end of the water tub in one hand; Lincoln had the other end in his good hand.

"You must be feeling better," Laura said, as the four of them met in the middle of the field.

Leroy noticed that the tub was full of clothes.

"I don't feel any worse," Lincoln said.

Laura placed the back of her hand against his forehead. "I don't feel a fever." She looked at Leroy.

"Just don't overstress or get heated," Leroy said.

"Right," Laura said with a slight smile. She glanced at Leroy and then back to Cindy and Lincoln. She looked in the tub. "You're washing clothes?"

"Might as well take advantage of the pond while we have it," Cindy said.

"Couldn't agree more," Laura said with a smile.

"I'll be sure not to get soap in the main body," Cindy said, looking at Leroy. "And we have plenty of room in the barn to hang everything to dry."

Leroy nodded as he and Laura began walking.

"Oh, and Rufus and Damon cleaned the rabbits and washed the potatoes," Cindy said.

"We'll get that stew going," Laura said over her shoulder.

At the barn, with the sky still overcast but with no rain, Leroy used some river rocks to form a firepit near the front entrance. Kneeling, he made a three-foot-diameter circle with the rocks. He then placed two groups of three rocks each inside the circle.

"What are the middle rocks for?" Laura asked.

"Cover the entire circle with the fire, and let it burn down a bit. Place the two pots we have on the center rocks."

"Smart," Laura said. "Less chance they'll spill."

"Uh-huh," Leroy said, as he continued to position the rocks just right. "About the pond."

"Yeah."

"Should we talk about it?"

"If you want to," Laura said. "I wouldn't have done it if I didn't feel something."

Leroy paused his work and looked up. "I feel the same way."

"That's all that needs to be said then," Laura said, as she started walking toward the trees behind the barn. "I'll gather some firewood."

Following a dinner of rabbit stew, when all the pots and dishes were washed and stored, everyone sat in a corner of the barn by the light of a single candle. While everyone talked, Leroy changed Lincoln's bandages.

"You look better," Leroy said. "How are you feeling?"

"Better," Lincoln said. "Shoulder's a little tight, but not as painful."

"We'll give you another day or two," Leroy said. "Make sure there's no infection."

"Why not just head out?" Rufus said. "We have the antibiotics if he turns for the worse."

Leroy glanced at Laura, who nodded, and then at Lincoln. "If he's no worse in the morning, okay," Leroy said. "Hopefully, he'll be even better."

After everyone retired to their corners, Leroy and Laura were left relatively alone.

"What happens when you reach Virginia?" Laura asked.

"When we reach Virginia," Leroy corrected.

"Okay, we."

Leroy took an awkward amount of time before he answered. "I don't know."

"Do you still plan to join up with the army, if there is an army?"

Leroy raised his chin and stared at the ceiling for several moments before he answered. "I don't know."

"Is there anything you do know?" Laura asked.

"Uh-huh."

Laura looked at him with anticipation.

"You and Cindy will be part of whatever I end up doing." He paused and stared at Laura. "If that's what you want."

Laura nodded. "It is."

CHAPTER 23

After two uneventful days of paddling and a walk around two dams, they found themselves floating under the Broadway Street Bridge in Little Rock with plenty of daylight to spare. Although the area was much less pedestrian than its former self, there were still more people out and about than expected.

"Why so many people you think?" Rufus asked, as he looked back at Leroy.

"I suspect people from miles around migrated here over the last two years," Leroy said.

"Probably right," Rufus said, as he looked up at the underbelly of the bridge. "More people, but still no vehicles."

"No gas," Leroy said.

Rufus looked in the distance and pointed to the bridge ahead. "I suggest we pull over just before the Main Street Bridge."

"You know the area better than I do," Leroy said.

Rufus got Laura's attention and pointed to the north bank, next to the end of the bridge. She nodded and started paddling in that direction.

Just past a line of barges, they beached the canoes on a rocky bank next to an overgrown grassy area and a few trees.

Leroy helped pull all three canoes completely out of the water and stood up next to Rufus and Laura.

"What's the first order of business?" Rufus asked.

Leroy scanned the area. His gaze came to rest on the gear-filled canoes. "We can't camp here, and we have more gear than we can carry in one trip."

"I think we should get the trading out of the way," Laura said. "Including the canoes."

Leroy nodded. He then scanned the area again and spotted two men walking down the paved road that ran alongside the river. "Be right back," he said, as he grabbed his rifle from the canoe and started off toward the two men. "Excuse me," he said, as he approached.

The two men stopped and faced Leroy.

"Where would a man go if he wanted to trade?" Leroy asked, as he stopped in front of them.

The taller of the two men pointed to the northeast. "The arena," he said, "that's where everyone goes to trade."

"They have boots and such?"

"They do," the man said, "pretty much anything you would need. Run by a man named Bill Custer. Heavyset, red beard, can't miss him." The man looked past Leroy at the others standing by the canoes. "What are you trading?"

"The canoes, maybe a couple of weapons, some ammo," Leroy said.

"They have more weapons there than they know what to do with, but they'll take the canoes," the man said.

"What kind of man is Bill Custer?" Leroy asked.

The two men looked at each other. "Fair enough, but you wouldn't want to cross him," the tall man said.

"Any law enforcement in town?" Leroy asked.

"Nothing official," the man said, "all died. Bill has kind of taken on that role as well. He and his men."

"Calls them deputies," the shorter man said.

The taller man nodded.

"Is it safe around here?" Leroy asked, as he glanced back at Laura and Cindy.

"Probably safer than it was," the tall man said. "But, you know, times are rough for everyone. Just be willing to protect what's yours."

"Thank you for the information," Leroy said, as he extended his hand.

The three men shook, and Leroy returned to the group.

"There's trading at the arena," he said, as he pointed.

Rufus looked at the arena. "Only a couple of blocks, do we split up the group?"

Leroy looked at Lincoln. "Can you carry one end of a canoe with your good arm?"

Lincoln bent down and picked up the end of a canoe and set it back down. "With a little help to get it up to my shoulder, shouldn't be a problem."

"We wear the backpacks," Leroy said, as he bent over and scooped up his pack. "Load the rest of the gear into one canoe which you and I can carry," he said, nodding to Rufus. "The rest can carry the two empty canoes. Just two blocks."

Everyone nodded, reorganized the gear, hefted the canoes, and started walking.

At the southwest side of the building they carried the three canoes up a grassy hill and lowered them to the ground next to a short hedge, overgrown with weeds.

Leroy surveyed the area and noted a few people walking in and out of the main entrance. Nearly everyone was armed with at least a pistol.

"Everyone arm up and wait here," Leroy said. "Let me check things out first."

"Maybe I should go with you," Laura said.

Leroy nodded and looked around at the rest. "Be ready, we have no idea what to expect here."

"We'll be fine," Rufus said. "The sooner we get rid of these canoes, the better."

Leroy led Laura to the front entrance, which consisted of several sets of double glass doors. Only the middle doors were open. They walked through the doors alongside two other men who were entering at the same time. Leroy got the attention of one of the men.

"How does this work?" Leroy asked.

The man, very tall and slender, pointed to a couple of tables set up facing them several yards away. Behind the tables stood rows of other tables heaped with various items of clothes, food, and gear. A few people walked up and down the rows. "Check in there, let them know what you have to trade and what you're looking for," the man said. "They'll direct you from there."

Leroy nodded, thanked the man, and glanced at Laura. They approached the far right table, behind which sat a young man, thirties, wearing a long sleeve shirt. When Leroy got closer, he could see that the man also wore a holstered pistol. He was writing notes with a pencil in a ledger.

"What do you have to trade?" the man asked without looking up.

"We have three canoes, a Winchester rifle, and the 30-30 ammo," Leroy said.

The man looked up at Leroy briefly, but spent much more time running his eyes up and down Laura. "Is that it?"

"Yes," Leroy said. "Three canoes and the rifle."

"What are you looking to trade for?" the man asked.

"A couple pair of good hiking boots and three winter jackets," Leroy said.

"The rifle won't get you much," the man said, "but we'll take the canoes. Where are they?"

"Right outside," Leroy said.

He gestured with his hands and gave a smirk. "Bring them in."

Leroy and Laura went back out the doors and rejoined the group. He began unloading the gear from the one canoe. "Rufus and Cindy need to stay here with the extra food, the rest of us will take the canoes and the Winchester inside. Shouldn't take too long." Leroy looked at Rufus and Cindy, in turn. "Is there anything you two need?"

"I have these boots and the parka," Cindy said, "I'm good."

"I have what I need," Rufus said.

Leroy put all the paddles, the Winchester, and its ammo in one canoe. "I'll be back for the other canoe in a minute," Leroy said, as he picked up one end of the canoe.

Laura picked up the other end and together they started off, followed by Damon and Lincoln with the second canoe.

They carried the two canoes through the doors and then put them on the floor in front of the table. Leroy left and returned two minutes later with the third canoe hefted over his head. He put it on the floor next to the other canoes.

The man stood up from his table, walked around, and examined the canoes. He looked at Leroy. "Okay, two pairs of boots and two jackets."

"Three jackets," Leroy said.

The man studied Leroy for several moments and then picked up the Winchester from the canoe. He examined the rifle closely. "Three jackets." He turned and pointed to the far right side of the building. "Boots and clothes are over there. When you find what you need, bring it back here."

The four of them walked up and down the rows of footwear and clothes until Damon and Lincoln had boots and a winter coat each and Laura had a suitable parka which turned out to be grey, with fur around the edge of the hood. They returned to the table with the items. The man behind the table examined the goods and gave his approval for the trade. Leroy shook hands with the man and left with Damon, Lincoln, and Laura trailing behind.

"How did it go?" Rufus asked when everyone was back together.

"Got what we needed," Leroy said. "Shoes and coats for the lads and a nice parka for the lady." He looked at Laura and smiled.

Laura winked with a smirk.

"Now what?" Damon asked.

Leroy glanced at the sky before he faced everyone. "We have a couple of hours. Put as much of this extra food as possible in our packs, carry the rest, and we head north toward the interstate," Leroy said. "We find a place to hole up for a bit to get organized."

"House or hotel?" Lincoln asked.

"Whatever we can find," Leroy said.

Everyone nodded, loaded their packs, and started off, carrying anything that wouldn't fit inside. They walked north on Magnolia. Commercial buildings soon gave way to an older community of nicer homes. Given the number of people out and about, they decided to keep walking. They entered an industrial area, crossed some railroad tracks, and entered another community, this time of modest homes. There were fewer people out and about, but still too many for Leroy's taste.

Leroy glanced over at Rufus, who was keeping pace. "How much farther to the interstate?"

"Half mile or so," Rufus said. "Mostly residential from here."

They walked out of the community of single-family homes, walked past a vacant school, and came upon two hotels across the street from a National Guard Armory compound. The area sat adjacent to Interstate 40 and included a number of fast-food restaurants, all vacant.

"Let's find some rooms in one of these hotels," Leroy said, "and then I'd like to check out that armory."

"The military vehicles?" Rufus asked.

"You never know," Leroy replied. "A running Humvee would be nice."

The hotels sat front-to-front, separated by a large parking lot. The building most north, closer to the interstate, was also closer to the armory. Leroy picked that hotel as their destination.

The glass lobby doors were closed and there was no broken glass, so Leroy had high hopes for the interior. They forced the doors apart with the small pry bar Laura still carried in her pack. All surfaces inside the lobby were covered in dust, but the interior was otherwise in pretty good shape.

Leroy set the contents of his arms, mostly commercial sized cans of vegetables, on the registration counter. He slipped his rifle sling over his shoulder, shifted it to one hand, and proceeded down the corridor to the first-floor rooms. Rufus, Laura, and Damon followed suit. Lincoln and Cindy took a seat on a sofa in the lobby.

Rufus used the pry bar to open the first room, which was ready for occupancy. He moved on to open more rooms, followed by Laura and Damon.

Leroy dropped his gear in the first room and joined the others.

Working from room to room they found three on one side of the hall and two on the other, closely grouped, that would serve them well enough. After everyone dropped their gear in the various rooms, Laura in the room directly across from Leroy's room, they all marched back to the lobby.

"I'd like to check out the armory with Rufus and Damon," Leroy said, "if the rest of you don't mind hanging here to keep an eye on our gear." He got no complaints, so he nodded at Rufus and Damon and the three of them walked out the lobby doors. They crossed the street, walked alongside the armory building to the back, and stopped at the compound's chain-link gate at the rear. Visible inside the fence were various military vehicles, arranged in rows. The gate was closed but not locked, so they entered.

"Why wouldn't others have checked out these vehicles long ago?" Rufus asked.

"I'm sure someone, probably a lot of people, did," Leroy replied, "but I'm hoping they found them inoperable."

"If they are not operable, how does that help us?" Damon asked.

Leroy slowed as he walked down a line of deuces and Humvees. "Before I was accepted to ranger school, I spent the first two years of my career in the motor pool. I know a few tricks that most people wouldn't know." Leroy stopped at an eight-passenger Humvee in desert camouflage. "Some of these have keyed ignitions, most don't," Leroy said. He looked inside the driver's side window. "This one does not."

Damon stood in front and leaned on the hood while Rufus walked around to the passenger side. He opened the door and slid into the seat.

Leroy opened his door, reached in and flipped the ignition lever to *run*. Not seeing the *wait* light illuminate, he flipped the lever back to the engine stop position.

"Batteries are dead." He then walked around to the passenger side and motioned for Rufus to step out.

Damon joined them on that side of the truck and watched through the open door as Rufus got out and Leroy stepped up to the opening.

Leroy reached to the front of the passenger seat and unhooked the two latches. He rocked the seat back, lifted the seat from its housing, and placed it on the ground next to the truck. He then turned back to the now-visible batteries. "Together they provide twenty-four volts," he said. "These look okay, wired right, just dead." He returned the seat to its former position and then scanned the yard. Adjacent to the rear of the building stood a large fuel tank. Leroy walked to the tank, followed by Rufus and Damon, and used a knuckle to tap up and down the side. "Nearly full," he said.

"Full of what?" Damon asked.

"Diesel," Leroy said. "All these trucks burn diesel."

"Isn't it too old to burn?" Rufus asked.

Leroy nodded as he looked around the vehicle storage yard. "There may be a solution to that." His eyes locked on a small metal storage shed in the far back corner of the yard. He marched off in that direction. He found the shed secured with a padlock, but made easy work of it with Laura's pry bar that Rufus carried.

Leroy swung the door open wide and stepped inside. He examined the various plastic containers and jugs stored on metal shelves until two at the end caught his eye. He picked one up and read the writing on the side.

"PRI-D, what's that?" Damon asked.

"Stands for Power Research, Incorporated," Leroy said. "The D is for Diesel. It's a fuel treatment meant to extend the life of fuel."

"But any fuel here is probably already unusable," Rufus said.

"It can also be used to refresh old fuel," Leroy said, as he replaced the jug. "It'll make it good again."

"What about the batteries?" Damon asked.

"That's no problem on a Humvee," Leroy said, as he looked around the shed. He shot Rufus and Damon two rows of white teeth. "Trust me, this will work."

CHAPTER 24

The next morning, Leroy stood next to the fuel storage tank. A five-gallon jerry can sat on the ground next to his feet and he held several layers of cheesecloth in one hand.

All eyes from the rest of the group stared at Leroy.

"Go through all that again," Damon said.

Leroy stared at the ground, massaging the back of his neck with his free hand. He looked up at the group. "We're going to filter the fuel in this tank through the cheesecloth and into the jerry cans. We then add about an ounce of the treatment to each can. While most of you are doing that, Rufus and I will be draining the fuel tank on the Humvee and cleaning out the lines."

"How do we know this will work?" Cindy asked.

"We don't know," Leroy said. "All we can do is try. It either works, or it doesn't. If it doesn't work, all we've lost is a couple of days." He looked at Laura.

She nodded almost imperceptibly and smiled.

The previous evening with Laura spending the night in his room flashed in his mind. "But it will work," Leroy continued.

"How many cans?"

"All of them," Leroy said. "I've scrounged sixteen cans from around the compound. Some are empty; some have fuel. We'll filter any fuel in the cans the same way we do the fuel from the storage tank. We start with the cans."

"What about our gear at the hotel?" Damon asked. "Shouldn't someone be over there watching it?"

Everyone laughed, except Damon.

"What?" he asked.

"I keep my backpack close to me at all times," Leroy said. "I suggest you all do the same. We can chance it on the rest of the stuff." He looked around at everyone. "No other questions, let's get started. Laura's in charge of the fuel filtering operation. Rufus and I will be at the Humvee." He looked around again for any questions. Seeing none, he nodded first to Laura, then to Rufus, and walked off toward the truck.

Having stopped work only once, around midday for lunch, by the end of the day all sixteen cans had been filled and treated. The truck's fuel tank and lines had been drained, and the tank refilled with treated diesel.

Leroy stood next to the open driver's door and faced the group, who all looked on. "Moment of truth," Leroy said.

"That it is," Rufus said, as he cocked his head.

Leroy turned to the door opening and reached inside.

"Maybe we should let the fuel set a while longer," Rufus said. "You said the treatment would take some time to refresh the fuel."

Leroy glanced back. "It's been long enough."

"What about the dead batteries?" Rufus asked.

Leroy held up his index finger without saying anything as he looked back inside the cab. He reached down to the floor and wrapped his hand around a steel cable with a lock attached to the end. He pushed the cable back through the firewall and gently pushed it in and out slightly until he felt some resistance. "Here goes," he said, as he took a deep breath and yanked the cable.

Nothing happened. Not a peep from the truck.

Leroy fed the cable back into the firewall, massaged it until he felt the resistance he was looking for, and yanked.

Nothing.

"Is this some special way of starting a Hummer?" Damon asked.

"It is," Leroy said. "When it works."

Leroy went at the cable, over and over, for a solid twenty minutes, resulting in a Humvee that refused to start.

Initially, everyone watched with great anticipation. But after the first five minutes or so, they each in turn moved to shady spots nearby, took a seat, and generally watched Leroy. Only Laura remained standing next to him, just out of his way.

"Maybe the fuel does need to sit longer," she finally said.

Leroy took a deep breath, exhaled, and turned to face Laura. His face glistened from sweat. Beads ran down his forehead and cheeks. He wiped his face with one sleeve. "That wouldn't stop the starter from at least turning over."

Damon walked over. "Can we push it to get it going?"

"That won't work with an automatic transmission," Leroy said. "I think we need those batteries charged so we can turn the engine over."

"How do we do that?" Laura asked.

Leroy pointed to a diesel generator at the rear of the building. "We drain the tank on that generator, fill it with the fuel, and see if we can get it started. It has a pull crank. There's a charger in the storage shed. We can hook it to the generator and charge the batteries."

"How long will that take?" Damon asked.

"A few hours," Leroy said.

"Maybe we should work on that tomorrow," Laura suggested.

Leroy wiped his face again with both sleeves and then looked at Laura. He nodded. "Okay," he said. "I guess we could all use a break."

"Especially you," Rufus said, as he walked up.

Early morning the next day found Leroy back at the Humvee, yanking the cable to no avail. About a half hour later the rest of the crew showed up.

"What about trying a different truck?" Rufus asked.

Leroy, bent over the driver's seat, let go of the cable and turned to face the others. Sweat glistened on his face. "We'd have to clear the tank and lines again," Leroy said. "Let's give the generator and charger a go." He walked off toward the generator.

Working together, they siphoned the fuel out of the generator's tank and replaced it with the refreshed diesel. Leroy pulled the crank handle several times. The generator turned over and puttered some, but would not start. Leroy let go of the handle, stood up straight, and massaged his neck. He looked at Damon. "Mind giving it a few pulls," Leroy said. "We need to pump the bad fuel through the lines until the new fuel cycles through."

Damon nodded as he traded places with Leroy. He grasped the handle and pulled, and then pulled again, and again. A full five minutes went by before Damon let go of the handle and stood up straight, breathing hard.

"Let me show you people how it's done," Rufus said, as he nudged Damon out of the way and took hold of the handle. He put one foot against the generator, looked at Leroy, winked, turned back, and pulled with one mighty effort.

In a cloud of smoke, the generator coughed and fired to life.

Rufus stood back and gestured with his hands. "And that's how it's done."

"After I did all the work," Damon said with a smirk.

Lincoln looked into the armory through a nearby window. "Hey, the lights are on in there."

Everyone gathered at the window to confirm the illuminated interior. Leroy then backed away and started walking toward the storage shed. "We need to remove the batteries from the truck," he said in a loud voice over his shoulder. "It's a twelve volt charger; we'll have to charge one battery at a time."

Rufus motioned for Damon to follow. They walked to the Humvee, gathered a couple of wrenches from the back, and began working on the batteries.

Leroy obtained the charger from the storage shed and set it up inside an alcove at the rear of the main building, next to an exterior outlet. He plugged the charger in, checked the reading on a gauge, and waited for Rufus and Damon to bring the first battery over.

Leroy hooked it up, checked the gauge again, and stepped back.

"How long?" Rufus asked.

"An hour each should do it," Leroy said. He then led Rufus and Damon back to the Humvee to help remove the second battery.

Laura, Cindy, and Lincoln stood nearby, observing the operation.

"While we're waiting," Rufus said, "why don't we drain the tank and clean the lines on a second vehicle. Just in case there's something wrong with this one."

Leroy paused with a wrench in his hand and looked at Rufus. "That's a good idea." He handed the wrench to Damon. "Finish this while Rufus and I get started on another truck."

Damon took the wrench, stared at it a few moments, and took Leroy's place.

Leroy and Rufus, joined by Laura, walked up and down the several lines of vehicles. "We need another eight-passenger version," Leroy said. He stopped and pointed. "Like that one."

Four hours later, with the tank and lines on the second Humvee drained and cleaned and both batteries charged on the first Humvee, they broke for a lunch prepared by Cindy and Lincoln. After lunch, Leroy, Rufus, and Damon reinstalled the two batteries into the first Humvee.

With everyone gathered around, Leroy took in a deep breath, exhaled, and flipped the ignition lever to *run*. The yellow *wait* light blinked on.

"That's a good sign," Rufus said.

Leroy nodded, paused until the light went out, and then pushed the lever over to *start*. The engine turned over for several seconds, but did not fire. Leroy let go of the lever and the engine stopped turning. He shook his head slightly side-to-side as he tightened his jaw. He pushed the lever over to *start* again, the engine turned over several more seconds, and suddenly coughed to life in another cloud of smoke. The Humvee ran rough at first, but then settled into a steady rumble.

Leroy let the engine run while he slid into the seat and examined the various instruments. The battery charge gauge needle pointed to green, which meant the alternator was charging the batteries normally. He ran the palm of his left hand around the steering wheel while he massaged the gear shift. He looked out the open driver's side door at the group smiling and giving each other high fives. The sound of the engine drowned out most of what they were saying, but Leroy got the idea. He smiled at everyone until his gaze focused on the scene behind them. His smile faded. He flipped the ignition lever to *stop* as he slid from the seat. The engine went quiet. His hand instinctively went to the butt of the Glock holstered on his hip.

The rest of the group turned in unison to their rear at the sound of clapping. The clapping from a single individual, a rather rotund man with a bright red beard, continued for several more seconds until he had everyone's attention. Five additional men stood behind the man. Each held a rifle, generally pointed at Leroy and his friends.

The man stopped clapping and smiled. "Very nice," he said in a deep voice. "Very nice indeed." He walked around the group and stopped at the open driver's door, next to Leroy. He smiled at Leroy. "Excuse me while I check out my new ride."

Leroy tightened his jaw as he stepped back a couple of paces.

The man slid into the seat and palmed the steering wheel. "This will come in real handy," he said. He then turned to Leroy and stuck out his hand. "Name's Bill Custer. I appreciate you getting my vehicle up and running."

"What makes it your vehicle?" Laura asked, as she stepped forward.

Custer raised his chin to the five men still pointing their rifles. His lips turned into a smirk. "They do."

CHAPTER 25

Leroy locked eyes with Laura and subtly shook his head back and forth. He casually looked around at his group. Only he and Lincoln were armed. He glanced toward the rear of the armory at the backpacks and long guns inside the alcove. He then looked back at Custer.

"You might be thinking," Custer said to Leroy, "that since you're in that army uniform, that this vehicle more rightly belongs to you." He turned and looked into the eyes of Leroy's people. Without turning back to Leroy he continued, "You would be wrong." He then turned back to Leroy. "Everything in this town, including everything in this armory, belongs to me and my men. Simple as that." He gestured to two of his men and then pointed at the weapons and backpacks.

The two men walked over and gathered the three AR rifles, Damon's shotgun, and Rufus' hunting rifle in their arms and returned to the formation.

Another man took Lincoln's pistol.

Custer lifted Leroy's pistol from its holster and then nudged Leroy toward the rest of the group.

Leroy stopped next to Laura. "What about us?" Leroy asked.

Custer twisted his lips to the left and flipped his hands in the air. "Free to go."

Leroy glanced at the pistol in Custer's hand.

"I'll hang onto the weapons," Custer said. He motioned with Leroy's pistol. "Gather your packs and be off. You have your new boots and jackets, so there's really nothing keeping you here." He pointed toward the interstate. "The highway is right there." His smile turned into a frown. "Get to it."

"Let's go," Leroy said, as he stepped off toward the packs.

The rest of the group fell in behind him.

One of Custer's men, a short middle-aged man with long hair, spoke up. "What about the women?"

Leroy stopped and turned to face Custer.

The rest of the group stopped and turned.

Custer smiled. "In fifty-six years of living I've learned something," he said, as he looked up and down at Laura and Cindy. "Don't leave a man with nothing to lose." He nodded at Leroy.

Leroy and the others turned and stepped off toward the packs. They gathered their packs and walked out of the gate, crossed a bit of overgrown grass, and stepped up on the pavement of Interstate 40. They began walking east.

"Are we just going to let them take our stuff?" Damon asked.

"For the moment," Leroy said, as he continued walking.

Leroy led the group a few hundred yards until a clump of trees stood between him and the armory. He made a sharp turn into the brush and stopped next to a large oak. "You still have that Glock?" Leroy asked, as he looked into Laura's eyes.

She nodded, slipped her pack off, and rummaged until the black pistol emerged in her hand. She gave it to Leroy. "What do you have planned?"

"Six against one handgun," Rufus reminded everyone.

"Two handguns," Cindy said, as she stepped forward with the revolver.

Leroy nodded. He led everyone to the other side of the thicket and took cover behind some thick brush, which gave them a view of the armory compound. Leroy and the others watched as Custer and his men hooked a trailer to the Humvee and loaded all the jerry cans full of refreshed diesel onto the trailer. They then all got into the Humvee and drove off.

Leroy stood up straight. "I think they'll take that fuel back to the arena and try to get the generator there going," Leroy said.

"The arena has a generator?" Lincoln asked.

"It does, for power outages and emergency situations," Leroy said. "Most stadiums are equipped for such emergencies."

"So what do you have in mind?" Rufus asked.

"I'm going to the arena, and if I see an opportunity, I'll drive off with that Humvee and hopefully our weapons."

"I'm coming with," Rufus said.

"Me, too," Laura said, as she took the revolver out of Cindy's hand.

"I can't ask any of you to go where I'm going," Leroy said. He looked at Laura. "Especially you."

Laura cocked her head to one side.

"You have a daughter to worry about." He then turned to Rufus. "I'd appreciate it if you would stay behind with Laura and Cindy." The serious nature of his request etched across his face.

Rufus nodded.

"What about us?" Lincoln asked. "Me and Damon."

Leroy looked at Damon. He expressed much less enthusiasm, but Leroy judged he was willing. He then looked at Lincoln. "How's the arm?"

"Fine," he said, as he swung it across his torso. His wince was almost imperceptible.

"Just Damon, if he wants to go," Leroy said.

Damon looked at Cindy and nodded.

"What do we do?" Laura asked.

"They won't expect us to return to the armory." He looked at Rufus. "Filter and treat more of the diesel. There's some left in the storage tank and some of the other vehicles still have jerry cans. You'll need to charge the batteries in that second Humvee."

"And then what?" Laura asked.

"If we're not back by the time you're done, I'd recommend you all head out."

Damon rubbed his face with both hands. "Why don't we all just filter the fuel, charge the batteries for truck number two, and leave?"

They all looked at Leroy expectantly.

"We need those weapons, for one thing," Leroy said. "Trust me, if Damon and I can't get the weapons without taking too much of a chance, we'll be back here to join you."

"If you're not back by the time we're finished," Laura said, "we'll wait longer."

Leroy closed his eyes and took in a deep breath. He exhaled. He nodded and looked at Damon. "You ready?"

"I guess," Damon said, as he reached for the revolver.

"Let them keep the revolver," Leroy said.

Leroy and Damon traveled at a fast walk until they were within fifty yards of the building. From a distance, they observed people walking in and out of the front entrance. They made their way around the building and finally took up a position on the north side, behind an Exxon station. There was no sight of the Humvee, but Leroy had his eyes on a concrete block, eight-foot wall surrounding an area that occupied the entire eastern quarter of the building.

"Has to be the maintenance area," Leroy said, as he darted off and came to a stop against the wall.

Damon pulled up next to him and leaned his back against the wall. "And we're going to jump this in broad daylight?"

"Yep," Leroy said, as he stood up and grabbed the top edge of the wall with both hands. He pulled himself up until his eyes were just over the top. Seeing no people or activity, he continued until he straddled the wall. He then bent over and extended his arm toward Damon. He motioned with his hand for Damon to take hold. When Damon took hold of the outstretched hand, Leroy pulled him up and helped him straddle the wall. Leroy then lifted his leg over the wall and jumped down to the concrete-covered yard. He then motioned for Damon to follow.

A few seconds after Damon's feet touched the concrete, the sound of a diesel engine starting from somewhere around the curve of the building broke the silence.

Leroy looked at Damon, raised a chin, and smiled. He then motioned for Damon to follow as he trotted to the building's curved outside wall and began inching his way around the curve. He passed three sets of double doors and slowed as the sound of the engine grew louder. Finally, thirty yards away, Leroy saw the source of the noise. Three men stood around the large generator, slapping each other on the back and laughing. The Humvee and trailer were parked nearby and there was a jerry can, presumably empty, at their feet.

Leroy pulled back, well out of sight. "Three men, all wearing sidearms."

"Great," Damon said. "Now what?"

"I can be on them before they know what's happening," Leroy said. "You hang back here until I have things under control."

"Sounds like a solid plan," Damon said, as he nodded. "I'll wait here."

Leroy drew the Glock. He checked to make sure the magazine was full and there was a round in the chamber. Satisfied, he inched forward again until the three men were back in sight. Two men had their backs to him. The third faced the direction from which Leroy would be running. A millisecond before he leapt, he heard the sound of a door opening behind him, just barely audible over the sound of the generator. He glanced back and saw Damon turn his head to the rear, then his body. He slowly raised his hands into the air. *Not a good sign.*

Damon glanced back at Leroy. His chin dropped to his chest.

Leroy couldn't see what Damon saw because of the curvature of the building, but he had a good idea. Leroy holstered his pistol, raised his hands, and stepped back toward Damon. Custer, holding a pistol, and two other men each with shouldered rifles, came into view. Their aim shifted to Leroy when he stepped next to Damon.

"I had a feeling," Custer said in a loud voice over the sound of the generator. He motioned with his pistol and pointed at the open set of double doors.

Leroy, with hands still raised, joined Damon. Together they walked toward the open door. As they passed Custer, he lifted the pistol from Leroy's holster.

Inside the arena, now lit by overhead fixtures blazing with light, the decibels from the generator immediately dropped to zero when one of Custer's men closed the door behind them.

Leroy scanned the lines of merchandise-covered tables and the few people browsing, now much more visible in the light.

"You just couldn't help yourself," Custer said.

"We just want our weapons," Leroy said, "and then we'll be out of your hair."

Damon had his eyes closed, chin down, and was slowly shaking his head side-to-side.

Leroy spotted the very weapons in question—the three automatic rifles, the shotgun and hunting rifle, Leroy's Glock, and Lincoln's M&P—laid out on a table a few feet away.

Custer walked over and nonchalantly placed Laura's pistol with the others. He then turned back to Leroy. "You do present a problem," he said.

Leroy glanced at his still-raised hands. He lowered them to his side. "Look, our destination is Virginia. There's a government trying to convene, probably at Mount Weather. We have no intention of staying here any longer than necessary."

A younger man perusing merchandise on a table a few feet away suddenly looked in Leroy's direction. "Did you say Virginia?" the man asked.

Everyone turned in unison to face the man.

"Yes," Leroy said. "Mount Weather, to join any military units that should have organized by now."

The man stepped closer to the group, looked at Custer, and back to Leroy. "I traveled here from there three months ago." He shook his head. "You won't find any kind of organization in Virginia."

"What do you mean?" Leroy asked.

"One cabinet secretary survived the plague out of all the others in the line of succession. Health or agriculture, I think. He did end up at Mount Weather. Tried to reorganize a government from there, but the various factions started squabbling. The whole thing fell into disarray again."

"How do you know all this?" Custer asked.

"I was there, a staffer for Senator Jamison."

"What happened then?" Leroy asked.

"The secretary was killed in a brawl at one of the meetings. I left soon after that."

"So you don't know what happened after you left," Leroy said. "Someone could have gotten things organized since then."

"Doubt it," the man said. "There just wasn't enough to get organized. Most did what I did. Went off on their own."

Custer turned back to Leroy. "Sounds like your plan has a fatal flaw."

Leroy rubbed his face with both hands, took in a deep breath, and exhaled. He finally looked up at Custer. "Doesn't change anything. Wherever we decide to plant ourselves, it won't be here. We'll be leaving, and we'll need our weapons."

"And the Humvee," Custer said.

"We'll walk," Leroy said.

The man from Virginia went back to examining the tables of merchandise.

Custer took a seat in a nearby overstuffed chair and motioned for his men to lower their rifles. "You can get another one running," Custer said, as he stared at Leroy.

Leroy stared at Custer for several moments. "Maybe," Leroy replied.

"You could stay here," Custer said. "I could use someone with your kind of talent."

Leroy twisted his lips as he paused for a moment. That was an offer he did not expect. Finally, he shrugged his shoulders. "I'll mention it to my friends, but I personally intend to move on."

Custer ran his fingers through his red hair. He stroked his beard as he contemplated the situation.

CHAPTER 26

Leroy and Damon walked into the armory compound carrying their weapons. They found the others hard at work filtering fuel. Batteries from the second Humvee were being charged to the sound of the generator.

Laura was the first to spot Leroy and Damon. She turned the valve off on the large storage tank and hurried to meet them. "What happened?" she asked, as she eyed the weapons.

"Custer had a change of heart," Leroy said. "He's keeping the Humvee and the fuel. We're free to leave with our weapons."

Laura breathed a sigh of relief as the others walked up.

Rufus took the hunting rifle and shotgun from Leroy's hands. "When do we need to be out of here?"

"He didn't say," Leroy said, "but I told him we would be gone soon." He looked at the six jerry cans lined up near the storage tank. "Just six cans?"

"I'm still removing cans from the other vehicles," Lincoln said. "Given the available fuel left, we should have ten or twelve cans."

"Does Custer know we're taking the fuel?" Laura asked.

"Not really," Leroy said. "He probably didn't expect there to be this much fuel left after he took the other sixteen cans."

Leroy walked over to the backpacks and dropped off the other weapons he carried. "The batteries charging okay?"

"Seem to be," Rufus said. "We should be done here in a couple more hours."

Leroy started walking, leading the others toward the second Humvee. "I'd like to move as soon as the truck is ready." He looked at Damon. "We should get the extra food in the hotel organized and ready to move."

Damon nodded and peeled off from the others.

"Are we still headed for Virginia?" Laura asked.

Leroy stopped at the hood of the Humvee and faced Rufus, Lincoln, Laura, and Cindy, who were gathered around. "About that."

The others looked on expectantly. Laura cocked her head.

"Met a man at the arena who said he traveled from Mount Weather a few months ago. He said there was an attempt to organize a government, but the whole thing fell into disarray. The acting president was killed during a brawl at one of the meetings."

"So what does that mean for us?" Cindy asked.

Leroy lifted his hat and scratched his head. He shook his head. "We could see for ourselves, or we could pick a different destination."

The others looked at each other.

"Or, Custer invited us to stay here," Leroy said. "He asked me to work for him."

"Is that what you want to do?" Laura asked.

Leroy shook his head. "No. Rather not stay here, but I'm open to what the rest of you think."

"We don't have to decide right this minute," Rufus said. "Let's get the rest of the fuel filtered and treated and the batteries charged. Hell, that truck might not even start."

"Sounds like a plan," Leroy said, as he motioned for Rufus to help him raise the hood. "Let's see if there are any obvious problems."

"We'll get back to filtering," Laura said, as she looked at Cindy and Lincoln.

Two and a half hours later, the mostly charged batteries were back in the truck, the tank was filled with the fuel treated first that morning, and thirteen cans of fuel were lined up next to the storage tank, now empty.

Leroy slid behind the wheel and flipped the ignition lever to *run*. The yellow *wait* light blinked on for a few moments. When he pushed the lever to the *start* position, the engine immediately began turning over. It continued turning without firing until Leroy let off the switch. He lifted his chin into the air and massaged the back of his neck. With his chin still in the air he reached out and pushed the ignition lever.

The engine began turning over. It rumbled on for several long seconds until, finally, the engine caught, coughed with a cloud of smoke just like before, and settled into a rough idle.

"Let's load up," Leroy said.

"Where we headed?" Laura asked.

Rufus pointed. "Over to the trailer so we can get this fuel loaded."

"That's not what I meant," Laura said.

Rufus grinned.

Leroy closed the door and stuck his head out the window toward Laura. "I'm thinking we drive to Memphis. A hundred miles. Two hours. We can talk about it on the way."

Laura nodded and began walking toward the alcove where the backpacks and weapons were stored.

Lincoln, Cindy, and Damon followed her.

Leroy and Rufus hooked up the short, open-air trailer and pulled over to the cans of fuel. They hopped out, loaded the cans, and helped the others load up the packs and weapons.

"Everyone jump in," Leroy said. "We'll pick up the food from the hotel and hit the road."

Twenty minutes later they were on their way down the interstate, east toward Memphis.

Leroy looked over at Rufus, sitting in the front passenger's seat. "Are we dropping you off?"

Rufus stared out the windshield for several seconds without answering. He finally turned his head and looked at Leroy. There was tiredness in his eyes. His forehead glistened. "If you folks don't mind, I think I'd like to hang with you."

Leroy glanced back at Laura and Cindy sitting on the bench seat, and then at Damon and Lincoln, each sitting on the individual seat to each side of the bench. Their backpacks and various items of gear, food, and weapons were on the floor at their feet.

Without saying a word, each person gave their approval with a nod or a slight raise of their chin.

Leroy turned back to Rufus. "Glad to have you," he said, followed by a smile.

"So we don't really have a reason to stop in Memphis," Laura said.

Leroy looked at Rufus.

"That's true," Rufus said. "Everything I need is here with me."

"So where are we headed?" Damon asked.

"If there's no organized government in Washington or Virginia," Cindy said, "I say we head to Florida, where it's warm."

"We could find a little place on the coast," Lincoln said. "Get a boat; do some fishing."

Leroy glanced back at Laura. "We could check out Virginia, and if there's no reason to stay we could head farther south. We have the time and we have the fuel."

"And we still have a jug of the fuel treatment," Rufus said. "We can always find more diesel."

Laura got out of her seat and stepped through the gear until her head was between the two front seats. "If we did find an organized government, what would you do?" she asked, looking at Leroy.

Leroy glanced at Laura. "I think Cindy had a good idea, except everybody and their brother will be headed for the warmest state. Those who can walk. I'm not sure Florida is a good idea. What do you say we skip Virginia and Florida and find a nice place in the mountains? Set up there for a while. Maybe grow some crops."

Laura put her hand on Leroy's shoulder. "I think that's an excellent idea."

Leroy placed his free hand on top of Laura's as he focused on the road ahead.

Two hours later everyone looked out the windows as they crossed the Mississippi River on their way into Memphis.

Leroy looked over at Rufus, who hadn't said much for over an hour. His head rested against the door's window glass. He looked asleep, except that his eyes were open. "You're back home, sure you don't want to stop for something?"

Rufus blinked, but otherwise didn't move or reply. His face and forehead were beaded with perspiration.

"Rufus, you okay?" Leroy asked.

"Pretty tired," Rufus finally mumbled. "Hit me all of a sudden."

Leroy glanced back and caught Laura's attention.

She made her way forward through the gear until she was between the two front seats. She placed a hand on Rufus' shoulder. "You don't look that good." She placed a hand against his forehead. "I think he's pretty warm. Might have a fever."

"Let's get through Memphis," Leroy said, "then we'll stop for a break."

Laura returned to her seat.

"Probably just a cold or something," Damon said.

"Probably," Laura agreed.

Leroy continued into Memphis, passing a few stalled cars and even a few people walking along the highway. They turned and gawked as the Humvee passed. Through Memphis with no problems, they continued a few miles past Arlington, where Leroy started looking for a place to pull over. He brought the truck to a stop in the median, next to a clump of trees on an isolated section of the road. Leroy cut the engine then looked at Rufus, whose position against the door had not changed. He glanced back at the others. "Let's get him over to the shade of that big oak," he said, as he opened his door and stepped out.

The others followed, and they all gathered at the passenger door.

Leroy opened the door and helped Rufus to the tree. He looked back at Damon. "Grab a tarp or something he can sit on."

Damon turned back to the Humvee.

By the time Leroy, with help from Laura, had Rufus at the tree, Damon ran up and spread the tarp. The three of them lowered Rufus to a sitting position, with his back against the trunk. Leroy stepped back as Laura knelt next to Rufus.

"Let's get him some water," Laura said, as she glanced at Damon.

Damon dashed off. He returned with a water jug and a cup. He poured some water into the cup and handed it to Laura.

"How are you feeling?" Laura asked, as she put the cup up to his lips.

Rufus took a few sips as he looked at Laura. "Weak as a newborn," he said, as he moved his head side-to-side. "It came on so quick. One minute I felt fine and the next I felt like a limp noodle."

"Ever had problems with your heart?" Leroy asked, as he hovered over Rufus and Laura.

Rufus shook his head. "Nope."

Cindy and Lincoln stood back from the group. Helpless to do anything except watch.

"I don't know," Laura said.

"Let's get him lying more flat," Damon said, as he stepped closer and knelt next to Rufus.

For the first time, Leroy saw worry on Damon's face.

Damon and Laura helped Rufus scrunch down into a prone position, flat on his back. As they did so, Rufus' t-shirt rode up a bit on his side.

Leroy caught a flash of something curious. He knelt next to Rufus and gently lifted the edge of Rufus' t-shirt.

An audible gasp emanated in unison from Laura and Damon.

Cindy and Lincoln stepped closer.

"What?" Cindy asked.

Leroy pulled Rufus' shirt higher, exposing a patch of bright red rash.

Damon fell back and immediately scrambled to his feet. "It's been two years since anyone showed signs."

Leroy lowered Rufus' shirt to cover the rash as he looked into Rufus' open eyes. Leroy blinked slowly as he shook his head back and forth. He pulled Laura to her feet as he stood and looked down on Rufus. "The symptoms are spot on," Leroy said. "Some people were carriers. Maybe it just took longer."

"Or maybe the bug mutated or something," Laura said, as she stepped back and hugged her daughter.

"You people don't need to fret," Rufus mumbled. "You're obviously immune."

"It's not that," Laura said, as she stepped back to Rufus and knelt next to his hip. "No one else was supposed to die."

"Who passed that law?" Rufus said. "We all die. It's just a matter of time. I'm just sorry I won't get to see what becomes of you good people."

Laura bent over and took hold of Rufus' hand.

Standing back several feet, watching Rufus and Laura, Leroy suddenly collapsed to his knees in the sand and leaves. He closed his eyes and tightened his jaw.

Laura looked back at Leroy. "What?"

Leroy ground his teeth as he blinked slowly. He then reached out and took hold of the hem of Laura's t-shirt. He raised it slowly as Laura looked down. The unmistakable beginnings of the plague rash came into view on Laura's left side.

She reached down and jerked her shirt up more, exposing more of the rash. She looked up and stared into Leroy's sad eyes for several long seconds before turning her head toward Cindy.

Cindy rushed forward. "Mom!"

Leroy caught Cindy before she reached her mother. "We don't know how contagious it is."

"Mom!" Cindy screamed, as she struggled in Leroy's arms. Tears ran down her cheeks.

Leroy looked past Cindy at Damon and Lincoln.

They both looked down at themselves, then at each other. They both raised the edge of their shirts. A rash on their trunks, similar to the one on Laura, was already beginning to form. They pulled their shirts down. Damon fell back against the truck; Lincoln's chin slowly sunk to his chest.

Leroy pushed back from Cindy while still holding both her arms. His eyes darted down to her waist. He dropped his hands to his side and stepped back to give her room.

Laura watched. Tears ran down her cheeks.

Cindy looked down at her waist as she slowly raised the edge of her shirt. She stared for several moments and then examined her opposite flank. She let the t-shirt drop as she looked at her mother, then Leroy.

Leroy lifted his shirt and checked both flanks. He looked up at Laura as he let the shirt's hem fall back down. He tightened his lips.

Laura stared into Leroy's eyes.

Leroy nodded with understanding.

Seven days later Leroy stood next to the Humvee's open driver's door and watched Cindy as she took a final look around the camp. Leroy glanced around the area as well. "I think we're set."

Cindy nodded, walked around to the passenger's side, and slid into the front seat. She turned her head to check the cargo area and then faced Leroy as he plopped himself in the driver's seat.

Leroy closed the door and placed both hands on the steering wheel while he stared through the windshield at the trees. He watched the leaves, just starting to turn their autumn colors, swaying in the breeze. He thought about all that had happened over the past few days, starting with Rufus falling ill. He would miss the old guy.

Cindy's voice broke the silence and his reverie. "Where to?"

Leroy glanced at Cindy and then resumed his gaze at the trees. With both hands he rubbed his whiskered face for several seconds. "Did I ever mention that I love to fish?"

"I don't think so," Cindy responded.

"It's a great diversion. It takes your mind off everything."

"Uh-huh."

Leroy continued staring through the windshield. "About ten years ago I spent a full two weeks just fishing. Every day. Me and two buddies from the unit. We rented a little cabin in St. Marks, Florida, a small, out-of-the-way fishing village on the Gulf just south of Tallahassee." He glanced at Cindy. "Wives, girlfriends, and kids weren't allowed."

"Sounds very manly," Cindy said.

Leroy nodded and tightened his lips as he stared at Cindy's face.

"And?" Cindy asked.

Leroy glanced in the cargo area and then turned back to Cindy. "Even if there is something brewing in Virginia, I don't think the army will miss one sergeant."

"Probably not," Cindy said.

"I say we head straight to St. Marks and do some fishing."

"I second that notion," came a voice from the rear. Laura's voice. Weak, a little mumbled, but clear enough.

Leroy and Cindy turned their heads in unison and gazed at Laura bundled in her sleeping bag on the cargo floor.

"I thought you were sleeping," Leroy said. "How're you feeling?"

"Drained but still alive," Laura said. She turned her head to the other bundle on the floor next to her. Only Damon's head stuck out of the sleeping bag. His chest rose and fell as he slept. "How's he doing?"

"Both your fevers broke last night," Leroy said. "It appears you two beat the odds. Not many who came down with the plague survived."

"Lincoln?" Laura asked.

Leroy's face turned grim. He glanced at Cindy and then back to Laura. "Afraid not. Just you and Damon came through."

Laura closed her eyes for several seconds. She opened them and looked at Cindy.

Cindy's eyes glistened. "I'll be okay, mom." She looked at Leroy. "The four of us will be okay."

"How far is St. Marks?" Laura asked.

Leroy turned his head back to the front. "We'll take it nice and easy. Lot's of rest stops along the way." He started the Humvee and pulled out to the highway. "Just rest," he yelled over the sound of the engine. "Drink plenty of water. Get your strength back." He glanced at Cindy and smiled. "Soon enough we'll be on the water. Fishing."

A REQUEST FROM THE AUTHOR

Thank you for reading *From Near Extinction*. I hope you enjoyed the story as much as I enjoyed writing it. I do have one request. I ask that you please take a few moments to enter a product review on your Amazon 'Orders' page. Independent authors depend on reviews to get their books noticed. And reviews also help make my future books better. A few moments of your time would be much appreciated. I look forward to reading your thoughts. —**Victor Zugg**

ABOUT THE AUTHOR

Victor Zugg is a former US Air Force officer and OSI special agent who served and lived all over the world. Given his extensive travels and opportunities to settle anywhere, it is ironic that he now resides in Florida, only a few miles from his hometown of Orlando. He credits the warm temperatures for that decision.

Check out the author's other novels—*Solar Plexus (1), Near Total Eclipse (Solar Plexus 2)*, and *Surrounded By The Blue*.

Made in the USA
Las Vegas, NV
16 December 2022

62912463R00194